ALSO BY EMMA LATHEN

Come to Dust
A Stitch in Time
Murder Against the Grain
Death Shall Overcome
Murder Makes the Wheels Go Round
Accounting for Murder
A Place for Murder
Banking on Death

WHEN IN GREECE

An Inner Sanctum Mystery by

EMMA LATHEN

Simon and Schuster

NEW YORK

Published by Simon and Schuster
Rockefeller Center, 630 Fifth Avenue
New York, New York 10020

FIRST U.S. PRINTING

SBN 671-20209-X
Library of Congress Catalog Card Number: 76-75871
Manufactured in the United States of America
by Mahony & Roese, Inc., New York

CHAPTER I

TIMEO...

WALL STREET IS the greatest money market in the world. This means, among other things, that it is a quivering communications network, plucking information from the air, putting it on high-speed tickers and speeding it to men who make or lose millions of dollars by knowing things before the rest of the world. The first tremor of turmoil at Bloemfontein sets gold dealers on Broad Street cabling branch offices in London, Geneva or Delhi. Gossip about a British cabinet minister can trigger frenzied activity on Blair Street. No banks in Vienna have failed recently, but Wall Street retains an indelible memory of what happened when one did.

In a word, Wall Street routinely deals with news that does not break into print. Intelligence crucial to the peace of the world, to the fortunes of men and the fate of nations is grist to the financial world's mill.

It does not form the subject of Wall Street's conversation.

"Damned cold for spring," said Tom Robichaux of Robichaux & Devane, investment bankers.

His luncheon partner was John Putnam Thatcher, senior vice president of the Sloan Guaranty Trust, the third largest bank in the world. As director of the Sloan's trust and investment departments, Thatcher probably dealt in knowledge more recondite than most. He agreed that it had been an unusual April.

"Rainy, too!" Robichaux grumbled over his deep-dish apple pie.

Tactfully Thatcher repressed a smile. The sodden spring had been oppressive, but in the past thirty-five years Tom Robichaux had been able to sustain his ebullience in the face of greater catastrophes, including the Great Depression and several divorce-court appearances. Thatcher suspected that Robichaux' peevishness stemmed from his failure to sell Thatcher on Bingham Corporation, producers of instant hair dryers.

But after they parted outside the Midtown Club and Thatcher began to stride through the clammy drizzle toward the Sloan, he realized he might be doing Robichaux an injustice.

First it was aged Bartlett Sims, still inflicting his sharp tongue upon Waymark-Sims.

"Filthy weather," Sims harrumphed, observing the pedestrian flow on Exchange Place with open contempt. "Haven't seen a spring like this for God knows how many years."

Thatcher moved out of the path of a flying wedge of secretaries and agreed that it was not a pleasant day.

"Day?" Bartlett Sims snorted. "More like a month! And don't try to tell me that the weather isn't changing. It's getting worse and worse. Just like most things."

With this, he stomped off. Thatcher had long since abandoned attempts to tell Bartlett Sims anything. He proceeded, reflecting that beneath the thin skin of concrete, steel and glass, Wall Street was not very different from the country store of his boyhood in Sunapee, New Hampshire.

"Well, the drought's over."

The voice in his ear belonged to Walter Bowman, the Sloan's large enthusiastic chief of research. He was just leaving the bank for a late lunch which would be devoted, Thatcher knew, to milking some acquaintance of inside information to be laid, like a trophy, at the feet of the Sloan's investment committee. When weather replaced dollars and cents in Walter Bowman's conversation, it was hypnotically powerful.

Or, Thatcher mused as he entered the Sloan's great lobby and gave the dog-like shake which had become habitual during this endless deluge, perhaps he was overhasty. Walter Bowman might have sound professional reasons for interest in the elements; the commodity market, for example, or firms manufacturing irrigation pipe.

But Billings, the elevator operator, certainly did not. In the brief voyage from the lobby to the sixth floor, he expanded his customary remarks.

"Good day to stay indoors, Mr. Thatcher."

"Yes, indeed," said Thatcher heartily as the pneumatic doors opened. He made his way to his corner suite of offices, past illicit drying umbrellas, and arrived to find his Miss Corsa waiting for him.

"Terrible weather, Miss Corsa," said Thatcher, removing his raincoat.

But although Tom Robichaux, investment banker, Bartlett Sims, broker, Walter Bowman, analyst, and Billings, elevator operator, might be farm boys at heart, Rose Theresa Corsa was a Wall Streeter to her very core. Dismissing weather as another one of her employer's frivolities, she reported the news that had just flashed over the ticker tape:

"There has been," she said precisely, "a revolution in Greece!"

Several hours later, Thatcher contemplated Charlie Trinkam and Walter Bowman, summoned for consultation. Bowman scowled as he put his personal information retrieval system to work.

"Blood doesn't seem to be flowing in the streets of Athens," he said, with an inquiring look at Charlie Trinkam.

Charlie shrugged. "As I understand it, it's a right wing group of reactionary Greek Army officers. They've just rolled in the tanks, and taken over! There hasn't been any sort of resistance, according to these latest reports!"

Charlie, one of Thatcher's senior staff, combined business ability and extracurricular gusto. His untrammeled pursuit of pleasure led him to worlds undreamed of by his conservative colleagues. At the same time, innate financial orthodoxy immunized him against the waves of enthusiasm that sometimes afflicted Walter Bowman. Usually, he was worth considerably more than his weight in gold to the Sloan. Oddly enough, he was currently its ranking expert on Greece.

With an apologetic look, Walter Bowman added that the news services were reporting thousands of arrests.

"Just who," he asked Charlie, "would they be arresting?"

Charlie began to enumerate. "The entire opposition in the election scheduled for next month. That includes the Central Union party, the trade unions, most newspaper writers, almost all intellectuals, half the civil service—oh yes, and a large part of the diplomatic corps, too."

"Perhaps it would be more efficient to concentrate on those the army won't arrest?" Thatcher suggested.

Charlie grinned. "You know these military types! The only ones they won't arrest are other colonels!"

"Charlie," said Thatcher threateningly, "we'd better make a lot of money out of Hellenus! This was your brainstorm!"

"Some brainstorm!" said Charlie ironically.

Three years earlier Charlie had, somehow, sniffed out an investment possibility, a multimillion dollar project to be located in the mountains near Salonika, Greece. In time this would include a multipurpose dam, extensive hydroelectric power installations and an ambitious transportation-communication system. Charlie had reported on this, the Sloan's investment committee had studied the situation and from such small beginnings had come conferences, negotiations, and preliminary agreements—all culminating in a consortium, that is, a temporary financial partnership between: the Government of Greece, the Sloan Guaranty Trust and Paul Makris & Son, International Development Engineers. Future financial aid was expected from several agencies of the United States and the United Nations.

Unbelievable as it may seem, this colossus, known as *Hellenus Company*, was a perfectly routine venture for a giant bank like the Sloan Guaranty Trust. Sloan money—to the tune of over thirty million dollars—was going to help Hellenus grow in the north of Greece, and help profits grow nearer home.

Nothing in the past year had shadowed this bread-and-butter goal; on a pilot project, large modern edifices were rising in areas previously reserved for goats. Provisional summaries, cost estimates and revised tax allowances all gave rise to endless conferences, but provided satisfaction to the interested parties. With the pilot project nearing completion, Hellenus stood ready to forge ahead and start yielding returns.

Charlie looked as worried as he ever could. "It's hard to tell what's up," he said. "Just that there's been this army takeover. Of course, Wilhouse wasn't happy about the political situation when he got back from his last trip..."

Thatcher was not inclined to take Wilhouse seriously. Almost everybody who had been commuting between Athens, New York, Washington and London had commented on the deteriorating political situation. The emergence of young Andreas Papandreou—sometime American citizen and professor of economics, who had left the University of California to assist his father in reorganizing Greece's largest political party—was regarded as so much fuel on the fire. But specialists, Thatcher knew, regarded all political situations with disapproval. Kings, parliaments, imperialism, independence—all were so many roadblocks between the Sloan and its single-minded pursuit of the lira, the pound, the peso or, as in this case, the drachma. Until bullets started flying, political ideology did not count.

"Well, we'll have to wait and see," said Thatcher. "It's a shame you're not in Athens, Charlie. Who's over there for us?"

Not that his colleagues wished Charlie ill, far less surrounded by Greek insurgents; but long experience had taught everybody that, during civil disturbances, floods and other cataclysms, it was helpful to have a top man representing the Sloan Guaranty Trust.

Charlie winced slightly. "Ken Nicolls," he reported.

Since Ken Nicolls was very junior indeed, nobody said anything at all. They did not have to.

Trinkam believed devoutly in nongeographic exploration. Since he was a bachelor living in considerable luxury—not a suburban husband with house, children, lawns and mortgages

—he had no reason to hanker after protracted business trips to Romantic Rome, Exotic Cairo, Fun-Filled Frankfurt or Swinging London. Even so, Charlie's responsibilities took him far too often to places he preferred leaving to vacationing college students or retired Peoria car dealers. The last two years had given Charlie Trinkam his fill of Greece.

On his last return, while he was sourly pointing out that business offices and Hilton hotels are the same throughout the world, he had glanced up in time to spot the gleam in Ken Nicolls' eye. Nicolls—tall, blond, seriously devoted to climbing the banking ladder for the sake of wife and infant son—was gazing straight at Romance.

Bouzoukis. Unspoiled villages. Flowers tumbling over whitewashed walls. Mimosa perfuming the air. A simple, hospitable peasantry. Wine dark seas. The isles of Greece, the isles of Greece!

"I thought it would do him good," Charlie said, sinking other, generous motives. "After all, it's just a question of routine for the next couple of weeks. The real horse-trading won't start until the consortium re-negotiation."

Walter Bowman hitched himself forward. "I don't know much about Hellenus," he said untruthfully, "but all this business of tanks rolling into Athens—you don't think that there's going to be a real civil war, do you?"

"With Greeks, you never can tell," said Charlie slowly. "But I wish I knew what the hell was going on at Hellenus right now."

CHAPTER II

PROCRUSTEAN BED

THE COUP D'ETAT found Kenneth Nicolls on location thirty miles north of Salonika, surrounded by Greeks, instead of the sixth floor of the Sloan Guaranty Trust. As a result, the event was less momentous to him than to John Putnam Thatcher and Walter Bowman. They had Charlie Trinkam, who had picked up an amazing grab bag of gossip and speculation in his many trips; when they finished with Charlie they had television bulletins and newspapers rich with analysis and speculation. They had reports from world capitals. They had protests from the American Economic Association. They had the comments of touring Greek actresses.

Ken had nothing to match, and had been feeling generally disgruntled even before the violence. He had set off on his first European trip for the Sloan in exaltation. Sternly reminding himself that he was a promising banker, not Lord Byron, he had taken his big news home to Brooklyn Heights and presented the trip as a professional plum and nothing else.

Jane, his wife, knew better. All she said was: "Marvelous! And you'll need a new two-suiter. You're going to be back in time, aren't you?"

"Mm? Oh sure," said Ken, dragged back from thyme-covered mountains to the imminent enlargement of his family. "I'll be back in three weeks."

"If you're not," said Jane Nicolls sweetly, "stay away for the next twenty-one years."

But anticipation had proved a good deal more gratifying than reality; after TWA finally transported K. Nicolls to Paris, Rome, and Athens, it seemed that the total upshot was to move him from one conference room to another. The Hotel

Britannia was as near exotic Greece and the romantic Mediterranean as he ever came and, as generations of well-heeled English and American tourists could have told him, at the Britannia both exotica and romance were kept on a damned tight rein. Otherwise, the Ministry of the Interior, the Bank of Greece, Paul Makris & Son, constituted Ken Nicolls' Greece, and pretty tiring he found it: long tables and break-even studies are the same throughout the world.

Nor did he get much opportunity to explore the night life he had read about; with Hellenus operations in progress for almost two years, the festive phase was long since over. The large cast of financial and technical experts had left wining and dining behind; some old-timers even invited Ken home for real American food. He trudged gloomily from garden apartment cookouts to dull hotel dinners with German cement specialists and hydroelectric experts, regularly retiring early enough to satisfy the most demanding wife. What little of Greece he managed to see was as he waited in front of the Britannia for the official car, or from that car's windows. Athens was crowded, colorful, busy. But then, so is New York.

Meanwhile the political cauldron boiled on without attracting his attention. The language he heard, in hotel and conference room, was English and nobody was using it to discuss Greek politics. Having been carefully briefed before he left New York, Ken knew that the election coming soon marked a confrontation between right and left. Otherwise, since the Greek alphabet was beyond him, the posters he saw defacing every available surface might just as well have been selling Coca Cola.

So, after two tiresome weeks, Ken was not sorry to leave Athens for the Hellenus site. The flight, in a Greek government plane, did not give him an opportunity to see the country. And Hellenus offered only the organized chaos of a huge construction site.

True, there were noble mountains in the background, but there are mountains in the background in California, too.

Visitors to Hellenus were housed in a low, rambling building like an inferior motel. As the Sloan's engineering experts could have told Ken, this was simply a supra-national large-scale enterprise. But Ken, noting the swarms of sun-blackened workers who sported colorful head wrappings, the eternal Greek bureaucrats, the endless representatives of many organizations, simply plunged into his work, regretting that it was not taking place on Wall Street.

On the morning of April 21, he presented himself at the administrative building as usual; there, he found the compound virtually deserted. The only sign of life was the cluster of guards intent on the radio. They looked up as he approached and burst into dramatic pantomimes, long, incomprehensible speeches and sweeping invitations to proceed, proceed. Then they returned to their listening.

Wondering if there was some Greek holiday he had overlooked, Ken went into the office set aside for his use and sat in solitary bewilderment for one hour before he was joined by the American field engineer assigned to the project.

"They're having a revolution," said Cliff Leonard briefly.

Startled, Ken stared at him.

"The way I get it," said Leonard, "the Army has taken over. They've sealed off Athens. I just tried to phone, and that's cut. One of my boys says they've thrown most of Parliament into jail."

He then went to a battered case and began pawing through blueprints.

Ken was impressed by this calm and tried to emulate it. "And what do we do?" he asked.

Leonard shrugged.

"It's none of our business. We finish this report. Might as well get it out of the way."

Privately, Ken thought this might be too tame a way to greet a revolution but, since he could think of nothing else, agreed. For several hours, he and Leonard double-checked specifications. By three o'clock that afternoon, he was coming around to Leonard's approach. Not a soul had disturbed the two men. Instead of the endless stream of Greek clerks and officials, of lawyers and civil servants, there was only empty and echoing silence.

"Makes it easier to get some work done," said Leonard. "Oh, oh!"

Ken looked up. There, in the doorway, looking curiously up and down, was Stavros Bacharias.

Ken rose to greet him, since Bacharias was the representative of the Ministry of the Interior with whom he had had most of his dealings. To his surprise, Bacharias broke into fluent apologies, murmured something about an appointment, then precipitately fled.

Leonard grinned sardonically and suggested adjourning to his quarters down the road.

"Maybe we'd better wait," Ken began. "Bacharias may want to talk to us."

"I've got a case of beer," said Leonard, hoisting himself to his feet. "And today, Bacharias won't want to talk."

The first three beers were washed down with a pungent description of the problems faced by the field engineer—from the impossibility of working with foreigners to the gross ignorance of American employers sitting back home. In fact, that third beer might have been the last if Nicolls had not made a discovery. Cliff Leonard was exclusively interested in coordinates and coefficients; the domestic problems of his host country bored him. He was virtually illiterate in the larger issues of foreign affairs. But his previous tours of duty had included Africa, the Caribbean and the Middle East. Willy-nilly, he had become a connoisseur of political upheavals. The National Radical Union and the Center Union party were nothing to him; he was, however, very practised on the street-corner aspects of the situation.

"Today, everybody stays home," he said. "If this take-over runs into resistance, then there's trouble. Maybe here, maybe some place else. No one can tell."

"And they think they're safer at home?"

"Well, what do you suppose?" Leonard asked. "If there was any real showdown, the Hellenus project would be one of the first targets in the north of Greece. I'd be surprised if there isn't a tank column up there, by now."

"But *you* went to the office today," Nicolls objected.

Leonard grinned as he backhanded blindly behind his chair for fresh beer. "Oh, I don't worry about the first column. It's when a second column rolls up with different ideas that the party gets rough."

Silently Ken brooded into his glass. Then he recalled their one visitor that day. "Stavros Bacharias came to the office," he pointed out. "Was he operating on the two-column principle?"

"Oh, no. Bacharias is different. The rank and file stay home. But Bacharias is in the ministry. He's a big shot. And big shots are all running around trying to find out whether they're in or out. It makes a real difference to them who's behind this rumble."

For the first time, Nicolls realized that the coup might make a real difference to him, too. He had worked with Stavros Bacharias for almost two weeks now and finally got on some sort of terms with him. He did not want to have to start afresh with someone else. He said as much.

"You'll probably know by tomorrow," Leonard shrugged. "If there's no shooting today, everybody will come back to work. Out of curiosity to see who's running the show, if nothing else."

Leonard's prediction proved accurate. On the next morning, April 22, Ken found the compound boasting its normal complement of humanity, in fact more than its usual complement. The guards at the lodge had been reinforced by the military in the shape of three soldiers at the gate and a single tank in the road outside. This display of armed might in no way affected the usual entrance procedure and Ken was passed through with due geniality. Perversely, now that there was no obstacle to performing the tasks scheduled for the day before, Ken no longer felt like work. What he wanted was an explanation of the political situation. But although most of the employees in the administration building spoke English, they showed no inclination to exchange views with an unknown foreigner in the shadow of the military. By early afternoon, when rumor reported that two union men had been arrested at the project during lunch hour, there were long un-Greek silences. Ken learned only that a military junta headed by a Colonel George Papadopoulos was in charge of the country and that the junta had issued a royal decree in the name of King Constantine, but that nothing had as yet been heard from the young monarch himself.

This information, meager as it was by Wall Street standards, represented the total harvest. Not surprisingly, Nicolls ended up accomplishing more than he expected to. Before he could become virtuous on the subject, a line to the outside world arrived with the return of Stavros Bacharias. The ministry man carried himself with a muted assurance which evoked one expert glance from Cliff Leonard and then the whispered appraisal:

"He's still in, but he hasn't gone up."

Leonard's standards were too high. For most people, still being in thirty-six hours after a military coup is enough. Bacharias at least was pleased enough to abandon the customary stiffness of a senior civil servant representing his Minister. He became positively affable. He was as unwilling as everyone else to discuss the broader implications of the situation: he was, however, willing to expand on domestic detail.

"Yes, Athens remains sealed off," he replied to Nicolls' inquiry. "The telephone exchanges are still reserving trunk lines for government priority calls. But I understand that the railroads at least will be running tomorrow. No doubt you will wish to return to Athens, when we have gone through these financial reports."

Kenneth agreed that he should return now that the task which had brought him to Hellenus was approaching its end. Tact made him refrain from expressing his real reason. He wanted to get some information about how the coup affected the future plans of the Sloan Guaranty Trust; preferably from the home office, at least from the foreign colony of financiers in the capital. Greece, he recalled, was an associate in the

Common Market, which would bring every Western European banker into the picture.

He need not have bothered with his explanation. Bacharias, a born Athenian, assumed that anybody in his right mind would, at all times and under all conditions, wish to leave the provinces for Athens.

"Yes, we must consider what is necessary in order to get you back," he murmured, weighing the pros and cons to himself. "Today, I think, is out of the question. And, if you permit, I would like to spend the evening with these projected capital requirements you have formulated. But tomorrow, if travel is permitted at all, we should be able to arrange something. If necessary, you understand, I can make a few calls."

Ken expressed profound gratitude, Bacharias produced stately disclaimers of any service. They parted, each satisfied that he had upheld national honor. Cliff Leonard, a skeptical spectator, was critical. All this unnecessary formality was, in his opinion, a cowardly truckling to outmoded standards and alien values.

"Still, you've got the magic touch, boy," he admitted. "Catch Bacharias going out of his way to do me a favor."

When you have made heavy inroads on a man's liquor supply, you cannot very well tell him that his open contempt for all foreigners, all bureaucrats, and all non-engineers is unlikely to win extraordinary courtesies from the Bachariases of this world.

"I expect he's just as glad to get rid of me," Ken said mildly. "His ministry would really like to have us deal with them in Athens and let them do the field work."

"Well," said Leonard disapprovingly, "if you're so hot on being buddy-buddy with the Ministry, why not do things that way?"

Kenneth stiffened slightly. "The Sloan," he said at his evenest, "likes to see where its money is going."

Surprisingly this made an immediate hit with Leonard. He launched into a story about a project in Central Africa which had inspired lavish support from both the Soviet Union and the United States for over two years before the discovery that it was more than inaccessible; it was fictitious.

On this note, Kenneth ended the day, dimly aware that one of his future difficulties was going to be charting a middle course between Bacharias and Cliff Leonard.

By the next morning it developed that Stavros Bacharias was steering an uneasy course himself. He had spent the evening as planned and, much as he disliked raising objections, he very much feared that one of Ken's figures was unacceptable. (This was scarcely surprising. In the course of eighteen months Bacharias had not once failed to overcome his dislike of objections when presented with a report of any kind. Understandably, it was now house policy at the Sloan to provide one red herring in every report. This sleeper was carefully designed to permit a specious defense which could, in exchange for acceptance of the rest of the document, be graciously waived.)

But Bacharias, to balance obstructionism in one area, was co-operating wholeheartedly in another. He hurled himself at the telephone. To Ken's untutored ear, the ensuing conversations sounded as if they began with a threat to assassinate the telephone operator and then unwound on an increasingly menacing note. At the end of two hours, long after Ken had adjusted his red herring, Bacharias cradled the phone and patted his lips delicately with his handkerchief.

"Good!" he said briskly in tones of one who had just completed a normal business transaction. "The schedule arranges itself very well. The Athens Express will run tonight. They are holding a ticket for you. I myself am spending the evening in Salonika so I can drive you to the station. You will be in Athens tomorrow morning without any inconvenience at all."

He was singing a different tune at seven-thirty that evening.

"I am afraid," he said dubiously, "I am afraid you will not have a very comfortable trip."

And that, thought Kenneth silently as he looked around, was the understatement of the year.

CHAPTER III

DRAGON'S TEETH

AT JUST ABOUT the same time, John Putnam Thatcher was far from comfortable himself. Charlie Trinkam and Walter Bowman were again in conference in his office. It was still raining. But these were not the factors ruffling his equanimity. He was on the phone to Mrs. Nicolls.

"... yes, of course, Jane. Ken will be in touch as soon as the lines are open," said Thatcher.

The telephone asked a question.

"No, no reason to worry," said Thatcher. "We're expecting the phones to be working again any minute. And according to the latest reports, there has been absolutely no violence. Whatever you may say about their social philosophy, these Greek colonels have been efficient. I understand, of course, that they have simply used NATO plans ... what was that?"

The phone spoke and Thatcher cast Charlie Trinkham—who should have been doing this—a look of reproof. Charlie was smug. He claimed he lacked the proper touch with wives; actually, they frightened him.

"Oh, it's quite simple, Jane," said Thatcher at length. "The center coalition was expected to win next month's election. So the Army has clapped everybody into jail and declared themselves the winners. What? Oh, yes, yes. Disgraceful. Of course, the Greeks have spared themselves campaign speeches, which is something ... What? No, this is purely internal. All Americans are safe. No, Jane, you are thinking of several other countries. No one has stormed the U.S. Embassy."

He rounded off this conversation in a soothing vein but, as soon as the call was concluded, his tone hardened.

"Jane Nicolls getting worried?" Charlie asked solicitously.

Thatcher glared at him. "Not at all. She has simply been unfavorably impressed by these newspaper stories."

Their tenor was not calculated to cheer; after weighing the annoyance and uncertainty inherent in the democratic process, the Army had decided that duty demanded suspension of the Greek constitution, removal of malcontents from the public view and purification of Greek life.

Not even American journalists found it difficult to follow these thought processes as explained by the junta.

Not, the colonels hastened to add, that purification of Greek life should be interpreted as antagonism to American tourists, American investment, American military assistance. Good heavens, no! Greek-American friendship must continue...

All this was enough for journalists, for political analysts, for concerned wives. The Sloan Guaranty Trust, predictably, wanted harder facts, particularly about the immediate outlook for Hellenus. Two years and several million dollars had already been committed. The Sloan wanted assurance that its $36 million was not going to be purified out from under it.

"It's a shame this got dumped in Nicolls' lap," said Thatcher mildly. Charlie Trinkam, he well knew, would have been in contact with New York if he had had to swim the Hellespont to get to a phone. But, Thatcher reminded himself, it takes years of seasoning to produce a Trinkam. And it was unreasonable to feel irate because a revolution that had caught Greece, NATO, Western Europe and the CIA off guard had not been pinpointed by the Sloan's research staff. "But in the meantime, let's see what we've got."

"It could be worse, John," Trinkam reported. "The Ambassador has already made a formal representation. The new Minister of the Interior, as well as Colonel Patakos, has assured him that the new regime welcomes Hellenus and will continue to co-operate in every way possible."

"What is that assurance worth?" asked Thatcher.

Charlie thought for a moment. "As far as it goes, it should be O.K. These colonels don't represent the sophisticated rightists of Greece. Oh, they're conservatives, all right, and they want to perpetuate the past. They're used to a few rich men running the country, and everybody else poor and respectful. They don't like change..."

Walter Bowman leaned forward.

"Look, Charlie, I don't know anything about Greece, but I would have thought that a huge power and development project would be the last thing they'd want. After all, nothing upsets the *status quo* more than a big shot of industrial growth. You know, the maids would rather work in factories, the lower classes start buying cars, people put housing developments in picturesque old villages. That always burns up the old guard. Everywhere."

Thatcher was amused by this condensed, but accurate, view of the social consequences of economic development.

"It's called Americanization, Walter," he pointed out. "Everybody hates it—everybody who has nothing to gain."

Charlie agreed. "Sure," he said. "But you're forgetting two things. Until it happens to them, every country thinks it's got built-in immunization. *Their* people could never act like Americans. They *like* being maids. Remember, Greece is damned poor. They haven't had any economic miracle yet. These military types don't really know what's coming. They think they can raise the standard of living without changing the social structure. They're pretty unimaginative. In fact, you wouldn't believe..."

"Oh, yes, I would," Thatcher cut in. "What's your second point?"

"The colonels are hysterically anti-communist," said Charlie. "They see a red menace in every suggestion of change—unionization, social security, an independent parliament. It's like McCarthyism to the nth degree. So naturally they look on the United States as their ally. I think they'll break their neck to keep Hellenus going. And more important, to keep American participation."

"Ah!" Walter Bowman pounced. "Because that's the main point. It's not going to do us much good if they decide to keep the Hellenus development, but expropriate our interest."

"I don't think so, but," Charlie shrugged, "we'll know better in a couple of weeks."

"That may be too late," Thatcher said grimly. He drummed his fingers on the table for a moment. "I wish to God they'd waited a month or two for their revolution. It couldn't come at a worse time for us."

"Yes," Charlie nodded. "A year ago would have been even better."

Bowman looked confused. "I don't follow that."

"It's simple, Walter. A year ago, they needed the Sloan's assistance desperately to get the pilot project off the ground. The international agencies decided to hold back money until the Sloan and Paul Makris really got the project started. Now the pilot program has gone well, almost spectacularly well. In two weeks we're going to negotiate our participation in the final program. If we'd already negotiated it and the consortium had agreed before this take-over, then the new Greek Government could get rid of us only by breaking faith with everybody—the World Bank, the Agency for International Development, and the others. Instead, look where we are! They could freeze us out without causing an international stink, and they could find other backers to take our place."

"Christ!" Walter Bowman was thinking of that thirty-six million dollars. "Do you think there's any chance they'll try it?"

"I hope not, but I'd feel a lot happier if we got some kind of report from Ken," Trinkam admitted. "If you don't mind, I think I'll get along and find out when we can expect some life from the Athens exchange."

Two hours later, he was back and his report was not reassuring. He had talked with several agencies in Washington and with the New York office of Paul Makris & Son.

"They've all heard from their people in Greece."

"Makris too?" asked Bowman. Governments were one thing. A commercial establishment was something else again.

"That's what they said," Charlie said irritably. "The lines are chaotic, but calls have been straggling through since this morning. What's more, they expect no delay in the consortium negotiations."

"Oh, they don't, eh?" Thatcher grunted.

It is a sad commentary on modern business practice that the prospect of the Sloan's partners opening communications with Greece and proceeding with Hellenus in the absence of a responsible Sloan agent put everybody on his mettle.

"Where the hell is Nicolls?" Charlie demanded. "That's what I want to know!"

"And we're going to find out." Stabbing the buzzer with a martial forefinger, Thatcher summoned Miss Corsa.

"Miss Corsa, the lines to Greece have been opened. I want Nicolls' hotel. Presumably he's not there. So, I'll talk to the manager." To Trinkam and Bowman, he said: "I suppose it's remotely possible that he's ill or something. They ought to know at the hotel."

"If his story is that he was too sick to telephone," Charlie growled, "he'd damn well better be unconscious!"

Thatcher made pacifying noises. "Well, we'll soon know," he said in one of the least accurate forecasts of his career.

Four hours later, Thatcher was again at the telephone. Miss Corsa, who had coped with overseas operators, a maniacally disorganized Athens exchange and several sinister unidentified persons, was resting.

"Hello?" said Thatcher. "Hello? HELLO?"

Miss Corsa had assured him that a responsible, English-speaking member of the staff of the Hotel Britannia was ready and waiting. The only response to his yodelling was expensive, transatlantic static and a distant wail.

Miss Corsa stirred slightly.

"HELLO?"

"'Allo! Wait please!" It was a breathy squeak.

"They said..." Miss Corsa began, but Thatcher waved her to silence.

"HELLO?"

Listening intently, Thatcher detected distant human voices, apparently arguing. There was a sudden loud crash.

"What did they say to you, Miss Corsa? Hello? HELLO?"

A different, but still frantic voice, burst onto the line:

"Wait, mister! Please!"

"Now, just a minute!" Thatcher bellowed.

To no avail. There was only electronic punctuation. This was the sort of thing that Miss Corsa normally spared Thatcher. For the first time, he began to get an accurate measure of the disruption obtaining in Greece.

"Confused, I suppose," said Charlie sleepily. It was long past normal working hours and he required bright lights to maintain evening sprightliness. "But they always are."

Thatcher was about to reply when a sudden explosion of noise temporarily deafened him. Hastily, he removed the receiver an inch from his ear, and heard:

"'Allo? Here, Lycurgos Diamantis, Assistant Night Manager of Hotel Britannia, at your best service."

"I am calling to ask," Thatcher began firmly, only to be drowned in another torrent of speech.

"Come to Athens, sir! Come to Beautiful Greece!" The phone spoke fair-to-middling American English with a Mediterranean gusto around the consonants. "We hold all reservations, just as normal. No danger! Beautiful! You are welcome! If you will please tell me your name..."

Searingly, Thatcher identified himself, disabused Mr. Diamantis of the notion that he was a potential tourist and demanded news of Kenneth Nicolls.

The phone was not downcast. On the contrary, Lycurgos Diamantis grew a shade more vivacious.

"Ah! Mr. Nicholas. He is a very, very nice man."

Mentally saluting Charlie Trinkam who had been dealing with Greeks for many months without showing signs of strain, Thatcher agreed and indicated that he wanted news of Nicolls' whereabouts.

"Aha!" It was a great light dawning. "One little minute, Mr. Thatchos..."

"Wait..."

But there was a delay, during which Lycurgos Diamantis

ascertained that Kenneth Nicolls was not currently in room 375 of the Britannia. The announcement was muted, tragic.

"What I am trying to learn," said Thatcher, very slowly, "is whether Mr. Nicolls left any information of where he was going."

"Oho!" said Diamantis, again on the upswing.

It took several frustrating moments to establish that no messages were immediately obvious at the desk, nor was there any evidence that the Britannia had arranged a sightseeing tour for Mr. Nicolls. On the contrary, with growing animation, Diamantis assured Thatcher that all of the Britannia's tourists, including 42 Pakistani industrialists, were safe and very, very happy. Diamantis showed an inclination to dwell on this happiness at length, but under prodding, promised to consult colleagues and leave urgent messages for Nicolls. He did this with conspiratorial zest, but his last words were on another subject.

"So please remember, Mr. Thatchos, all Greeks very much like Americans. No reason to not come. See Athens! The Acropolis! Delphi! We will arrange many interesting expeditions, with car and driver..."

Without compunction, Thatcher hung up and, for the first time in many years, mopped his brow.

Charlie grinned at him. "They're a gabby bunch," he said.

"Nicolls is probably trapped somewhere, being talked to death," said Thatcher. "I think that what we do now is wait for him to get in touch with us. In the long run, it will save time. He's bound to get through soon."

He was not the first man to recoil before the onslaught of Greek volubility.

Athens might be very very beautiful, but the Salonika railroad station was not. Dismayed, Ken Nicolls and Stavros Bacharias came to a halt.

"I had not considered... that is... the grounding of planes and these restrictions," Bacharias faltered.

As well he might; the wholesale disruption of transportation in Greece had left the Salonika terminal a howling maelstrom.

Thousands of people paced, stood, slumped, sat, talked, ate and slept. They were on the benches, on the floor, against the walls. All of them radiated a stubborn endurance. Silently Ken followed Stavros Bacharias. The older man led him to a newspaper kiosk.

"Reading material," he suggested, looking around with undisguised horror. "I think you had better prepare yourself. There is certain to be a long wait, a very long wait. I will go to the office to see about your ticket..."

"Don't you want me to go along?"

"It would be better if you remain here. There may be some difficulty." Bacharias was grim. "I had not realized the extent of the crowd. And I had hoped to get you a berth. But now—" He shrugged to end the sentence.

In spite of his common sense, Nicolls found his spirits rising when he examined the kiosk. There were periodicals in English, German, French, Italian, Spanish. And now that he cocked his ear critically he could distinguish amidst the great choral rushes of Greek, antiphonal responses in more familiar languages. This was reassuring. So, too, was the fact that the stallkeeper, who had heard him speaking with Bacharias, addressed him in English.

"It is better to get a book, no? You will want to read a great deal."

Kenneth decided to prepare against all contingencies. He bought the thickest paperback novel available in English, the *New Yorker* and *The Economist*.

"I am going to run out of the *New Yorker* and *Der Spiegel*," the stallkeeper predicted.

"It's good business for you," Kenneth offered.

The stallkeeper duplicated Bacharias' shrug. Then, having established amicable relations, he suggestively advanced a round contribution can as he handed Nicolls some change. Kenneth, embarrassed as always by the smallness of satisfactory contributions in Greece, dutifully dropped in his three drachmas. The stallkeeper handed him a little metal lapel ornament.

"Put it on," he urged. "Then you won't be bothered again."

Kenneth examined the pin first and noted approvingly that it was the sign of the International Red Cross. Now was no time to be advertising himself as a contributor to the Center Union party.

"And a word of advice," the stallkeeper continued. "Keep a hand on your suitcase. The baggage thieves are laying up for their old age tonight."

Ken had been in banking long enough to know that every event, no matter how apocalyptic, finds a reflection in local business practices. He was gripping his case firmly when Bacharias hurried up with a buoyant step.

"It is satisfactory," he reported. "Unfortunately there was no question of a berth. But here is your ticket for a reserved seat. Thus far, there is no announcement of any delay in departure time. Let me show you the waiting room. And then I am afraid, discourteous as it must appear, that I have an engagement."

Warmly, Nicolls rejected the proffered apology. "You have been more than generous with your time and trouble. I have imposed on your good nature." Leonard should hear me now, he thought.

Bacharias sketched delight at having been of service, walked with Nicolls to the waiting room, pointed out the most strategic spot for an alert response to the announcement of the Athens Express and took his leave.

Mentally calling down blessings on the head of an old hand at the Sloan—the one who had advised him to travel with a suitcase which could be sat upon—Kenneth upended his valise near the wall. He had no faith in the punctuality of the Athens Express tonight, nor in the reserved status of his seat. When that train was called, there was going to be a mad stampede which had nothing to do with silly little arrangements by functionnaires. And the train would go out with people hanging from the window sills. Ken flexed his shoulders against their rigid support. His faith lay in a different direction. He was young and strong. Also, he thought as his eyes surveyed the other participants in this mob scene, he was not encumbered by small children, elderly relatives, or miscellaneous household possessions. (Why, he asked himself, did the current emergency make it necessary for that woman over there to carry a large black stove with her?)

A polite Greek voice sounded above his left ear. It came from a small, brisk man busily inserting himself into the space between Nicolls and an adjacent pillar and, no doubt, represented apology for intrusion.

Kenneth edged over companionably. "I'm sorry," he said, ready for conversation, "but I don't speak Greek."

The little man's eyebrows went up. "You are a foreigner? Involved in this?" He spoke English with a fluent competence and a thick accent.

Kenneth was pleased with his luck. All urban Greeks of a certain education speak some foreign language. Too often it was one that Kenneth did not.

He disposed his legs more comfortably and tried to induce a chatty atmosphere. "Foreigners, too, can be caught up in Greece's difficulties," he reminded his companion.

"Of course, yes. How stupid of me. And you are an American, are you not?"

Kenneth knew that this assumption did not evidence an ear for accents, but simply an eye for dacron suits. "Yes. Originally from California," he amplified.

"Ah, California. Then you have something in common with us."

"Yes, we both live in lands of sunshine," Kenneth agreed, not feeling inclined to go into the distinctions between Northern California and Southern California. "But I have left California behind me."

"Naturally. Now you are here, and on your way to Athens. But I hope you have seen some of the beauties of Salonika."

This, as a matter of fact, was Kenneth's first entrance into the city. He had arrived at the airport and been driven straight to Hellenus. And from what he had seen of Salonika so far, he could do without any extension of his knowledge.

"Unfortunately the press of business has prevented me. On my next trip I certainly hope to do so," he said courteously.

"And you must allow me to be your guide," was the polite response. "I am in a favored position when it comes to antiquities. You will find me at this number any day."

The large calling card which on the Continent passes between two professional or business men within seconds of their meeting, was produced. Nicolls furnished his own and then read with interest that his new acquaintance was Dr. Elias Ziros, Senior Archivist at the University of Salonika. The acquaintance, however, was to be short-lived.

"I am afraid I must ask you to excuse me," the archivist murmured. "I see a friend of mine over there, and he seems to be having some difficulty."

It would be exceptional if he were not having difficulty in this madhouse, Nicolls thought, as he settled himself to wait for what the heavens would bring. The fates brought first a married couple on his right, far too preoccupied with their own spitting quarrel to have any time for strangers. Then there came a pallid youth who certainly spoke no English, though it was by no means clear from his total silence and unchanged expression whether he spoke anything at all. After ten minutes of restless straining at some metaphorical leash, the youth departed. It was just as a woman who looked hopeful was disposing her suitcase that Kenneth was again hailed from above. He looked up to find an assortment of soldiers standing before him. The Greek phrase was repeated impatiently. Inspired by the mute performance of his last neighbor, Kenneth simply shook his head. A flush darkened the officer's face. Suddenly the woman, with a quick frightened intake of breath, hissed one word:

"Passport!"

She, too, could recognize a dacron suit.

Kenneth obligingly produced his passport. The officer took one look and frowned.

"American?"

"American."

The officer mentally solved whatever problem he had encountered and spoke briskly.

"You are under arrest. Please follow my men."

With that he turned and marched abruptly off, leaving Kenneth goggling in his wake.

"Arrested!"

He was still gasping as he was unceremoniously hauled to his feet, spilling a welter of reading material at the feet of the lady.

"You had better go with them," she intervened once again.

And go with them, Kenneth did. He was too shocked and incredulous to resist. He was hustled out to some sort of baggage yard before he could recover his breath. When he did recover his breath, it did him no good. The soldiers spoke no English. Nor were they in the mood for questions, it seemed. For when they arrived under the brilliant arc lights, they found another threesome—two more soldiers sandwiching a burly Greek carrying a black medical bag. The doctor was rapidly shouted into silence. He looked as confused as Kenneth felt. They stood in a shuffling, clanking silence as their party was slowly augmented, each time by a threesome. It was with the sixth trio that the officer in charge made his reappearance and Kenneth saw his first familiar face. The figure dwarfed by two soldiers was that of the Senior Archivist, Dr. Elias Ziros. A livid bruise down the side of his face and the heavy panting of his guard suggested that Dr. Ziros was as energetic as he looked.

The officer barked a crisp command into the shadows outside the pool of light. A long black shape moved slowly forward. Kenneth had never seen one before, but he knew that this was Greece's version of the paddy wagon. More unintelligible commands followed. The soldiers lined their charges up in a single file which threw grotesque elongated shadows on the metal siding of the truck. The guards prepared to step aside. Suddenly Kenneth was infuriated at his own docility.

"Now look here—" he began to storm.

A hard hand clamped down on his shoulder in a paralyzing

grip. He swung his head angrily to one side and the guard raised his other hand to strike.

It was then that the single shot rang out.

Ken and the guard stood as if turned to stone. For two long breaths, Kenneth was rigid, convinced in that sickening moment that the shot was a reply to his own insubordination. Then he realized that the others were looking down at the ground.

Looking at Dr. Elias Ziros, sprawled at their feet with half his head shot away.

CHAPTER IV

CLASSICAL RUINS

NOBODY IN THE vicinity of the Sloan Guaranty Trust was wielding firearms, but the situation there was deteriorating as well. Hellenus and the Sloan's investment seemed safe. Still, the news from Greece did not have a happy impact.

The colonels continued their wholesale transport of political opponents, union officials and ex-diplomats to filthy, overcrowded prison camps—and silence. They banned beards and classical plays; they lifted the citizenship of those of their nationals who did not support them. (Those of their nationals abroad, needless to say; those in Greece either kept their mouths shut or ended up in prison.) They banned miniskirts.

"I wish to God," said Thatcher wearily, "that people would stop this nonsense about profits to be made in Pago-Pago and Timbuktu! The best place in the world to make money is the United States! I wish I could get that across to everyone at this bank!"

Walter Bowman and Charlie Trinkam were both familiar with Thatcher's dislike for the new wave in banking. Moreover, they both appreciated the merit of his old-fashioned position. But there are styles in banking as well as haute couture; the Sloan Guaranty Trust was an international power these days.

And as such, Charlie Trinkam pointed out, this meant they had to steel themselves. "After all, John, if the State Department can stomach this, we can!"

Thatcher did not waste more time shooting down that proposition. Instead he reverted to a more immediate concern. The Hellenus situation was critical and the Sloan appeared to have no acting representative on the spot. In the normal course of events, this would have been serious enough; with final ratification in the offing, it was beginning to be more than that.

Kenneth Nicolls had still not been heard from. Fifth Avenue speciality store buyers had relayed tidings of their own safety and the continuing availability of Arachova rugs; domestic science teachers were assuring Congregational authorities that all was well at Patras; stunned parents of smart jet setters were learning that Glyfada was still magnificent.

Under the circumstances, the Sloan Guaranty Trust was disappointed in young Mr. Nicolls. But nobody was bothering with that now; first on the agenda was getting somebody to Athens.

Unfortunately there were other calls on the bull pen. Charlie Trinkam was due to represent the bank at important meetings in Caracas.

"Bah!" said Thatcher, becoming more xenophobic by the moment.

"Everett's in Istanbul," said Charlie quickly. "His bond issue should be just about tied up. Why don't we alert him to stand by, and get over to Athens as soon as he can?"

This, in turn, produced a cable from Turkey.

ANKIST BONDSET STOP PREPATH STOP MAKRIDOUBTER STOP INFOSEEK STOP GABLER

"Oh, for God's sake!" muttered Charlie when Thatcher passed this document on to him.

Everett Gabler's admirable frugality was frequently tinged with parsimony. One of the passions of his life was testing the outer limits of cable code.

Not that translation was difficult; the Ankara-Istanbul monorail debenture arrangements were nearing satisfactory culmination. Gabler was available to move on to Athens. He wanted to know what was going on.

And, being Gabler, he could not help reminding those present of his frequent and bluntly phrased doubts about Hellenus and, more significantly, about Paul Makris & Son. Gabler's doubts were so often in evidence that they did not always carry much weight; this, however, did not keep Everett from citing their presence on the record with great regularity.

"I'll airmail Ev a letter, filling him in," said Charlie resignedly. He had already heard Everett Gabler's views on the whole subject. "Makridoubts! I don't know what Ev has against Paul Makris!"

But he did know, just as Walter Bowman did and John Thatcher did. Paul Makris & Son was a firm of great respectability and financial integrity. Otherwise the Sloan Guaranty Trust and others, including two governments, would not be associated with it. Certainly Makris & Son in Manhattan was an impressive collection of engineers, accountants, consultants—all housed in simple, expensive elegance. Makris' legal affairs were handled by Carruthers and Carruthers, one of Wall Street's doughtiest and staidest law firms. Thatcher knew that Makris Ltd (London) and Makris et Cie (Paris) must be similarly impeccable. Charlie Trinkam had already assured him that Makris & Son (Athens) was the very model of the modern international firm.

It was, despite Everett, all open and aboveboard, as it had been for many years.

Yet, adhering to Makris & Son was the whiff of something else, something elusive, quicksilvery, ephemeral. Was its flexibility too supple for Wall Street? The quickness that had something of the cobra's strike about it? Thatcher had heard others besides Everett Gabler hint darkly that the Makris empire was like an iceberg, seven-eighths hidden from view.

Thatcher himself continued to believe, quite privately, that Paul Makris, who was small, sallow, totally bald and pleasantly reserved, encouraged this reputation. It was worth millions.

"No matter what Everett thinks about Makris, he'll go in once the negotiations begin! Now, I propose to forget about Greece for a while!"

They scattered, returning to their routine chores and wrenching their attention away from Greece according to ability. The looming menace of Caracas and volatile oil interests made it reasonably easy for Trinkam. Walter Bowman got caught up in a complex and felonious situation unfolding, with SEC assistance, on the American Exchange.

But John Thatcher was scheduled to lunch in the executive suite with the Sloan's president, Bradford Withers, and to think of Withers was to think of foreign climes. Temporarily at loose ends, he was currently occupying his magnificent offices at the bank, but he was certainly the prize world traveler on the premises.

"Greece?" Withers asked vaguely, interrupted in his measured denunciation of New York weather. "I make it a point to drop in whenever I'm in the vicinity. Did I tell you about the time Carrie and I were having tea with the king?"

Realistically, Thatcher wrote off Withers as a source of useful information. This was a shame, he thought; given normal perceptions and a very mild interest in banking, Withers could justify his endless peripatetics by producing a serious challenge to the research department's intelligence-gathering prowess.

But Walter Bowman and his staff were in no immediate danger.

"... seemed like a very nice chap," Withers was saying.

Hastily, Thatcher apologized and asked who this particular nice chap was.

"That economist fellow they've arrested. He had just come back to Greece when Carrie and I were there, and we had tea with him and the king! Now he's in jail! He didn't look like a radical to me, John, although they tell me he taught up at Harvard before he went out to California."

Thatcher was not fool enough to interject a comment.

"Some of our Greek friends told us," Withers confided, "that all the trouble began when the young man picked up an American wife!"

As might be expected, this told Thatcher more about Bradford Withers and Carrie than about the reform movement in Greece.

Later that afternoon, however, he was privileged to get more useful tidings.

Looking mildly pleased, Miss Corsa announced an overseas call.

"Nicolls," Thatcher told himself with pleasure. He liked to see the Sloan's young men performing creditably. Not even garbled remarks from London and Geneva dulled this satisfaction.

It was certainly a wholesome American voice that ultimately greeted him. But it did not belong to Kenneth Nicolls.

"Mr. Thatcher? This is Riemer, from the Embassy. The Ambassador asked me to get through to you, sir. Something rather strange has come up here, and we thought you should be informed immediately."

"Yes," said Thatcher encouragingly.

Riemer, distant and mildly apologetic, was also, it seemed, desperately tired. At any rate, he had trouble forming sentences.

"It's the police. I mean the civil police, not the military. We've just had a visit from them..."

"Go on," Thatcher said tightly.

There was a buzz. Then Riemer said:

"They want to question Kenneth Nicolls about a murder."

"What!"

"Now, we're not altogether sure of what has happened," Riemer said earnestly, "but the story seems to be that the police—the civil—oh, I already explained that, didn't I—well, the civil police have found a corpse!"

Now it was Thatcher who could not form a sentence.

Riemer continued.

"Shot, as I understand it. Well, it's all very confusing, but the police say they want to know about a business card they found on the body. 'Kenneth Nicolls' it says 'Sloan Guaranty Trust.'"

As the crumpled body of Dr. Elias Ziros lay untidily on the asphalt, confusion reigned in the baggage yard of the Salonika railroad station. It was fully a minute before Kenneth could think clearly enough to realize that not one of the soldiers held a gun. At the same moment that his own jarred faculties returned to life, the officer exploded into action. Barking at his subordinates, he himself ran to the body, now lapped in an enormous pool of blood. The subordinates, in their turn, barked.

Kenneth did not understand a word, but a rifle butt in the kidneys is an infallible communication device. Almost without knowing it, he was being propelled into the wagon. His fellow prisoners were less recalcitrant. Once they grasped the fact that someone out there was shooting prisoners, their desire to put sheet steel between themselves and the world outstripped that of their captors. The doors banged closed within seconds of Kenneth's entrance, a heavy metal bar dropped into place and they were in motion.

There was no light in the interior of the wagon and no windows. The five prisoners were in total darkness. To add to their discomfort, the driver switched on his siren and proceeded to take the corners of downtown Salonika with demonic abandon. His passengers caromed off the walls and off each other like so many billiard balls. Even when they were all on the floor, the sudden sharp tilts piled them mercilessly into one corner after another.

Kenneth Nicolls tried to persuade himself that these things could not possibly be happening to him. He was a respectable banker, progressing steadily, if not brilliantly, in his chosen profession. His evil genius at this point was prompted to recall some of the folklore of the Sloan Guaranty Trust. It was Innes, the bank's South American specialist, who had escaped, by the skin of his teeth, achieving international fame as the first Wall Street banker to be shot by Venezuelan security forces as an anti-American revolutionary. Innes, himself, had been less concerned by the closeness of his brush with death than by the implied criticism of his appearance.

"I ask you, in God's name I ask you," he had stormed upon his safe return, "do I look like a guerrilla?"

For once a question couched in these terms could be answered without evasion. Innes, in Homburg and charcoal grey, did not look like a guerrilla. Incongruously Kenneth was reminded that he himself was getting to look more and more like a desperado. Now that he came to think of it, all his spare clothing, like his reading material, reposed at the feet of an unknown lady in that hellish railroad station that they were so rapidly leaving behind.

It was not until they were on the Athens–Salonika highway that conditions in the truck improved enough to permit speech. He was indebted to an English-speaking neighbor for the information.

"They are taking us to Larissa," said the unknown alertly. "That is military headquarters for the North of Greece. There they will undoubtedly shoot us."

This calm declaration produced a howl of protest from a further corner, a howl that resolved itself into a torrent of yet another unfamiliar language. Finally the speaker controlled himself and resorted to English.

"They cannot shoot me! I am a Turk! An innocent Turkish tobacco buyer. Istanbul will never tolerate such an atrocity."

Kenneth's neighbor, who had appointed himself an all-purpose translator, spoke briefly in Greek. His fellow-countrymen responded vigorously.

"They say that if we are to talk of atrocities, Istanbul has much to answer for."

"Are we then in the nineteenth century?" demanded the Turk passionately. "No! I repeat, my government will not permit this!"

More Greek.

"They say," said the interpreter with bright detachment, "that that is not how things are done anymore. The Greek Army saves itself unnecessary trouble. They do not tell Istanbul they are going to shoot you. First, they shoot you. Then they apologize to Istanbul and say it was all a mistake. They mistook you for a Greek. What government is going to waste time protecting the rights of a dead national? It would be wasteful, deplorably wasteful."

The Turk became inarticulate in his protestations. He could scarcely have felt worse at this disclosure of Greek practices than Ken Nicolls. For one glorious moment there had been a vision of a warm, protecting American ambassador. That vision died a quick death. Where, thought Kenneth savagely, is our much-vaunted technical progress? In the nineteenth century, an Englishman could fall afoul of the Ottoman Empire and, in spite of the weeks necessary for communication, London would learn of his peril and dispatch a leisurely gunboat which would arrive in time to effect his rescue. And rightly so, thought Kenneth, whose views on gunboat diplomacy were becoming more imperial by the minute. But now, in the midst of radio, telephone, nuclear submarines and Telstar, what happens? He was going to be shot out of hand and then the Greek Army would explain that all along they thought he was Andreas Papandreou. Unless, of course, they had already shot Papandreou, in which case it would be embarrassing to explain away two of them. But they had made some six thousand arrests already. There was an almost unlimited number of Greeks, undesirable in the eyes of the present *de facto* government, for whom Kenneth Nicolls could be conveniently mistaken.

The interpreter was trying to calm the Turk by the force of pure reason, never a wise proceeding.

"You saw what they did to the old one, did you not? Shot him out of hand. Why, then, do you say they cannot do it to us?"

"That poor old one," declaimed the Turk emotionally. "I was speaking to him ten minutes before he was shot. I even gave him my copy of *Der Spiegel*."

Kenneth's head swung up suddenly. He broke in without hesitation. "But I spoke with Dr. Ziros only about twenty minutes or so before I was arrested. Quick, ask the others, if they had anything to do with him."

The interpreter was so excited that he almost forgot his self-appointed mission. "But I too... no, wait, I must tell the others."

The babble of interest presently arising made it clear that Kenneth had hit the nail on the head.

"They say they all spoke with him at the station. The doctor here had coffee with him at the snack bar. And I myself met him at the information window. That is very good." The interpreter sounded genuinely pleased. "You have given us a reason for this occurrence. Why should the military go into a crowded railroad station, seize four Greeks, a Turk and an American at random and proceed to shoot them? It is nonsensical. But now we know that it was not at random. They simply watched Elias Ziros, then seized him and everyone with whom he spoke. That explains everything!" he ended on a note of triumph.

Nicolls was unable to join the triumph. He did not want reasons; he wanted rescue.

"It is monstrous!" said the Turk roundly.

A rumbling from the medical man expressed equal disapproval.

"He is from Athens," the interpreter explained. "He says what can you expect from Macedonians and Thessalonians. They are all barbarians. I am a Macedonian myself. I understand the problem. It is all because the coup was made by the colonels instead of the generals."

"I'm afraid I don't understand," said Ken wearily.

"It is simple. Everyone has a coup ready to prevent Papandreou from winning the May elections. That is, everyone on the right. The National Radical Union party has a coup ready, the king and the generals have a coup, and these miserable colonels have a coup. Now, if the king and the generals have their coup, what happens? Everything stays the same, is it not so? The party stays in power, the king stays on his throne, the generals and the colonels stay generals and colonels. So everyone is happy! No one is nervous! There is no need to shoot!"

"But," said Ken, faint but pursuing, "if Papandreou was going to win the election, then most of the electorate is unhappy."

"Oh, that!" said the other airly. "People may want something new, but they don't become genuinely unhappy unless you take away what they already have. And that is what has happened. Look! The party people are in jail. The king doesn't know what's going to happen to him. And even a general knows something's wrong when the colonels are running the country."

"Yes, yes, I can see that."

"So what happens? The generals want to crush the colonels, the colonels know it and are nervous. The result is that we get shot! Now what kind of a coup is that?"

"A totally unsatisfactory one," Ken had no hesitation in replying.

This satisfied his companion, who then diverted the stream of his lucidity to the other Greeks. Ken was left to the only constructive exercise he could think of, namely reviewing his formidable life insurance coverage for the benefit of his wife and children. He was certainly not going to waste the few remaining hours of his life trying to penetrate the thickets of Grecian politics. As part of his conscientious preparation for his first overseas assignment he had reviewed the economic and social reforms proposed by the younger Papandreou, and they had not startled him by their wildly Marxian flavour.

But he was through with that kind of idiot conscientiousness. Cliff Leonard knew nothing about Greece. He would emerge from the coup alive. A little of that sort of detachment might mean some hope for Nicolls. This was an avowedly rightist government. He was a representative from the bastion of capitalism. If he got the slightest chance, he was going to have to push himself as a bloated capitalist, a prop to fading monarchies and *arrivist* military juntas. Being from America wasn't going to get him anywhere. Being from Wall Street might possibly save his neck.

This possibility he did not care to measure in statistical terms. It would probably work out at something like one in ten thousand. The overriding probability was that he would be hauled out of this wagon and shot before he could find anyone who spoke English. Nicolls set his teeth grimly. He had damn well better shout, then. It might bring the odds up to two in ten thousand.

It was just as well that Kenneth had set his teeth. It would have helped if he had braced his legs as well. Suddenly, without warning, there was a tremendous jolt which brought them all sliding forward in their billiard game again as the truck smashed to a halt. Then, even more terrifying, the whole body of the truck seemed to rise on its springs and leap lightheartedly up and down like a joyous young elephant trying out pogo sticks. The steel plating groaned and cracked like pistol shots as the successive stresses weakened its fabric. Then there was one last furious report, and a cool lash of air entered with a view of starlit sky. One of the rear doors sagged drunkenly from its remaining hinge.

Shakily they began to rise and make their way backward, clutching at smooth walls for support.

"I don't know what this is all about," the interpreter whispered, his brightness finally and entirely deflated, "but me, I leave while I have the chance."

He spoke for all of them. Willing shoulders pushed the half doors open. For a moment they hesitated, trying to make out how much the truck was canted over in the uncertain light. Then, as they dropped to the ground, it heaved galvanically upward to meet them.

"Oh, my God," screamed the Turk in startled horror. "It's an earthquake!"

CHAPTER V

O ATTIC SHAPE!

"... *a tremor of three on the Richter scale,*" read Charlie Trinkam aloud. "*Fordham University experts say this indicates moderate-to-severe earth tremors rather than a major earthquake* ..."

Walter Bowman was pursuing another account. "Here, listen to this!" he interrupted, "*According to Greek military authorities, there have been many casualties, although the exact number is not yet known. Communications have been disrupted. The injured and homeless* ..."

He continued through ruined bridges, impenetrable passes and blocked roads while Charlie located the follow-up story in the inner portions of the *Times*. "... *the Red Cross, medical teams and aid from nearby U.S. military installations airlifted to stricken areas* ..."

Accompanying this melancholy recital was steady pelting rain.

"Yes, yes," said Thatcher, gazing at the blurred window pane. "I gather that a small portion of Greece has been shaken by an earthquake—oh, all right, Charlie, a moderate-to-severe earth tremor. Frankly, I cannot see why it has made such a large impression."

On balance, Thatcher was inclined to worry more about the announcement that Kenneth Nicolls' business card had been found on a body in the Salonika railroad yards than about seismological oddities. No explanation immediately suggested itself, but Nicolls' unavailability was now something more than one of the inevitable disadvantages of doing business abroad. Possibly it was more menacing. The U.S. Embassy agreed. No sooner had Mr. Riemer relayed his tidings than mighty wheels began turning, telephones began ringing and officialdom was alerted. But unfortunately, while questions were raised in many circles, answers were not forthcoming.

"Ziros. Elias Ziros," repeated an aide of Colonel Patakos. "Outrageous! But my government knows nothing! No, nothing at all!"

The American Embassy sternly told itself that what happened to Greeks was not its proper concern. It continued to express anxiety about Kenneth Nicolls.

"How do we know?" screeched the aide. "We find his card on a body! Then he disappears! No, we know nothing of where he is. Yes, of course we seek him! But these are busy days! We seek many people..."

Private enterprise, like the Government, was worrying about Kenneth Nicolls. In the Athens office of Paul Makris & Son, a man gaped at the phone unbelievingly.

"And he's from the Sloan? You're sure of that?" he demanded.

His informant produced solemn assurances.

"And the Army simply drove away? There's got to be more to it than that. It sounds like a conspiracy to me."

The informant said it usually was these days.

"You're going to have to find out," the man said firmly. "And fast!" He put down the receiver with an authority that bordered on incivility.

But there his decisiveness ended. For a moment he stared blankly out the window, many thoughts revolving in his mind. Going to a row of file cabinets by the wall, he removed a folder and studied it, looking for something that was not there. The frown on his face deepened steadily.

Without knowing it, he started to scrawl a list on the desk pad.

Hellenus—sixteen million!
Sloan
Coup d'état
May 17
Demetrios?

As he finished the last word, the point of his pencil broke and he threw it from him with an impatient exclamation. Then, reluctantly, as if it were something he had been putting off, he reached for the phone and started to dial a number that set a buzzer ringing in a palatial villa twenty miles from Athens.

"Paul?" he asked, then broke off. It was a moment before he went on jerkily. "It's come. What you were waiting for. The Army arrested a man from the Sloan. And Demetrios!"

"Aha!" the telephone said thoughtfully, then asked if he knew more.

"Not yet. If he is still alive, we will soon hear. You know we can trust Demetrios."

"I hope so. I hope so very much."

When it was borne in upon the Sloan Guaranty Trust that one of its young men was currently being hunted by the Greek Government, Thatcher thought that George C. Lancer, Chairman of the Board, might forget his commitment to international peace. Indeed, at one point, Thatcher found himself defending the current state of affairs.

"No, no, George," he told his fulminating chief. "I'm convinced this is a simple mixup, of some sort. Of course, George! The Greek Government has assured us most solemnly that they will contact us as soon as they locate Nicolls. No doubt this unfortunate earthquake has made communication... er... even more dubious..."

"Let them," George Lancer growled, "let them harm one hair of his head!"

Scratch a foreign policy thinker, Thatcher reflected, and you find John Paul Jones.

Yet despite his soft words in the board room, Thatcher was not happy with the latest turn of events. Nor was Charlie Trinkam.

"It sounds to me," Charlie said glumly, "as though somehow Ken stumbled into one of their goddam political messes. But what the hell was he up to?"

"And," asked Walter Bowman, raising the question nobody wanted to contemplate, "where is he now?"

Charlie was beginning to feel the burden of guilt. "How is Jane Nicolls taking this latest?" he asked.

"She's a level-headed young woman," said Thatcher evasively. "Naturally, she's concerned. But she's taking heart from the Embassy reports that no Americans have been hurt in the earthquake. And I haven't felt it necessary to inform her about this—this murdered man!"

"I should hope not!" said Charlie Trinkam, horrified.

Pityingly, Thatcher looked at him. "Charlie, we might as well be realistic. We may have to break even worse news to Jane Nicolls."

Distraught, Charlie ran a shaking hand through his hair.

"Why the hell? ... Listen, I'll scrub this trip to Caracas. I'd better fly to Athens to find Ken myself. God knows what the Embassy is doing. And things are beginning to look lousy."

He was offering himself as a human sacrifice. Or, perhaps a hostage to uncertain Greek fortune. Thatcher was patience itself.

"Charlie, you're going to Caracas if I have to put you on the plane myself," said Thatcher. "God knows what's going to happen to Hellenus! I don't want a Greek revolution to play havoc with our South American operations, too! Now, why don't you two get some work done while I check around again..."

In short, by virtue of the prerogatives of seniority, Thatcher managed to speed Trinkam and Bowman back to their desks. He could do without their keening and lamentation. His own predilection was to reduce complexities to manageable proportions. But, such simplification left him more disquieted than he cared to confess. Rightly or wrongly, he could dismiss Greek political upheaval as irrelevant. Rightly or wrongly, he could dismiss Greek earthquakes as fortuitous. Yet pruning only emphasized the stark outlines of the basic question:

Where was Kenneth Nicolls?

Thatcher swiveled around to gaze bleakly at the continuing

downpour. If Nicolls had fallen before revolutionary bayonets or before seismic disaster, then all the telephone calls in the world were futile; there was nothing that the Sloan Guaranty Trust—or anybody—could do.

Quite automatically, Thatcher turned back to his desk and to his responsibilities.

"Miss Corsa," he told the intercom without emotion, "will you send off that cable to Gabler? Tell him to proceed directly to Athens. We'll forward instructions about Hellenus. And circulate the usual memos, Miss Corsa."

Almost immediately, he was back staring at the endless gray of the New York afternoon. No matter what happened to Kenneth Nicolls, the Sloan Guaranty Trust and Hellenus must continue. Having taken steps to insure this, Thatcher returned to the problem at hand.

One trouble, among many, was the number of lips mouthing the same meaningless sentiments.

"No Americans are involved."

Come hell or high water, that was about the best the Athens Embassy could do.

"Progress at Hellenus is expected to continue."

So said governments, economists and assorted technicians.

"Greece is peaceful, happy and welcomes American tourists."

And was that the way a colonel should talk?

"Bah!" said Thatcher disagreeably. A brief review of the pronunciamentos from the other side shed no further light.

"Free Papandreou!"

"Democracy is Dead in Greece!"

What he needed, Thatcher realized, was a disinterested, fresh, and above all, different view of Greece.

No sooner had this notion visited him than he was struck with one of those sudden unwelcome insights into exactly where his duty lay.

Without enthusiasm, Thatcher returned to the intercom.

"Miss Corsa, will you please get my daughter for me?"

"Of course, those saddles take some getting used to," Cardwell Carlson was saying. Click. Click. "Here's a good shot of Agnes. We're going up to Mychrovladas to see the ruins." Click. Click. "Oh, here's a good one. That old fellow is the man who owned the donkey. Now this will amuse you..."

Thatcher shifted slightly in the darkness of his daughter's large recreation room and reflected philosophically that all of this was his own fault.

Professor Cardwell Carlson, now happily installed amidst several thousand dollars worth of photographic equipment, was training brilliant pools of color onto the large screen. He was the noted classicist of Columbia University, editor of a new edition of Menander, indefatigable contributor to Studies in Classical Epigraphy and well known as a controversialist in the columns of *Die Fragmente der Griechischen Historiker*.

He was the father of Dr. Ben Carlson, Laura's husband; he was fundamentally an admirable man, kindhearted to a fault, generous, enthusiastic and even-tempered.

He was also appallingly long-winded.

When Thatcher joined family holiday gatherings he tended to devote most of his attention to his grandsons.

"Now, here's our hotel room in Sparta," Carlson was saying happily.

Laura had more of her late mother in her than she realized, Thatcher reflected. She was genuinely delighted to inject a dinner for the grandparents into her busy life, but she did want to know why. She had already assimilated her father's very moderate appreciation of Cardwell Carlson's extended analyses of whatever situations were current.

"Oh, Greece!" she had said upon hearing Thatcher's cautious explanation. "Father Carlson knows all about Greece."

At the time, these words struck Thatcher as ominous. But as usual, reality outstripped his direst forebodings. Upon learning of Thatcher's interest in Greece, Professor Carlson had taken the trouble to equip himself. In addition to large and cumbrous machines, which he lugged in from the car with unfeigned pleasure, he had brought slides.

Thousands of them.

Laura had produced an excellent dinner, deftly dispatched the children to distant places, borne off her mother-in-law (both ladies having seen the slides before) and left the gentlemen with coffee, brandy and a veritable library of transparencies, each one of which elicited happy memories and exhaustive explanations from Cardwell Carlson.

Thatcher had now been part of a colorful wedding party in Crete—"You've never seen such dancing. Here, let me go back. Look at those coins. The women, you see..." He had eaten delicious *dolmades* in a taverna in Nauplia—"Otto of Bavaria, you know. Beautiful harbor. It's a shame that I overexposed this one..." He had uncovered a third-century thimble in excavations near Mycenae—"There, down in the corner, you can see that little spot, can't you? Well, just a few minutes later, Pezmoglu brought up..."

Now he was climbing a mountain aboard a donkey. Sidesaddle.

"Yes, yes," said Thatcher, duty bound to prove that he was awake at intervals. "I can see that it is a spectacular country. What I wanted..."

"It's unbelievable," said Cardwell Carlson, causing Greek Islands to pound after each other in a dazzling kaleidoscope of blues. "Of course, you can't really catch the color, even with the best of film. Now here. You see that door? Well, that door was really more of a crimson. Not the coppery color that I've got here..."

When, at long last, the lights came on, Cardwell Carlson rested from his labors, refreshed himself with a brandy, and moved on to analysis of the Greek ethos.

"...a truly simple, unspoiled peasantry. Why, John, as you walk along a village street, small children come out to give you flowers. Poor as they are, they want to share what few things they have. You know, of course, that the word for stranger is also the word for guest."

"Of course," murmured Thatcher drowsily. He was trying to muster enough energy to ask Carlson about the less exclusively rural aspects of modern Greece. But Ben's father, frowning into the brandy, swept on:

"I have always deplored the overemphasis on the mercantile aspects of the Greek character," he said with classroom judiciousness. "In part, I've always thought, it was because of the tremendous energy of the Greeks in America. I don't know whether you've ever realized, John, but most of them have tended to go into business."

Perhaps feeling that this was beyond Thatcher's grasp, he expanded: "I mean, they haven't become farmers."

"So few people have," said Thatcher with admirable self-restraint.

"But I feel that this has distorted our view of Greece," Carlson ruminated. "Perhaps putting undue emphasis on the materialistic. But in Greece—and Agnes will bear me out—there is still a strong sense of the spiritual, non-material basis for values. There is a real disposition to explore human relations. I have seen a simple, humble peasant stopping to smell a rose..."

For a rocky spread of land notable for its lack of fertility, Greece seemed to be strong on flowers, Thatcher reflected. Not that he believed for a moment that the inhabitants of the country spent as much time sniffing blossoms or distributing them to passing strangers as Carlson believed. But then, he did not believe the word picture that was slowly unfolding; a happy, healthy peasantry, breaking into colorful dances at the drop of a handkerchief; noble intellectuals indifferent to sordid gain and advancement; brawny sailors who dreamed only of returning to their native isles.

Thatcher should have known all along. Asking Cardwell Carlson about labor conditions, hydroelectric plants or taxes in Greece would simply be unkind. As far as Cardwell Carlson was concerned, if you couldn't record it on film, it wasn't Greek.

"...my one fear," said Carlson, just as the ladies rejoined them.

"Oh, what was that?"

"I wouldn't like to see Greece Americanized," said Cardwell Carlson.

"But why are you interested in Greece, John?" asked Agnes Carlson, a plump and efficient creature who managed her husband kindly and thoroughly. "Are you thinking of making a trip?"

"At the moment," said Thatcher with truth, "nothing could be further from my thoughts."

By the next morning, Thatcher saw Charlie Trinkam off to Venezuela with real relief. As news of earthquake victims trickled across the wires without uncovering a Ken Nicolls or anyone who sounded remotely like him, Charlie might have been expected to grow slightly less lugubrious. On the contrary, he seemed to be taking the position that no news was bad news; Thatcher in fact suspected that he was harboring saintly thoughts about devoting the rest of his life (and earnings) to the avuncular care of Jane Nicolls and her children.

Ignoring the atmosphere of incipient martyrdom, Thatcher produced the cable just received from Everett Gabler. Deciphered, it reported that Gabler was ready to depart for Athens. He was going to interview the police, and everybody else he could find. He wanted preliminary drafts of all agreements that Nicolls had been carrying. He would keep in touch.

Thatcher rather hoped that this impressive combat readiness would spark the competitor in Trinkam. If it did, it was only briefly.

"I'll bet the food will play hell with Ev's stomach," said Charlie, cheering for a moment. "But, you know, that's what Ken said. That he'd keep in touch. I hope to God that Ev doesn't drop into a pit, too. Now, listen John, you'll keep me up to date, won't you? I can always jet back..."

"You don't want to miss your plane," said Thatcher, firmly escorting him out into the hallway and as far as the elevator. "You will be the first to hear any good news."

"And bad news too," said Charlie Trinkam.

"Oh, get out of here!"

When Thatcher got back to his office, he addressed an editorial aside to Miss Corsa. "I certainly hope that the bright lights of Caracas bring Trinkam back to his senses."

Miss Corsa, who disapproved of bright lights on principle, honored Mr. Trinkam for his feelings in the matter of Mr. Nicolls' inexplicable disappearance. But she had well-founded doubts about overnight conversions. She compromised by looking rather reproachful. Whatever she might have been going to say was forestalled. Walter Bowman burst into the office behind Thatcher. Something had restored his normal spirits. As Thatcher suspected, it was a piece of news.

"John," he said portentously. "One of my people has just picked up a rumor. Paul Makris is back in town."

Miss Corsa had, after all, borne the brunt of the local discomfort caused by the Greek imbroglio. She turned the full force of her redoubtable personality on Bowman and punctured his pretensions with a few well-chosen words.

"As I was about to say, Mr. Thatcher," she reported, "I've just taken a message requesting you to call Mr. Paul Makris, at your convenience."

Bowman was too big a man to let this stealing of his thunder deflect him. He plunged into active speculation.

"I wonder what that means," he said. "You know, I had the impression that Makris himself was in Athens. Not that you could get anything out of his office. They keep pretty close-mouthed about his comings and goings. But he wants you to get in touch, does he? I wonder what that means."

Among other things, it meant lunch. Two hours later, Thatcher sat across the table from Paul Makris. They were in the unexotic quarters of the Bankers Club and Makris, a spare contained man, had greeted Thatcher with standard business courtesy. It was all a great relief from the Byzantine suspicion prevailing at the Sloan. But, Thatcher noticed, they were drawing attention. Makris always did.

The phenomenon of Paul Makris would not have raised so much speculation on Wall Street if he had appeared on the American scene in one of the two standard ways—arriving on

Ellis Island as a penniless youth in the twenties or steaming into New York Harbor in the owner's suite of his oil line's flagship.

Instead, he had arisen like a phoenix after the Second World War. Not from ashes, however, but from a modestly prosperous trading business in Beirut. The original small office in New York had grown into a world-wide empire, much respected up and down the Street. Makris, himself, remained a man of mystery. True, he spoke excellent and idiomatic English. But he was said to speak five other languages as fluently. What could be more sinister?

Thatcher was inclined to think his colleagues were succumbing to a romantic stereotype. Wall Street had simply forgotten that there are middle-class Greeks.

"I thought we might meet informally to discuss Hellenus," said Makris with a faint smile. "I know our subordinates have everything in hand. But there are a few things I felt I'd like to discuss with you."

While Thatcher was not one of those who saw Machiavellian cunning writ large on Makris, or on Makris & Son, he still did not believe that Paul Makris was the man to delegate responsibility for multimillion dollar projects.

"I'm delighted to discuss Hellenus with you," he said neutrally. "As you perhaps know, Everett Gabler is on his way to Athens and he'll be representing the Sloan in the final negotiations next month."

"Ah," said Makris. Now this was no more than a slight indication of information received. But since Wall Street is not a community in which people frequently indulge themselves this way, Thatcher thought he saw one reason why Paul Makris was looked upon as a strange and enigmatic figure. Well, he was not going to play that game.

"Of course, you will have heard that at the Sloan we're having communications difficulties. We haven't heard from our representative in Athens since the Army took over. Everybody assures us that there is no likelihood of serious mishap."

Makris concentrated on an indifferent shrimp cocktail. "Yes,

I had heard something about your Mr. Nicolls. It is very strange. Although from all that I hear..." he broke off for a moment, then continued, "but Mr. Nicolls is one reason that I wanted to discuss things with you, Mr. Thatcher."

Thatcher listened with care as Makris went on:

"I have myself been out of town for the last few days." Makris very deliberately did not say where he had been.

Had Thatcher been a lesser man he might have countered with an *Ah* of his own.

"... but of course, because of my special interest in Greece, I do keep in touch with developments. It now appears that Hellenus will be able to continue, without any radical changes occasioned by this new regime."

Thatcher, in turn, picked his words carefully.

"That certainly is our impression, and I am glad to hear you say so as well. But it may be too early to make assumptions of that sort. There has been a total overthrow of the government, with political prisoners, censorship and suspension of the constitution. It seems to me that it would not be surprising to expect more changes—of one sort or another—in the next few months. I am not certain where any such changes will leave Hellenus."

Makris looked up at that. "You think so? Interesting, very interesting. But of course, at the moment we are committed to Hellenus..."

"It is certainly too late for us to pull out now," said Thatcher.

"Indeed. Oh, indeed. But, as I was saying, at the moment our investment in Hellenus seems safe enough. You agree? Good. That is why I am... slightly concerned about this one unsettling feature."

Thatcher suddenly sensed wariness. For some reason, Makris was projecting extreme caution. Thatcher hastily repressed a smile; possibly someone over at Makris & Son had warned Makris that John Thatcher of the Sloan was a deep one, an international banker, a man to be approached with utmost caution.

"Am I correct then in assuming that you have not heard from Athens today?" Makris asked suddenly. "No? Then your Embassy will no doubt be in touch with you soon. Or perhaps your Mr. Gabler when he arrives," said Makris, crumbling a roll. "But I have associates in many places in Athens."

"I do not doubt it," said Thatcher.

"Last night," Makris said, "somebody broke into the Hotel Britannia, into the room of your Mr. Nicolls. Oddly enough, nothing was stolen. As I understand it, the room was simply searched. According to these . . . er . . . reports . . . it would appear that somebody was looking for something."

It was Thatcher's practice to maintain silence in the face of totally meaningless data. But now, with Makris' close-set eyes unblinkingly fixed on him, some response was necessary.

"I wonder what it could be," he said without emphasis.

Makris looked at him quickly, then, as quickly, away.

"I am sure you do, Mr. Thatcher. Just as I do."

CHAPTER VI

THE MOUNTAINS LOOK ON MARATHON

CAUGHT BETWEEN TWIN perils of earthquake and firing squad, Kenneth Nicolls and his fellow prisoners did not linger at the scene of the crash. They could see that the cab of the wagon had crumpled against an uprooted tree leaning across the road. The Greek doctor, after fumbling for several moments through the twisted window frame, announced that the driver and guard were dead. Then he leaned further inside. When he re-emerged from the cab he was holding a dark object which clinked dully metallic as it glanced off the door jamb. Suddenly the interpreter hissed and gestured frantically backward. Far down the darkened highway, regularly spaced headlights heralded the approach of a military convoy. With one accord the five men dived for the embankment by the road.

In his first frenzied rush, Ken was conscious of nothing but approaching menace—the threat of more soldiers, more guns and, if the action of the Greek doctor had any meaning, more shooting. He hauled himself up the embankment, hand over hand, snatching blindly at stubby undergrowth, sometimes missing and slipping back on the shale underfoot, but always thrashing out for a new hold. Only when he fell to his knees did he realize that he was over the top. Without pause he rose to a standing crouch and set forth in a broken run. The ground was uneven. One arm protected his head from the branches that whipped aside under the impetus of his charge and then swung back, scratching and grating along his sleeve. He fell several times, but thrust himself up and forward in one unbroken movement, driven by his fear of a search party fanning out from the site of the wreck.

He never knew how long that first insane dash lasted. Conscious thought returned only when he fell for what must have been the fourth or fifth time. When he tried to regain his feet, he fell immediately.

"Hell! Now I've had it. Something's twisted or broken, and I can't run anymore."

Almost with relief, he lay full length, his laboring lungs gasping for air, his pulses hammering in his chest and throat and head. Only when the roaring subsided did he make a discovery.

It was not he who was unsteady: it was the earth itself. The tremors that he attributed to his own weakness were being reinforced by tremors from the ground he was embracing. Then he remembered what the approaching convoy had made him forget. He was in the middle of an earthquake. Cautiously he raised himself on one elbow. He tried to remember what it had been like in the truck. Even allowing for the force of the collision, that had been a longer and mightier shock. With luck, the earthquake was abating. Or, he thought grimly, gathering itself for the final, devastating blow.

Shaken, he rose first to his knees, then to his feet. He could not protect himself from the elements. But they were proving to be a godsend, as far as his human enemies were concerned. The earthquake had made a good start by wrecking that damned paddy wagon. Now it was undoubtedly raining rocks and trees onto the road. With luck, the convoy had been halted. At the very least, any search for him was more complicated. The only course open now was to count his blessings and forge ahead, getting as far from that highway as possible under the shelter of night. Tomorrow morning, if he was still alive and at large, would be the time to think.

Belatedly, he realized he must avoid the perils of a circular course and scanned the dim starlit sky. But Kenneth Nicolls was a city man; the stars to him were a decorative lacy display, not a navigational aid. He ended by placing his dependence on a steady ascent, always aiming for high ground. Twice he was interrupted by additional tremors, but they were mild compared with what had gone before. He regarded them almost gratefully as long as he could think at all. But his stumbling run became a dogged walk, then a drunken lurching.

"I've got to keep going until morning," he told himself.

But an hour before the first pinkness streaked across the east, exhaustion brought him to his knees. After two or three attempts to rise, he rolled over, surrendering himself to a blackness darker than the surrounding night.

It was high noon when he woke to pain, and a raging thirst. His last act had been to slide into a clump of scraggly trees with a carpeting of undergrowth, so that only now was the sun penetrating his retreat. In confusion he tried to take stock of himself. His suit was a motley of rents and tears held together by a mass of dust, blood, and creases. Memory came rushing back, and with it came caution. Quickly he scanned his surroundings. But the stony landscape slumbered peacefully in the sunlight, devoid alike of sound and movement. He levered himself upright and essayed a cautious movement. He realized that his limbs however stiff and aching were in working order. There was nothing to prevent his proceeding at the pace of an arthritic and elderly man.

"But move where?" he asked himself.

That question answered itself. His first need was water. Within half an hour he was kneeling beside a spring freshet that tumbled briskly over moss-covered boulders in a hidden fold of the hillside.

Drinking greedily, he realized he had been lucky so far. He could not hope to move stealthily over this countryside in full daylight. The Greek Army was probably quartering the hills this very minute. And there were no long vistas to warn him of a search party. Soldiers could be within arms' reach before he knew it. On the horizon a man with binoculars could be waiting patiently. Every time Ken budged, he risked observation. A single glance would tell any hidden watcher that the missing American had been found. The safe course was to travel by night.

Ken passed the afternoon, holed up by his stream in a convenient thicket. As the hours passed he learned that the countryside was not as deserted as it seemed. Two men in country clothes passed, loping along silently, intent on some errand. The afternoon silence was broken once by a woman calling musically in the distance. An approaching clatter, some time later, resolved itself into a boy running with a stick in his hand, rubbing it against tree trunks and the spiky shrubbery. All this Ken watched, but he himself came in for attention only once. While he was listening to the woman, a friendly butt pitched him forward on his face. Turning, he found himself being inspected by a very curious and smelly goat. She obviously identified him as an alien intruder into her world and a welcome novelty. For several agonized moments, while Ken feared that someone would come looking for her, she considered settling down with him. But his rigid aloofness defeated her interest and she finally ambled placidly off, in search of other excitement.

With the first shadows of sunset, Ken saw a finger of smoke rising vertically in the still, breathless air. Earlier he would have been appalled at the closeness of a habitation. Now he was acutely aware that he had not eaten since the previous evening. There could be no question of a night's travel without food. He must avoid the Army, but he could not hope to survive without human contact.

When twilight was well established, Ken made his way toward the smoke. As far as he could tell, his appearance at the open door of the plain stone hut was greeted with exactly the same enthusiasm as his appearance at the gates of Hellenus, back in the good old days. There were the same broad smiles, the same sweeping gestures of invitation. Four suddenly-shy children were shooed off, and the black-clad woman retreated inside. The husband, apparently settling down to an aperitif on a stone bench against the front wall, hospitably poured a second glass of the local retsina wine.

Ken attempted a few explanatory sign movements, but these were waved aside with much laughter. His host seemed to be urging patience on him and Ken suffered a pang of social embarrassment. Did he think that this uninvited guest was howling for a quick dinner? Mortified, Ken retreated into a somber silence that remained unbroken for a quarter of an hour. Then one of the children returned, escorting a robust man of about seventy.

In unmistakably American accents, the newcomer identified himself as Louis, cousin to the lady of the house.

"Came back from Gary, five years ago. I retired from the mills," he explained. "Looks like you had some trouble last night. Car smash?"

Yes, Kenneth agreed truthfully, he had an accident on the toll road when the earthquake sent a tree down in front of his car.

"You look all in." Louis was sympathetic. "Put your feet up! Rest! You'll feel better after dinner."

The family displayed an instinctive courtesy when the food was placed on the table. They were all too familiar with the symptoms of hunger and fatigue. Conversation was a family affair until Ken had finished his large bowl of vegetable stew—a dish in which he identified only the lentils and olive oil. But as he sipped the last of his wine, Louis began to relay the gist of the remarks. They were discussing the earthquake, quietly commenting on the human traffic occasioned by the disaster—there were the homeless moving to temporary relief stations, the bereaved searching among the victims, there were construction crews and road engineers, there were soup kitchens and first aid stations.

As strength returned, Ken paid more attention, and a picture of the countryside emerged. For the first time he realized that the earthquake had not been a personal event in his own isolated predicament. It had been a public event affecting thousands beside himself.

He pricked up his ears. He had pictured himself—disheveled, homeless, wandering—as a unique pheomenon. But apparently the landscape was overrun with figures superficially like him.

With this realization came a return of sanity. He had been a fool to think of hiding out in the countryside. He was incapable of living on the land—on this land, he doubted if anyone could. He would simply wander around, becoming progressively weaker, until he was picked up. No, his safety lay in making a break for the Embassy in Athens while Northern Greece was still in the throes of upheaval. What had they been saying in the paddy wagon? The Army could avoid trouble by shooting him out of hand. It was quite another thing to wrest him from the wing of the American Ambassador.

For the first time, Ken began to take an intelligent interest in his geographic surroundings, cursing the intellectual snobbery that had made him study maps of Delphi and the Parthenon and left him ignorant of his environs.

Louis was happy to oblige. There were two principal roads from Salonika south to Larissa. The new tollway along the coast, which Ken had left so abruptly, was the main artery for through traffic and the only high speed road in Greece. But there was the older, inland route, passing through Verroia and Kozani. It was along this route that the commercial and social life of the inhabitants centered, as it always had. Here movement tended to be local, assisted by country buses and aged farm carts. Ken had made his escape inland not far from the junction of these two roads. Louis regarded it as natural that Ken should wish to proceed via the inland road.

"It is only three miles from here," he said. "And I'm going there in the morning. Come with me. When we reach the highway I must turn north, but there will be a bus for you going south to Verroia."

Ken went to sleep that night on the floor of the hut in a mood of confidence. There was no insuperable bar to a modest progress southward by a series of local buses. It would be a circuitous route, and therefore all the less likely for a fugitive on the run. And somewhere there would be a phone. Of course he could not use it himself. He would need a post office with an operator who spoke English—unlikely in these parts and far too dangerous. The police could save themselves the trouble of combing the hills. They had only to alert the exchanges for an American trying to reach the Embassy.

But there was Louis, going into the local market village to the north. And there was more. Almost the only personal possession which had remained intact, throughout Ken's arrest and flight, was his wallet. Among the miscellany of professional cards, there was the card of an attache at the Embassy, complete with his residential phone. There was also a very comfortable wad of Greek currency.

Good!

While he himself was escaping to the south, Louis could call Bill Riemer and pass a guarded message. At least it would be a life line.

With a shudder, Ken recalled the huddled body of Dr. Elias Ziros.

He could use all the life lines he could get.

The United States Government, the Greek Government and the Sloan Guaranty Trust were not the only ones interested in what was happening to Kenneth Nicolls.

There were others, among them Stavros Bacharias, Under Secretary to the Ministry of the Interior before the coup. He was still in office although there were now a new Minister, several new undersecretaries and a new public relations officer who wore the uniform of the Royal Artillery and was, to all intents and purposes, illiterate in three languages.

Bacharias, like most civil servants these days, was treading very warily. At his sumptuous office in Athens he was indefatigably and ostentatiously busy with apolitical matters such as: projected analyses, including sealed bids, concrete subcontracts, electric power substations. He eschewed the pleasant habits of an earlier era; he had no coffee sent in at midmorning. He lunched alone. He did not initiate condescendingly kind inquiries to his secretary about her family and activities.

Bacharias carried his circumspection into off-duty hours. Since he was quieter than most Greeks, his wife in their pleasant high-ceilinged apartment on Amalia Street did not notice much difference. The servants did. The domestic life of the Bachariases remained formal and old-fashioned as ever. But dinners—and like many Greeks of his age and class, Bacharias entertained at dinner as often as four times a week—were very different. Instead of the twelve to twenty guests that had been customary, Bacharias carefully pared his list to comply with recently promulgated laws. Accordingly, once his wife had withdrawn with the ladies, Bacharias and his guests constituted a gathering of five men, just within the letter of the law. (Like all Greeks, they realized that those charged with enforcing the laws would never count women as part of an unlawful assemblage; do not Greek fathers have children *and* daughters?)

"Well, Stavros," said one guest, a large fleshy man who had known Bacharias all his life. "And you are busy down at your office? Many new pieces of paper?"

A lawyer, he affected a mocking weariness that was the Greek version of sophistication.

"There is a certain increase," Bacharias agreed, passing the nut bowl. His Greek was curiously like his English, a shade pedantic. He used the precise formulations of *katharevoussa*, the language of the educated, even in informal discourse.

Not so another guest. With gusto, he used the earthy domestic language of the common folk.

"All this horse shit!" he exploded, cracking a walnut. "Little soldiers in uniform. Yagh! What difference does it make? The trouble with Greece is that there are too many little soldiers! Too many papers! Yes, Panayotis, too many lawyers!"

Bacharias smiled but it was his third guest who replied: "Easy to say, little Georgios! You sit on your lands and expect the world to stand still, as you have done! No, we make progress!"

"Progress! Pfa!"

They were all old friends who could say to each other what none would confide to his wife. Yet, Greek indirection being what it is, their intimacy did not spark the kind of political discussion expressly forbidden by the regime; on the contrary, since they knew each other so well, it was unnecessary.

"So, Stavros," said the oldest man present, once the First Counsellor at the London Embassy. "Do you face new problems?"

Bacharias waited until the maid put a tray of liqueurs on the table.

"There are, as is to be expected, difficulties. Take this missing American..."

His guests, who had heard about this before, made encouraging noises.

"I left him in Salonika," said Bacharias absently searching a dish of pastries. "First he was arrested. Then they were taking him to headquarters for questioning. Routine enough in its way. But now—poof! Who knows where he is! Oh, it is strange, but it could be very important!"

"How could such a thing happen!" asked the agriculturist angrily. "These little colonels are impossible! No system! No arrangement!"

The diplomat asked if anyone knew where the American was.

"No one," said Stavros Bacharias. "You cannot imagine how discouraging it is. Already, the Americans have begun with questions..."

"The Americans!" said the landowner robustly.

"And," Bacharias continued implacably, "ultimately the colonels will do something. I worry about it. Perhaps I myself should be doing something more. Ah, these are difficult days!"

"Exactly," said the lawyer, rising. "Stavros, you are too conscientious. This American, for example. We all know you did what you could. Who can blame you for what happened to him after you left him? These are violent days in Greece."

The diplomat nodded energetically. "Oh, indeed, indeed," he agreed. "Just today, I heard of Dino Stamatis—you know him, the poet—he was found, floating face down in Gythion Harbor!"

"Tsk, tsk, tsk!"

"Who killed him—and why? Will the world ever know?" the diplomat asked histrionically. "No, Stavros, remember, a revolution has taken place. It is not for you to worry! But for others. You have done what you could."

Stavros Bacharias, however, had the soul as well as the outward appurtenances of the civil servant.

"Philosophically, I accept what you say, my dear Dr. Frangos. But, I would sleep happier tonight if I knew where Mr. Nicolls is—and what he is doing."

The lawyer took a turn around the room. "That, of course, does you credit."

But the farmer, in fact a large landowner from Sparta, said: "Stavros, Stavros! You are too much citified. Your father would not have talked like this! Nor your Aunt Virginia! Now, you are learning to worry! Come back to the country! That way you learn to live with what Nature brings—with life and death!"

This produced a round of laughter, and one of those argumentative exchanges that ultimately descend on all Greek gatherings.

At Hellenus, work was going on as usual. Functionaries bustled around with folders and blueprints; the grounds were dusty with jeeps and trucks; workmen swarmed, shouted and worked. The sun beat down.

Cliff Leonard, who had never seen anything more beautiful than Ames, Iowa, wiped sweat from his brow.

"Yeah? So, what else?"

The very small dark man opposite him broke into lucid, Oxford-accented speech. Leonard listened. Then, as was his wont, he thought. (This habit, had he but known it, threw all his foreign contacts into paroxysms of anxiety.)

"I don't like it," he said finally.

The Greek spoke brilliantly, nervously and at length.

"Sure," said Cliff Leonard. "Listen, Nicolls was green, but he wasn't anybody's fool. And he works for the Sloan. So don't give me that hot air about his getting lost. I've had calls from the Embassy. What the hell happened, I wonder."

The Greek spoke again.

Leonard looked down at him. "Look, buster, you got your problems and I got mine. But don't try that line. Something funny's happening. I better do what I can."

He strode off. The Greek, cleverer, more voluble, and more devious, watched him with suddenly narrowed eyes.

"Yes, you may be troublesome, Mr. Leonard," he said. To himself.

CHAPTER VII

THE LABORS OF HERCULES

THE OBJECT OF this widespread interest, Kenneth Nicolls, was limping along the inland highway southward to Verroia. So far, events were proceeding according to plan.

"Sure, sure!" Louis had agreed when they parted, "I will call this Mr. Riemer for you. He'll be worried about his car. I will give him your message."

Louis had accepted the cryptic message without a blink. Ken had congratulated himself on his plausibility. Little did he know that Louis was congratulating him on his act. To Louis, it was quite clear. The young American, by handing over ten times the cost of the phone call, had found an unexceptionable way to repay his hosts for their hospitality without wounding their sensibilities.

But physical discomfort was threatening Ken's sense of well-being. The final collapse of his shoes, never designed for cross-country work, had been accomplished by the stony track along which Louis had led him immediately after breakfast. Nor had Louis' final words been comforting. The hours of the bus to Verroia were not fixed with any precision. Ken was to march steadily southward and, sooner or later, the bus would overtake him. But steady progress demands willing feet. By now a substantial amount of debris, of an unyielding nature, had collected between his split shoe soles and the tattered remnants of his socks.

A large shaded rock proved irresistible. Ken decided that he could wait for the bus sitting as well as walking, and he could seize the opportunity to empty his shoes. With the weight off his feet, he realized for the first time that it was a beautiful morning, bright, cloudless, and cool enough to be refreshing.

The road also met with his approval. It had come through the earthquake better than its coastal companion, perhaps because, along this stretch at least, it ran level between the fields without overhanging rocks and trees. Ken allowed his newly-freed foot an invigorating stretch while he upended its shoe and started to dislodge some of the more tenacious sediment.

His absorption was so complete that the jeep had stopped directly by his side before he was startled into awareness. He was looking straight into the eyes of three Greek soldiers.

The volley of Greek questions which ensued did nothing to reassure him.

He shrugged. It really made very little difference to him what they were saying. When hoping to pass as an earthquake victim, Ken had not bargained on an eyeball-to-eyeball confrontation. His worst fears were confirmed when the driver, after peering intently at the jacket so recently brushed into respectability by Ken's hostess, turned to his sergeant and unleashed a torrent of Greek ending in the word *American.*

The sergeant, in his turn, leaned out to inspect the evidence. Then, with all the signs of effort, he searched a limited English vocabulary and, banishing his fierce scowl, laboriously intoned one word.

"Friends?" he questioned tentatively.

It was not what Ken had expected, but he wasn't looking a gift horse in the mouth.

"Friends!" he declared enthusiastically. Maybe they would all shake hands and offer each other cigarettes, he thought.

But no, that was not to be. The sergeant issued a sharp command, boxes were shifted, and Ken was motioned into the rear seat. He hung back for an instant, but the gestures became unmistakably minatory. Ken remembered the rifle butt last time. He obeyed, sadly stuffing his foot into its shoe and hoisting himself aboard.

He was still puzzled by that initial offer of friendship. Of course, it might be simple Old World politeness. They wanted him to know that, even though they were going to shoot him, they bore no personal malice. More likely, the sergeant had made a simple linguistic error. He might have thought he was asking if Ken were a gangster, in which case Ken's hearty confirmation would explain the immediate summons to the jeep. Or could there still be a ray of hope? Maybe things were not as bad as they seemed. But, whatever the situation, Ken's heart sank when the jeep swept into a U-turn and started back toward Salonika.

Within an hour they were roaring past a post office. At exactly that moment, inside the post office, the supervisor of the exchange was saying firmly:

"But no! All long distance lines have been commandeered because of the earthquake. Do you think yours is the only accident to be reported? No private calls are permitted. Absolutely none!"

Cousin Louis shrugged philosophically. He had done his best. And that young American had only wanted to be generous, anyway.

Two hours later Ken Nicolls was in the same state of doubt. The lack of a common language relieved him of the necessity of sustaining a role, but it made the acquisition of information impossible. He had cautiously offered his cigarette pack, and the offer had been accepted by both privates. After a good deal of careful consideration, Ken decided that the sergeant's refusal proved nothing. Either sergeants didn't smoke with prisoners, or this particular sergeant didn't smoke cigarettes.

But clarification was at hand. The jeep, which had been charging up a dirt road for forty-five minutes, suddenly breasted a hillside and slid to a halt beside an encampment of tents, trucks and ambulances. A bright banner flapped in the wind proclaiming:

AMERICAN FRIENDS SERVICE COMMITTEE

Before Ken's feet touched the ground, the jeep was reversing to turn. A harassed bald man with a clipboard darted forward.

"Thank God!" he exclaimed. "We've been expecting you since last night. You've no idea how shorthanded we are."

Grasping Ken's elbow, he started to propel him toward the largest of the tents, chattering briskly about tetanus vaccine and morphine ampoules. Suddenly he stopped dead in his tracks and stared at Ken's jacket.

"But you don't belong to us," he said sharply. "You belong to Jamison!"

"Jamison?" Ken queried weakly. With approval he noted that the jeep was out of sight.

"Well, you're Red Cross, aren't you? Jamison's in charge of the Canadian detachment. But they're thirty miles farther north!"

"I'm sorry," Ken murmured, letting the tide sweep him where it would.

"And if you think we're going to ferry you up to him, you can think again," the bald man said accusingly. "We've got enough on our plate right now. You can help out here."

A less preoccupied man might have been suspicious of the readiness with which Ken abandoned any hope of reaching Jamison. Instead his new-found employer put Ken to work within minutes. The next few hours were such a bustle of unloading crates, checking invoices, and carting supplies to the field hospital that Ken had very little time to consider his situation.

But two things were obvious. The insignia of the International Red Cross, which he had pinned so casually to his lapel in the railroad station, was responsible for his acceptance as a relief worker by both Greeks and Americans. And he had reached temporary sanctuary. True, when the first turmoil of crisis began to subside, someone was bound to discover that an irregular had managed to add himself to the roster. In the meanwhile, he could very profitably use the time to consolidate his position.

The first item on his agenda was raised by a co-worker, an old hand of twenty-two and a veteran of previous campaigns.

"Boy, you must be new here," he said after a disparaging

glance at Ken's battered footwear. "For this kind of work, you want boots!"

Ken wanted more than that. Within two days, during which he worked harder and for longer hours than ever before in his life, he effected a transformation in his appearance. He was picturesquely unshaven and had acquired, piece by piece, the unofficial uniform of the Quaker camp—a white shirt, faded chino pants, and field boots, augmented at night by a grimy sweatshirt emblazoned *Swarthmore.* Surprisingly, he looked years younger, the kind of irresponsible youth to which no bank in its right mind would entrust weighty affairs. He also finished a detailed account of his predicament addressed to the American Embassy in Athens which was now in the pile of mail waiting for a pick-up truck.

An extended stay with the American Friends Service Committee was out of the question. The bald man with the clipboard was, unfortunately, an administrative precisionist, and Ken's unorthodox position was a thorn in his side. In spite of willing labor and lack of complaint, Ken was deluged with promises of transport north. His sense of security was further undermined when, on the second morning, he was helping unload supplies in the soup kitchen. A cook was hovering about, urging them to concentrate on dried eggs and dried milk.

"I want the high-protein stuff," he explained. "We're beginning to get the bad cases, the ones who had trouble getting here."

Ken, remembering the condition of yesterday's refugees, was appalled and said so.

"It always happens," a knowledgeable helper remarked. "By the third day after a disaster, the ones who had to crawl are showing up."

The cook agreed. "Say what you will, these Greeks are tough. Look at that old man over there. Seventy, if he's a day, and he carried a grandson with a smashed leg at least ten miles."

Ken looked over at the hero of the hour. He was a gnarled old peasant, sitting at one of the board tables, slumped over a bowl of soup in the lassitude of exhaustion. Then Ken's eye travelled to the old man's neighbor, and he stiffened. There, breaking a piece of bread and chatting to his companion with bird-like vivacity, was the little Greek interpreter of the paddy wagon. For a moment Ken wondered if he could be mistaken. But no, he had ample opportunity to examine the man under the brilliant arc lights at the Salonika railroad station while they waited for the additional prisoners to be rounded up. And while his clothes were now ragged and disheveled, he had obviously used the relief station's soap and water to restore a good deal of his former spruceness.

Ken realized that he had forgotten all about his fellow prisoners the moment he parted from them at the coast road. Presumably they too had been crashing around in his vicinity during the initial stage of his flight. But certainly, by the time he had fallen during the second series of tremors, he had effectively separated himself from them. He remembered the unearthly quiet and the placid sky when he had risen. But if they had survived, they would all have had the same thought as Ken. Safety lay in becoming an earthquake victim. And they were all better equipped to play the role than Ken. The interpreter, if he recalled correctly, was even a Macedonian.

Remaining at the relief station seemed less and less attractive. Whatever the odds for a successful escape, they were going to be lessened by being in the vicinity of other fugitives. Ken faded unobtrusively out of the kitchen tent, hoping that the sprightly interpreter had not spotted him. He was determined to seize the first opportunity for a break to the south.

His chance came shortly after nightfall. A party of Greeks had been dug out of the ruins of a collapsed house in which they had been buried for over three days. Two men were in critical condition. To add to the confusion a young woman was on the brink of childbirth. The camp was pandemonium. The bald man rushed back and forth, diverting people from their normal duties and pressing them into service.

"You!" he barked at Kenneth. "You'll have to drive the ambulance. I don't have anyone else I can spare. We'll give the two men emergency treatment here, but they'll have to go to Larissa for surgery. It's their only chance. We'll radio ahead so the hospital will be ready."

Kenneth's heart leaped. Larissa was a good solid one hundred and twenty miles south of Salonika, and it was his gateway to Athens. He would drive the victims to the hospital, then he would shed the doctor and medics companioning him and proceed in his new guise.

The bald man continued with his conscription. The mail clerk, summoned to serve as midwife's assistant, hastily jammed the outgoing letters into their pouches. In his confusion, he included Ken Nicolls' letter with the mail destined for the Friends Service Committee headquarters in Philadelphia.

There, it was faithfully forwarded by sea mail and arrived in Athens four weeks later.

Ken had no trouble evading his companions in Larissa. On the contrary, they all trailed off in the wake of the stretchers to somewhere in the depths of the hospital. But their approach through the deserted streets of the city had warned Ken that he must not appear in public until the daytime bustle of town life had commenced. The only visible figures had been patrolling soldiers. A solitary male, loitering aimlessly, was sure to be stopped and questioned. He needed someplace under cover where he could pass the two or three hours before breakfast time. And the hospital would not do, lest his Quaker friends reappear and demand his return.

A cautious tour of the grounds showed him what he wanted. Like most hospitals, this one had an all-night cafe nearby which served the needs of the night shifts. When Ken entered, he knew he had found the right place. The hospital was working on an emergency basis these days, and the cafe was thronged with medical personnel, relief workers, and relatives waiting for word about victims. A group of medical students made room for him at their table and Ken foresightedly ordered food as well as drink.

The students spoke English and were interested in conditions up north. Ken relaxed and took part in a general discussion of earthquake casualties. He himself was waiting for transport, he explained. The students were obliging. He could wait in their lounge, if he liked. Nothing could have been better. They had risen and were just leaving when one of the students brought the conversation closer to home.

"Incidentally, you haven't seen an American called Nicolls, have you? He's not a relief worker, he's some sort of businessman."

Ken was thankful that he had just passed into the shadow of the street. His face could not be seen.

"No," he said, striving to be casual. "I haven't seen any businessman."

"I suppose not." The student sounded regretful. "Somebody should warn him. There's a car load of tough types looking for him. They were going round the city this morning. I heard them at the bus station."

The other student chimed in. "They were even asking at the hospital this afternoon."

The silence was too prolonged to be casual. Could they possibly know who he was? Ken took a deep breath.

"It sounds serious. Were they official, these toughs?"

The first student snorted. "Official! Who knows what an official is these days?"

The second student broke in on these incautious utterances. "It does not matter. But it is political, that is certain. Being an American, you might come across this Nicolls. We thought you might pass him a word of warning."

"American? Oh, no," said Ken instantly. "I'm Canadian."

"Canadian?" The student was politely incredulous.

Kenneth reached for corroborative detail. "I'm with Jamison's bunch. Red Cross."

"Jamison? Oh, of course, they are way up north, aren't they? I—"

He was interrupted brusquely.

"Jamison? Good heavens! What are you doing, sitting around here? You must have got the time wrong. Come on!"

After that, events moved rapidly. His new friends grabbed him by either elbow and set out at a dead run for the hospital yard. Before he knew what was happening, they were shouting excitedly at a large, high-axled truck, just pulling out into the street.

The truck braked to a halt, everybody screamed at each other, willing hands were extended over the tailboard. With people in front of him pulling, and people in back of him hoisting, Kenneth tumbled into the cavernous interior. The driver engaged his clutch, the students called good-bye, and once again Kenneth had started on the long haul to the north.

Elasson lies thirty-seven miles north of Larissa. During those miles Kenneth had ample time for thought, most of it unpleasant. First, there was this continual regression northwards, farther and farther from his goal. Second, and a good deal more disturbing, was the news of the medical students. A carload of unidentified toughs combing a city for him? Why?

Ken had seen a good deal of Greece since his arrest. And he was at the moment neither hungry, exhausted, nor shocked. For the first time, he was perilously close to being furious. He had seen truckloads of Greek soldiers moving into the disaster area. He had heard the political news being discussed by Greek-speaking Americans and English-speaking Greeks.

In the last week, two events had shaken Greece, a coup d'etat and an earthquake. The military junta was working hard to achieve international recognition and pacify the country. Under these conditions it was inconceivable that an American, picked up because of a casual contact in a railroad station, should be the subject of an intensive and unrelenting manhunt. Ken had expected trouble at check points, yes. No doubt there were long lists of people due for arrest if they tried to board a plane from Salonika to Athens. It would be no trouble to add his name to such a list. But he wasn't important enough to justify the man-power being used. And he could tell why it was being used, too. Somebody was determined to bottle him up in Larissa and prevent his entry into Athens. There was virtually no other route to the south, short of traversing the entire country to the west coast.

And now he came to the most bewildering feature of the situation. Six men had been arrested. One had been shot, and five had escaped. Yet the carload of toughs was searching for only one man, Kenneth Nicolls. The students would surely have mentioned other subjects of inquiry. This would have been understandable on the assumption that the other four had been recaptured. But Kenneth had seen the Greek interpreter with his own eyes. He knew to a certainty that the little Greek was still in the friendly shelter of the Quakers at the very moment questions were being asked in downtown Larissa.

Kenneth shook his head wearily. A short twenty-four hours ago, he would not have believed that he could look forward to capture by the Greek Army. But he liked the sound of the Army better than the sound of unidentified hooligans. Then, that car at the hospital! Somebody realized a missing American could disappear most effectively in the midst of Americans. It was a matter of time before that car would be making a circuit of relief stations. Right now, a Red Cross camp was the worst possible place for him.

He reverted to his original idea. Local buses, surrounded by local people, and if possible wearing local clothes. That was his kind of travel. He looked around; his companions were all asleep. He could leave the truck as unceremoniously as he had entered.

All he knew about Elasson was what he had gathered from the road signs. That told him it was big enough to have a bus service and that they would soon be there. Moving slowly and silently he made his way to the tailboard without disturbing the occupants and watched the road unfold under the early morning sun. He was not going to repeat his mistake of Larissa. No city streets for him until eight o'clock in the morning. Then he could go about his business of finding new clothes and learning time-tables.

Accordingly he waited until they had passed through Elasson proper. He was afraid to wait too long, knowing that the driver would pick up speed once on the open road. It was on the outskirts therefore, when the truck slowed for a turn, that Ken let himself fall lightly to the ground near some bushes where he immediately took shelter.

The whole movement was so quick that it was unlikely the driver could have seen him in a rearview mirror. The sound of gears shifting upward and the lumbering progress of the truck testified to his success. Ken paused to survey his surroundings.

Not surprisingly the most significant object in sight was the mountain range to the north. Ken was in the foothills of Mount Olympus. Other than that, there was nothing noteworthy. The homesteads were not yet agricultural, these were townspeople who lived here. But their houses sprawled over grounds which measured several acres, and the landscaping fervor of American suburbs had not invaded the area. There was a satisfying amount of rough land, in its natural state.

Ken, choosing a comfortable spot, which was not overlooked from any house, settled himself. He intended to review the situation; instead he dozed off. He was awakened by the general bustle in the neighborhood to find a satisfactory amount of movement. Children were going to school, housewives were going to market, men were going to business. He walked along the road to the town center, secure in the conviction that only his clothes made him an object for comment. Once he had a nondescript suit and a rough shave he would be indistinguishable in a crowd. Ken quickened his pace. Clothes first, then the shave.

There was no difficulty in finding people who spoke English. The difficulty lay in making them believe that an American college boy wanted to buy a second-hand Greek suit. Even the proprietress of the shop, to which he was at length directed, shared the general skepticism. She persisted that he really wanted Greek folk costume. It took time and effort to resist her attempts to turn him into a large, blond, fully-accoutered evzone complete with frilly skirt.

Kenneth finally extracted what he wanted, a faded grey suit of poor workmanship which was exactly what he had in mind. His self-congratulations came to an abrupt end when he reached into his hip pocket.

He had lost his wallet.

CHAPTER VIII

STILL UNRAVISH'D

EVERETT GABLER WAS the Sloan's oldest trust officer, its most conservative, and its most cantankerous. Any departure from normalcy roused in him foreboding, suspicion and concern for his digestive well-being. It might have been expected, therefore, that arriving at the Hotel Britannia amidst the furor created by the violation of Ken Nicolls' room would have plunged him into blackest gloom.

Quite the contrary. Never at a loss for objects of censure, Gabler now experienced an embarrassment of riches. From the outset, he had foreseen disaster in the Hellenus project. And what did his first six hours in Athens prove? The Greek Government which had put the whole deal together was plainly incompetent, as witness the fact that most members of that government were now languishing in prison. Kenneth Nicolls had proved unworthy of his trust, as witness the fact that he had abandoned his post and become involved in a police investigation. The American Embassy in Athens was derelict in not producing Nicolls—or his remains—on demand. Everything was deplorable, utterly deplorable. Everett Gabler was suffering from the giddy exaltation of a confirmed gambler with a nine-race winning streak. It was too good to be true.

On his first afternoon in Athens he was content to terrorize everyone within reach and accept, relatively mildly, the fact that the Greek police were not going to be available until the morrow. Retiring to the arms of a chastened Hotel Britannia, he passed the evening familiarizing himself with every scrap of paper which could, in any way, affect the Sloan's interest in Hellenus. Then, after a revivifying night's sleep, he arose and came bouncing along to the Embassy, the light of battle gleaming in his eye.

He had the immeasurable advantage of starting fresh on the problem of Kenneth Nicolls. With a successful negotiation in Istanbul behind him, an abundant supply of first-class yoghurt around him, and unlimited opportunity to find fault in store, he was in top form. Happily he acknowledged Bill Riemer's introductions with the murderous satisfaction of a world champion greeting second-rate challengers.

And a sorry lot they were. Bill Riemer, himself, was no credit to his country. The exigencies of foreign service being what they are, he was immaculately shaved, laundered, and pressed. Unfortunately the splendor of the packaging merely emphasized the deficiencies of the product. It was now over a week since the coup d'état. Riemer had not had a night's sleep or a sit-down meal in that period. Three days ago he had merely looked gaunt and hollow-eyed. Now he seemed to be in the throes of a fatal disease. He was husbanding his remaining energy to achieve two goals. One, the Greek police officer was not to be publicly embarrassed. Two, certain disturbing information was to be conveyed to the representative of the Sloan Guaranty Trust.

Police Captain Philopoulos, although in better physical condition, was in yet worse plight. Whenever a coup d'état or revolution succeeds, the police of the country are left in an anomalous position. They try to maintain ordinary standards of law and order, going about their business of writing parking tickets and apprehending burglars with one hand as it were, while the other hand remains motionless in the face of far graver breaches of decorum. No policeman has ever given a parking ticket to a tank—successfully. The Greek police were no exception to this rule. The file which Captain Philopoulos had opened on the case of Dr. Elias Ziros recited the bare official facts: namely, that, at 8.55 on the night of April 23, a baggage porter had notified the police that a body had been found in the rear yard of the Salonika railway station. The file was scrupulously silent on other details: namely, that at 8.20

a contingent of the Greek Army had rampaged through the station making arrests with abandon, that the principals had withdrawn to the rear yard, and that shortly thereafter an army truck had roared off into the night leaving behind a bullet-ridden corpse. Under the circumstances the Greek police did not feel they could do themselves justice in investigating the death of Dr. Ziros. Naturally Captain Philopoulos had no intention of discussing these unofficial details with his present companions. However, he realized that several thousand people in Salonika had witnessed the Army's descent on the railroad station and had since been talking of little else. It was to be hoped that the Americans were still ignorant of these unpalatable facts. It was certain that the fourth man present in the room was not.

Stavros Bacharias was also in an unenviable position. His Minister, mindful of the junta's emphasis on continuing American investment, had instructed him to cooperate to the hilt with the American Embassy and the Sloan Guaranty Trust in their search for Ken Nicolls.

"But," his Minister had said with awful emphasis, "without in any way prejudicing our cordial relations with the police. I know, my dear Bacharias, I do not have to remind you of the respect we all owe to the leaders of the Greek Army."

His Minister, being no fool, had then waved him out of the office without enlarging on these instructions.

In other words Bacharias was to support the dignity of the new Greek Government, protect the police from awkwardness, and satisfy the Americans. And if anything went wrong, it would all be his fault.

If his Minister was so eager for American investment, Bacharias could only wish he would do some of the dirty work himself. Quite apart from the fact that no amount of cooperation was likely to recommend a country where bankers disappeared into thin air.

It was with a noticeable lack of enthusiasm, therefore, that he opened the proceedings.

"Captain Philopoulos is familiar with the search for Mr.

Nicolls," he announced stiffly. "He has kindly agreed to give us what little information he has."

Philopoulos eyed his would-be protector with misgivings. When the sacrificial-goat aspect of his assignment had startled him into protest, he had been advised that he could look for support to the man from the Ministry. He was not impressed by what he now saw, but then, policemen rarely are. Manfully taking the bull by the horns, he plunged into the heart of the controversy.

"At the request of Mr. Riemer, we have succeeded in tracing Mr. Nicolls' movements down to the evening of April 23," he began.

Gabler pounced instantly.

"It is now the morning of April 28."

Riemer suppressed a groan but Captain Philopoulos nodded. He was not himself unmindful of the gap. Stolidly he forged ahead. "Mr. Nicolls left the Hellenus site with Mr. Bacharias. Together they went to the railroad station in Salonika where, I understand, Mr. Nicolls intended to take the night express to Athens."

"That is true," Bacharias corroborated. "I left him in the main waiting room."

"Conditions at the railroad station were very confused," said the police captain with a wholesale avoidance of thin ice. "I do not know whether you realize, Mr. Gabler, that all travel to Athens had been halted during April 21 and 22. This train was the first available means of transport in almost three days. Conditions were not normal."

"I am to blame," Bacharias reproached himself. "Never should I have left him alone."

Gabler turned from one to the other in high irritation. "I do not understand," he said severely. "That the station should be unusually crowded is comprehensible. But that scarcely suggests that it was a dangerous locale in which to leave an adult man who contemplated nothing more hazardous than a railroad trip."

"Mr. Bacharias is too harsh with himself. Of course he could not have anticipated any danger," said the Captain promptly, storing up grace in heaven. He had a feeling he was going to need Stavros Bacharias any minute. "Unfortunately we now know that, long before the Athens Express finally arrived, at least one murder was committed in the immediate vicinity."

Gabler, in Istanbul, had never learned the specifics of the police inquiries about Nicolls.

"A murder? In the station?" He was scandalized. His tone made it clear what he thought of a country where that went on. God knew, the American railroads were unsatisfactory, but they had not yet sunk to this level.

"No! Not in the station!" The Captain's outrage equalled Gabler's. At least, he thought to himself, the Army still had enough decency to retire to the baggage yard when it wished to stage a massacre. "The body was found outside, in a yard directly adjacent to the station."

"But Mr. Bacharias left Nicolls inside the station." Gabler put his finger unerringly on the weak spot. "How can this murder be connected with him?"

Philopoulos explained about the discovery of Ken's visiting card on the corpse. He had rehearsed a little speech for the occasion, and every sonorous phrase in his vocabulary was pulled out to magnify the event into a personal connection between the two men. Things would be so much easier if this American could be led to believe that young Mr. Nicolls had become involved in some personal imbroglio of a Greek friend.

Unfortunately, quite plausible swindlers had been trying to lead Everett Gabler to believe things for years. With each suave sentence, the myopic little eyes behind the rimless glasses grew harder. Everett found it difficult enough to believe the evidence of his senses. Flight of fancy never had any appeal for him. He waited impatiently for the Captain to finish.

"One does not offer professional cards to friends," he explained waspishly. "One offers them to strangers. It is perfectly clear what happened. Dr. Ziros and Mr. Nicolls met inside the station, where they fell into conversation and exchanged cards. Then Dr. Ziros went outside, where he unfortunately met his end. That has nothing to do with Nicolls. And," he concluded with a return to the pedagogic manner, "one does not leave a railroad station when one is in momentary expectation of a train."

"Normally, no," Captain Philopoulos said distantly. After all, he salved his conscience, no one could regard a military raid as normal.

Gabler misinterpreted the Captain's reservations.

"Do you mean you suspect Mr. Nicolls of participation in this murder?" he demanded.

"Not at all," Philopoulos replied.

Gabler narrowed his eyes suspiciously, and the Captain produced further particulars.

"Mr. Nicolls' movements in the station have been traced in some detail. Mr. Bacharias, a porter, and a policeman all report that he was carrying a small suitcase."

"And what does that mean?"

"The post-mortem revealed that Dr. Ziros was shot with a rifle from a considerable distance."

"A rifle, at a distance?" Bacharias was surprised and hastened to cover his surprise. "I did not know that. It is not a city murder, somehow."

Captain Philopoulos was far too able an officer to allow his grin to surface. So the man from the Ministry thought he knew everything, did he? Well, he was not alone in his surprise. The police, too, had expected to learn that Dr. Ziros had been shot by a service revolver held to his head.

"There is no reason to suppose that Mr. Nicolls acquired armaments during the brief period in which he was last seen and the body was discovered," the Captain continued sedately. "Particularly as he was a stranger in the city, unfamiliar with our language."

"I should think not!" Gabler said roundly. Nicolls might be young and wayward, but Everett was not going to sit still while it was suggested that members of the Sloan passed the interval of waiting for trains in playful sniping. "This simply confirms my original contention. There is no connection between Dr. Ziros' murder and Mr. Nicolls' disappearance. How then do you explain the latter?"

Captain Philopoulos rolled his eyes at Stavros Bacharias like an imploring dog. Now, if ever, was the time for support.

Faithful to his instructions, Bacharias intervened. "We could consider the situation at the railroad station in greater detail later on, perhaps. But there is one element in the problem with which you may not be familiar, Mr. Gabler. There was a major earthquake in northern Greece on the night of April 23. If Mr. Nicolls did, in fact, leave the Salonika station, then his subsequent disappearance becomes much more readily explainable."

Now in Manhattan, the earthquake had been characterized as a severe tremor. In Turkey, where they know about earthquakes and take a parochial pride in the home product, the newspapers had spoken of slight tremors. Everett Gabler knew perfectly well that city structures had not been crashing to the ground. But he was fully alive to the tension between Philopoulos and Bacharias.

And he was growing more alarmed about Ken Nicolls. He had expected to find incompetence, face-saving, and genuine ignorance as to the whereabouts of the Sloan's missing employee. Instead he was met with evasion, palpable red herrings and furtive glances.

Very well. If certain information would not be forthcoming in the police captain's presence, he was ready to dispense with that presence as soon as possible. Therefore, he launched into expressions of gratitude, listened in noncommital silence to promises of further efforts and was shaking hands with the relieved Captain Philopoulos within ten minutes.

As soon as the door closed, he turned to Stavros Bacharias. "We were going to discuss conditions in the railroad station," he said uncompromisingly.

Bacharias retained his posture of alert cooperation, but his glance at Bill Riemer was a mirror of Philopoulos' earlier appeal. Riemer rubbed his hands over his red-rimmed eyes before he spoke.

"You know, Mr. Bacharias," he said at length. "Even here in Athens, there have been rumors about what was going on in that railroad station."

Bacharias accepted the inevitable. After all, most of the people in the station had been en route to Athens. It was too much to hope that the scandal would remain localized.

Carefully neutral, he described the descent of the Army, the six or seven arrests, the sudden departure of everyone involved. There were rumors, he admitted sadly, that several foreigners had been included in the haul.

Now that he was receiving information, Everett Gabler was far too experienced to interrupt. True, his face assumed an expression of shocked disapproval. But, then, that was the expression it normally wore.

"Please accept my assurance, Mr. Gabler," Bacharias said earnestly, "I would never have suggested that Mr. Nicolls contemplate traveling that day if there had not been every indication normalcy had been restored."

Everett did not reply. He knew full well that an unforthcoming response will often elicit information. A nervous speaker will talk to banish silence.

His tactics paid off. Stavros Bacharias unbent still further, his stiffness yielding before the desire to justify himself.

"The trains were being permitted to run. This meant that Colonel Papadopoulos regarded the crisis as over. There was no longer any need to seal off Athens. Everyone in that railroad station considered it safe to travel. I did not imagine that a businessman, particularly an American, would have any difficulty." He spread his hands. "I was not alone in my error. It seems that even leftists did not think there would be trouble."

Gabler abandoned the glasses he had been industriously polishing. "Leftists?" he asked.

"Dr. Ziros." Bacharias spoke reluctantly as if he had said more than he intended. "It is officially reported that he was a socialist. They say he was an agitator, an anti-monarchist."

"We are not interested in Greek politics. We merely wish to locate Mr. Nicolls," said Gabler, returning to his point with the tenacity of a terrier.

Bacharias shook his head mournfully. "I can only offer you every good wish and promise you our sincere cooperation. But, alas, I cannot hold out high hopes. It is now the 28th, and there has been no word."

Sad-eyed resignation had never been Everett Gabler's strong point. At his most militant, he replied:

"We are certainly not going to let the situation rest here. Our investigation has only just started."

And apparently it was starting right now. What Stavros Bacharias had assumed to be the end of his ordeal was only the beginning. With impeccable politeness, Gabler cross-examined him about his last moments with Ken Nicolls. An hour later the man from the Ministry was only too happy to escape on a final wave of condolences.

His departure brought the first expression of the morning to Bill Riemer's tired face. Amusement tinged his voice as he said:

"You'll get more out of Stavros Bacharias than any foreigner ever has before. He's on the defensive now, and I expect you mean to keep him there."

Gabler shook aside these irrelevancies.

"But we haven't learned anything useful. In fact, we don't seem to have learned anything you didn't already know." Everett paused to examine Bill Riemer. He was prepared to modify his preconceived opinion of the Embassy. As he frequently said, he lived in a world of babbling imbeciles. Riemer's ability to hold his tongue was outstanding. But Gabler withheld judgment. It might turn out that the man was simply asleep on his feet.

"Oh, I wouldn't say that," said Riemer thoughtfully. "I didn't know that Dr. Ziros was a socialist."

"Why wasn't the Sloan informed of this disgraceful scene at Salonika?" Everett shot out suddenly.

Riemer shook his head gently. "We didn't know ourselves until yesterday."

There was a long silence. Finally Gabler paid the enormous compliment of asking an opinion.

"Do you think the Army's actions in the railroad station explain Nicolls' disappearance? We have no evidence that he was one of the men arrested."

Now that they were all in the family, so to speak, Riemer allowed himself the luxury of a gigantic yawn and stretch. Then he slumped in his swivel chair and examined the ceiling.

"I'm afraid that there is one more point which I didn't want to raise before our visitors." He tapped a pencil unseeingly on his fingernails. "There is an American engineer up at the Hellenus project. He came in to see me yesterday. In fact, he's the source of the rumors about the arrests in the station. But he had another item of information. On the morning of April 24, the Greek Army sent a patrol car out to Hellenus, looking for Nicolls."

"And the people at Hellenus never saw fit to mention this?"

"Be reasonable, Mr. Gabler. There were a lot of people asking Hellenus about Nicolls on the 24th. We were, ourselves. They probably thought it was just routine. But by the time the rumors reached Cliff Leonard, he began to put two and two together. He didn't like what he came up with."

Gabler digested this information.

"But," he said in exasperation, "but that implies..."

"Yes." Riemer was almost apologetic. "It implies that, if the Army ever had Nicolls, they seem to have lost him."

Gabler returned to the Britannia in a far less buoyant frame of mind than he had left it. He wanted time to mull over his discoveries of the morning. He wanted to dispel the vision of Kenneth Nicolls disappearing into a bog of inexplicable circumstances. He wanted to recharge the batteries of his spleen. Most of all, he wanted an opponent. Allies never did Everett Gabler half as much good as a target.

He received unexpected help as soon as he set foot in the

lobby. The manager awaited him, with half a dozen aides-de-camp spread out in battle formation. The manager was a small man who normally comported himself with a stately dignity. Now he was literally dancing with suppressed fury that struck answering sparks from Gabler before a word had been spoken.

"Aha! I have been waiting. I have to report to you an unparalleled outrage!" The manager rang up the curtain with slow, venomous articulation.

"Yes?" Gabler saved his powder.

"After breakfast the maid, Cassandra, comes to me in unimaginable woe!" Three thousand years of dramatic tradition brought the manager to an artful pause. Then, he picked up his tale on a quickened tempo. "She tells me that Mr. Nicolls' room has again been broken into. She describes to me the horror, the devastation! She tells me of her shock and terror. She weeps!"

Gabler had no time for Cassandra's sensibilities. He was urging his numbed faculties into attack. "Again? But this is outrageous, Mr. Tsaras!"

"It is indeed an outrage of which we speak," Tsaras hissed. "Who is this Mr. Nicolls? Is the Hotel Britannia then a den of thieves? Do we cater for gangsters and mobsters? Mr. Nicolls has been absent for a week, and twice, twice, brigands have broken down our doors!"

Gabler met fire with ice.

"I am shocked that you can speak of a repetition of this event as if it were in any way Mr. Nicolls' fault."

"Repetition!" Tsaras paused, then gave an affected laugh. "Ha! It is more than a repetition. This time there has been outright theft, wanton destruction. It is a progression! Who can tell what these assassins will do next! Will I arrive to find Cassandra and Iphigenia slaughtered? Lying in their gore? I announce to you that I can no longer be responsible!"

"That will scarcely alter the situation. You have already been irresponsible." Gabler did a little artful pausing himself. "There has been grossly inadequate surveillance of valuable personal property."

Tsaras sucked in his breath sharply. The litany of all hotel managers on such occasions rose automatically to his lips. "Guests are requested to deposit valuables in the hotel safe."

"That in no way relieves the manager of the duty to take ordinary precautions," Gabler said sternly. He instantly followed up his advantage. "I myself will view the scene. If necessary I shall demand a police investigation with full publicity. I may even speak to the Greek Tourist Bureau."

Tsaras paled. He knew he had gone too far.

"You will see with your own eyes," he promised. "Then you, too, shall weep. It is not a robbery, it is a desecration."

Everett Gabler did not go so far as to weep. But the scene on the third floor speedily wiped away his satisfaction at having routed Tsaras. The Britannia's clean-up operation had gone into effect too soon for him to view the aftermath of the first ransacking of Kenneth Nicolls' room. But he had received descriptions. The first effort had dumped out the contents of drawers and closets, rolled up the carpet, pulled down window-shades and reversed mattresses.

But, as Tsaras truthfully reported, this was not a repetition, but a progression. Of Ken Nicolls' possessions, there was not a sign. Clearly they had been bundled into his suitcases and carted off bodily. Of the hotel's possessions, there was plenty of sign. Every upholstered piece of furniture had been torn apart completely. The floor was inches deep in tufts of white stuffing. Mattresses, curtains and denuded chairs lay about like the jetsam of an immense tidal wave. Even the television set had been gutted.

In the shock of actually seeing this destruction, resentment and hostility drained away. Gabler and the manager stared at each other blankly.

"But it must have taken hours!" said Gabler involuntarily.

"Yes," said Tsaras grimly, "either that or very many men."

Within three hours Everett Gabler was sitting in the Athens office of Paul Makris & Son. This interview was the direct result of his internal communings after he had retreated to his own room at the Britannia. By now Everett had firmly rejected any straightforward explanation of Ken Nicolls' disappearance. He could have been seized innocently by the Greek Army on the night of April 23. He could, even though this required a greater stretch of the imagination, have been shot by them. But that would have been the end of the episode.

Instead there was a continuous and feverish interest in Ken Nicolls and his belongings. There were inquiries at the project site hours after his fate should have been known to the Greek Army. There were these repeated intrusions into his hotel room, capped by the wholesale removal of his belongings. And, most disturbing of all in Gabler's eyes, there was the failure of the Hellenus people to report Army interest in Nicolls at a critical time.

While Hellenus was a patchwork of many interests, at the site north of Salonika there were only three principals—the Greek Government, the Sloan Guaranty Trust and Paul Makris & Son. Two of them were actively looking for Kenneth Nicolls on the morning of April 24. Did the third already know where he was?

"And so we are naturally disturbed, very disturbed," Gabler was saying after a suitably edited recital of the search for Ken Nicolls and the second invasion of the Britannia. He had rigidly suppressed all reference to the Army search for Nicolls.

The chief representative of Paul Makris in Athens met even Everett Gabler's standards of orthodoxy. Conservative tailoring, fluent English, dignified restraint were all just as they ought to be. Perversely, this only increased Gabler's suspicions. By rights, the office of a Greco-American adventurer, however successful, should smack of flamboyance. No one would ever accuse Peter Chiros of flamboyance.

"We had heard of the first search of Mr. Nicolls' room," Chiros now murmured, "but not of the second. It is understandable that you should be distressed."

This was not very helpful. Gabler probed further.

"It has been suggested to us by the Greek Government that

Mr. Nicolls might have met with an accident during the final stages of the coup, on the night of April 23, to be precise."

Peter Chiros, sitting squarely at his desk with blazing white cuffs exposed to the correct quarter of an inch, did not indulge in restive movements or involuntary signs of emotion.

Nor did he shake his head when he replied.

"I do not think that is reasonable. Even supposing that the Greek Government were responsible for his death, in the long run it would be less embarrassing to produce his body, with a carefully embroidered explanation of course, than to permit the affair to drag itself out."

"And you think that enough time has passed for that?" Gabler had resigned himself to the fact that Chiros would answer questions; he would not volunteer explanations of his own.

"You have heard the statements of the junta. They say they are anxious to encourage American investment, is that not so?"

"So I understand."

"This would not be the way to do it."

"So you don't think the Greek Government has anything to do with this?" Gabler persisted.

Chiros raised his eyebrows deliberately.

"I do not think *you* believe it, Mr. Gabler, and I agree with you."

Agreement was not what Everett Gabler was looking for.

"Then there is the matter of the hotel room. You called them searches."

"Certainly," said Chiros calmly. "Even if Mr. Nicolls' possessions have now been stolen, it is apparent that somebody is looking for something."

"But what could he have that would interest anybody? All his Hellenus papers were duplicates freely available to everyone concerned."

"Mr. Gabler, I think it would be rash to assume that anybody except Mr. Nicolls knows exactly what he had."

Gabler could finish the unspoken half of the sentence for himself: *exactly what he had or exactly what he was up to.*

Automatically Gabler rose to the defense of a colleague. "Mr. Nicolls stands in very high repute with the Sloan. We are assured that he would act always in the best interests of the Sloan."

Chiros prepared to rise. "That may be true. But doubt might exist as to what those interests are. I am sorry not to have been of further help to you. We share your concern at these mysterious events. And we would certainly share your relief if Mr. Nicolls were to reappear in Athens."

Chiros escorted his visitor down in the elevator to the front door with undiminished courtesy. If Gabler cared to inspect the project site, every attention would be paid to his wishes. Paul Makris & Son would be delighted to arrange a tour.

"No, Mr. Chiros," said Gabler grimly. "I do not anticipate leaving Athens for some time. Certainly not until Kenneth Nicolls has been located."

Rarely had Everett Gabler made such an erroneous prediction. Mulling over suspicions roused by this desire to remove him to the north, he approached the curb of the crowded street and signaled to a taxi on the other side. The taxi driver abandoned his inspection of the passengers alighting from a bus just behind him and waved his accord. The gesture drew the attention of several of the passengers. Thus there was a multitude of witnesses for what happened next.

Without any warning a black Fiat that had been idling at the curb half a block down from the entrance to Paul Makris & Son shot forward until it was directly under Everett Gabler's nose. As if synchronized by a stop watch, two doors flung open and two men appeared. The one in front of Gabler threw a blanket over his head and fell back into the car. The one in the rear thrust Gabler into the back seat and hurled himself on top of the writhing blanket. With the same smooth motion, both doors closed and the driver, who had not budged throughout, shot the car forward under the bemused stare of Peter Chiros, the taxi driver, and a dozen assorted bus passengers.

CHAPTER IX

EUREKA!

HARD AS GREECE was proving to be on Kenneth Nicolls and Everett Gabler, it was, in many ways, harder on Miss Corsa. Given the nature of events, it was she who relayed each unsavory development to John Putnam Thatcher.

"There was a call, Mr. Thatcher," she announced as he returned from a long conference with George Lancer.

"About Greece?" he asked wearily. "If it's another report of no progress, just file it and forget it!"

Miss Corsa persevered. "Yes, it's about Greece."

"Of course it is," said Thatcher. "What else could it be? If I'm not getting cables from Greece, I'm in conference about Greece."

Miss Corsa had no time to waste. "It's from the State Department," she told him. "They called to report that they have been informed by the Embassy in Athens..."

"Oh my God! So many channels and so little information!" Thatcher snorted.

Pointedly, Miss Corsa ignored this and reproduced a message announcing a second forcible entry into the Hotel Britannia. Again somebody had scoured Nicolls' room. The Embassy was insisting on vigorous police action with a review of the activities of hotel personnel.

Thatcher absorbed this, meaningless as it was, and involuntarily recalled his luncheon conversation with Paul Makris.

"There must be some sort of mistake," he said.

Coldly, Miss Corsa assured him that the message was absolutely accurate as it stood.

"Hmm," said Thatcher. "Well, God knows what it means, but we'd better get in touch with Gabler."

"I've tried," Miss Corsa said, fatigue in her voice. "I haven't been able to contact him."

"He's probably cornered King Constantine and is busy giving him the third degree," said Thatcher absently. "I wonder... do you think some of these Greeks have confused Nicolls with someone else? After all, he isn't carrying diamonds—or atomic secrets! Why are they breaking in and searching his room—after killing him, for all we know, and turning out his pockets! Why are—"

"Mr. Thatcher!" Miss Corsa cried out warningly.

Too late. From behind him came a small moan. Thatcher turned. To his horror he found himself face to face with a young red-haired woman, in an advanced stage of pregnancy.

Jane Nicolls was staring at him with equal horror. Her coppery curls, carefully brushed into a tumbled swirl, accentuated the bluish pallor around her lips. She made a valiant attempt to maintain her self-control. Then:

"You haven't... you haven't heard any news?"

"My dear!" said Thatcher, simultaneously cursing himself and hurrying to her side. "Of course we haven't. I was simply speaking in the heat of the moment."

She rewarded him with a wan smile. "I was so frightened," she said with a sigh. "I came because I had to find out..."

Suddenly she broke off. Her expressive green eyes went blank for a moment. She put out a hand to steady herself against Thatcher's arm.

"Let's go into my office," he said anxiously.

Her grasp on his arm tightened. She took a sharp breath.

A hideous suspicion dawned. Thatcher looked closely at her, then searched many years back in memory. Enlightenment came.

"Good Lord!" he exclaimed. "Here, sit down, Jane. Fine, now don't you worry. Miss Corsa, I'm going to need some help..."

Miss Corsa started to rise.

"No, no, the phone," Thatcher directed her hurriedly.

"Call the nurse! Call the limousine! Call the hospital! I'm afraid that we're about to have a baby!"

The next six hours were busy enough to enable Thatcher to do what he had been claiming he wanted to do, namely, put Greece totally out of his mind. It was doubtful, however, that he was suitably grateful since this entailed frenetic activity inappropriate to his age and station.

"After all," he said, quite late that night to an amused Lucy Lancer as he assuaged his near exhaustion with brandy in the Lancers' apartment, "I have been through this three times before. That seems to me—and seemed to me at the time, I might add—enough for one man!"

George Lancer tactfully refilled his vice-president's glass but Lucy asked:

"How are they?"

Austerely Thatcher reported that mother and daughter were doing fine and braced himself for the usual sentimentality that accompanies birth.

"How much did the little girl weigh?" Lucy cooed.

Thatcher sincerely admired Lucy Lancer, but he knew about feminine foibles from his own wife and from his daughter Laura. He had long since learned to be kind, but firm. After exchanging a speaking look with George, he said:

"Lucy, I do not know how much the baby weighs. Please bear in mind that, through no fault of my own, I have been forced to race through the streets of New York..."

"In a limousine, John," Lucy reminded him. "It could have been a taxi."

"What difference does that make?" Thatcher began, but recollected horror brought him to a halt.

In the limousine he had assumed that his chief problem was getting to the hospital in time. Hospitals, after all, were expressly designed for these emergencies. Miss Corsa, thank God, could be relied on to alert the hospital, the obstetrician, and the Nicolls' home on Brooklyn Heights. With clenched jaw Thatcher had sat out the ride uptown, alternatively calculating their progress through heavy traffic and the alarming rate at which Jane Nicolls' spasms were accelerating. He had forced words of encouragement through dry lips and patted a hand whenever it was available. When he had, at last, surrendered the expectant mother into professional hands, he had wiped his brow and congratulated himself that the worst was over.

The chauffeur, who had been silent throughout (he had been praying for the absence of all traffic jams) joined in his relief.

"In the nick of time, if you ask me, Mr. Thatcher," he beamed.

"Thank heavens!" said Thatcher devoutly. "But she'll be all right now."

"I'll have to move the car. You want me to find a place to wait?"

"No, no. That's all right. I'll stay here. You go back to the Sloan. And, Sam!—Good work!"

Sam grinned cheerfully, touched his cap, and pulled out into the street. Thatcher, now that he could catch his breath, asked for the nearest phone booth. The decent thing, he decided, would be to get the addresses of the grandparents so that he could announce results as soon as they were available. But Miss Corsa proved strangely elusive.

"I'm so sorry," the switchboard operator said over and over again, "but Miss Corsa's line is busy."

Finally, sounding shell-shocked, the operator said disbelievingly: "Miss Corsa says you'll have to wait, Mr. Thatcher. She has some important calls to make."

Stunned, Thatcher obediently left the number of his pay phone and prepared to wait his secretary's pleasure. Dimly he realized that the atmosphere, if not the event, was familiar. It had been over thirty-five years since this last happened to him, but he remembered that, in questions of childbirth, all women tended to dismiss all men as distracting non-essentials. With some justice, perhaps. But still, it was going a little too far when his secretary relegated him to the position of importunate suppliant. Particularly when she was safe at the Sloan while he, so to speak, was in the battle line.

When the phone finally rang, he advanced with a few well-chosen words at the ready. But Miss Corsa beat him to the punch.

"Mr. Thatcher, how is Mrs. Nicolls?" she asked anxiously.

"Fine!" said Thatcher at his brusquest. "Now look here, Miss Corsa—"

"Good. Don't let her worry about the baby."

"What do you mean? Don't let her worry about the baby. What else do you suppose she's worrying about?" he demanded.

"I don't mean your baby," said Miss Corsa with uncharacteristic confusion. "I mean our baby."

Thatcher took a deep breath.

"Maybe we had better start again from the beginning," he suggested with iron control. "How many babies are you expecting?"

"Oh, Mr. Thatcher, I'm sorry. But it's so upsetting. I'm talking about the baby in Brooklyn Heights. There's no one there now, except the cleaning woman. And she has to go home before *her* children get back from school."

"Ah!" At least Miss Corsa had not gone round the bend. But it was irritating to find her occupied with trivialities.

"Well, Miss Corsa," he said out of the depths of his experience thirty-five years ago, "you'll just have to find another woman to come in for the night. Then, when you've done that—"

It was Miss Corsa's turn to exercise control.

"Yes, Mr. Thatcher," she said repressively. "I have already made eight calls on the subject. But that's all right. I think that the wife of one of the junior trust officers will be able to stay the night if necessary. And I have spoken with Mrs. Nicolls' mother in Boston. Unfortunately the planes are rained out, but the train should get her here before midnight."

Feeling vaguely guilty, in fact feeling as if it were all his fault somehow, Thatcher humbly asked for the phone number of the senior Nicolls in San Francisco. He knew that, nature being what it was, if the limousine had been delayed by fifteen minutes, Jane Nicolls would have had her baby on the spot. On the other hand, now that she was safe in the hospital, it would be hours and hours before there was issue.

Reconciled to the need for patience, and armed with the San Francisco number, he had proceeded to the obstetrics waiting room. There he had opened the door and stared, appalled.

Unbelievably, the room was populated entirely by minors.

He remembered the waiting room of thirty-five years ago. He had been exposed to it three times. It had always contained a motley collection of men—trim, taut executives; big, sweating blue-collar workers; tidy, worried little clerks—but all of them, indubitably, *adults*. And what did he find here, for Christ's sake? Schoolboys! There were two of them, with book bags at their feet, actually doing homework! And every single one of them, it seemed, had a transistor radio slung over his shoulder. Thatcher tried to get a grip on himself. Was that so surprising? Our boys in Vietnam were taking their radios into the front lines—where presumably they had other things to occupy them. Why not into a waiting room? Grimly Thatcher sighted a chair, somewhat isolated from its fellows, and began to pick his way over shambling limbs.

It was at this point he had realized that the occupants of the room were staring at him with mass disapproval.

"Lucy," he complained savagely to his hostess, "I had to pace around that room with a bunch of teenagers who looked on me as a dirty old man!"

George Lancer could no longer contain himself. He broke down and howled.

John Thatcher reviewed his afternoon and identified the culprit. "Charlie Trinkam is going to pay for this!"

George commented that it was a shame that Charlie had not been on duty.

Lucy pointed out that Charlie, a born bachelor, would certainly have fainted at a critical juncture. "There's nothing so helpful in these things as experience." She looked severely at Thatcher. "And, John, I am thoroughly ashamed of you. Think of that poor girl! Worrying about her husband, then having to go through this!"

Gloomily Thatcher replenished his glass. In point of fact, he had been able to think of nothing else. As soon as it became apparent that Jane Nicolls was in no danger and that the tiny daughter—six pounds eight ounces and exuberantly healthy, although he was not going to indulge Lucy with that information—had an endearing pink halo, it became unbearably cruel that young Nicolls should not be at their side. That he should be missing—or dead.

Lancer shook his head. "What was that business about his room, John?"

"It was ransacked, for the second time. This time, his belongings were stolen as well."

Together they pondered this.

"But why are people ransacking Nicolls' room ad infinitum?" George asked the world at large.

"I was thinking," Thatcher said sadly, "before today's little adventure, that somebody is making a bad mistake. Somebody thinks Nicolls has something of value. They... killed him, searched the body, didn't find anything, then searched the room twice..."

"Oh, no!" said Lucy in soft dismay. "Not with the baby..."

Lancer cleared his throat. "I don't like to ask this, John, but is there any chance that Nicolls *was* up to something?"

He was not impugning Ken Nicolls' personal integrity. The Sloan Guaranty Trust employed no one, in any capacity, with whom smuggled heroin or counterfeit currency was remotely conceivable. But it was simple realism, nonetheless; every firm with international operations knows all too well that various arms of the U.S. Government stake out patriotic claims and act, so to speak, as free loaders, turning bona fide businessmen into couriers—and worse.

"And it saves them money, too," said Thatcher irascibly. Cloak and dagger, like cops and robbers, irritated him immensely when played by adults. "I don't know, George. I do know that nobody ever approached Charlie."

"But Nicolls is younger and idealistic," said Lancer obscurely. "Washington swears that they didn't..."

"But would Washington know? The CIA seems to have seceded from the nation," Thatcher said brutally. Things were looking blacker and blacker. "There's only one thing. These searches."

"Well?"

"Why two of them? Doesn't that suggest more than one group, looking for whatever it is?"

But he got no direct answer. Instead, George rumbled "Makris" suggestively enough to tell Thatcher that here was another adherent of the Mephistophelean Makris theory.

"Do you think Paul Makris could have anything to do with Nicolls' disappearance?" George asked deeply.

Thatcher tried to be honest. "On the face of it, no. So far he's been scrupulous with us about Hellenus. But there's no denying that he has all sorts of irons in the fire in Greece. I do get the impression he knows more than he is saying." He paused, then added: "I also get the impression that he is suspicious of us."

"Us?" said George Lancer, genuinely indignant. The Sloan's contribution to world peace and understanding was precious to him. "Why should he be suspicious of us? Good God, even this new Greek Government trusts us."

In the distance, a telephone trilled.

With rare pessimism Thatcher said, "George, I don't have any answers. All I know is that I am beginning to fear the worst. Everett will move heaven and earth to find out what's happened to Nicolls, but I'm not sure that will be enough."

The houseboy materialized in the doorway.

"Mr. Thatcher? A Mr. Makris would like to speak to you, sir."

Thatcher arose. "Something new," he said. "And in the very nature of things, bad."

The voice on the phone was low-pitched, almost hesitant.

"Ah, Mr. Thatcher. I am sorry to disturb you, so late. But, I have just received news that I think you will want to hear."

"Of course," said Thatcher, smothering a yawn. He did not waste time inquiring how Makris knew where to find him. He would not be surprised to learn that Makris had already sent a bouquet to Jane Nicolls. "No, you are certainly not disturbing me. We are eager for any news you may have."

Makris was strangely apologetic. "An employee of mine, in Athens, has just called."

Thatcher made an encouraging noise.

"Improbable as it may seem," said Makris in an odd voice, "it appears that yesterday your Mr. Gabler was kidnapped, in broad daylight. He has not been seen for twenty-four hours."

By pure act of will, Thatcher kept his voice free from any emotion.

"Improbable indeed. Er... tell me, do you have any more details?"

Makris did not have many. "According to my men in Athens, nobody—that is, nobody official—knows anything about it."

"Do you believe that?" asked Thatcher bluntly.

"At the moment," Makris said slowly, "I do not know what or whom to believe."

"I see." Thatcher paused, then said merely, "I need hardly ask that you relay any further information you receive."

With unimpaired politeness, Paul Makris agreed that he would.

After mutual courtesies, Thatcher put down the receiver. He hesitated a moment in the decorous elegance of the Lancer hallway, trying to digest this latest outrage. Then, suddenly invigorated, he rejoined his hosts and described the conversation.

George was almost incoherent. "Ev... Kidnapped? For God's sake, I'll call Washington! We'll send in the Sixth Fleet..."

Lucy, examining her guest, was more perceptive.

"John, you're relieved, aren't you? You're not so worried any more?"

Thatcher considered this. "You're right, Lucy. I am relieved, although I don't know why!"

But by the next morning, he did. With quick decision, he was explaining the situation. Stunned, Walter Bowman, for once, was not taking things in.

"They've kidnapped Ev?" Bowman repeated. "*Ev?*"

"That's what Makris says," said Thatcher checking a list, pressing the buzzer for Miss Corsa, and tearing open a cable. "And this does, too," he added, tossing the flimsy across the desk to Bowman.

The U.S. Embassy in Athens now sounded demented.

Bemused, Bowman read. "Ev! Why would anybody want to kidnap Ev?"

"Exactly the point," said Thatcher bracingly. "Ah, Miss Corsa. Now let's see . . . we're going to be busy. Oh yes, flowers for Mrs. Nicolls . . . oh, you've already done that . . . good! Now, send off this cable to Trinkam, first thing. He's to drop everything and get back as soon as possible. Good. Now when you're through, hurry back."

Bowman bewilderedly stared. "John. Will you tell me . . ."

Thatcher cut in. "Listen, Walter, this kidnapping proves it. Somebody is gunning for the Sloan—not for Ken Nicolls. Obviously, if they've gone after Everett as well, there's a chance that Nicolls is safe . . ."

Some unknown perversity stirred Walter Bowman.

"John, hold it! What if neither of them is safe?"

Thatcher looked up, a glint in his eyes. "That's what I'm going to find out!"

Miss Corsa reentered to the accompaniment of protests from Bowman.

"I'm going to Greece," said Thatcher martially. "There's some method to all this madness! These are not mistakes! This is a deliberate attempt to discredit the Sloan, for some reason or other. And by God, it's not going to succeed. I'm going to Athens as soon as possible..."

"No!" Bowman yelped. "John, for God's sake! You can't go! They may both of them be lying dead somewhere! We don't know what's happening..."

"Miss Corsa," Thatcher demanded, "you heard that? I'm..."

Unmoved, Miss Corsa admitted that she had heard. She did not add that most of the sixth floor had heard as well. Then:

"I've already made your reservations for you, Mr. Thatcher. You're leaving at six this evening."

So much for instant decision. Thatcher smiled to himself.

"If I were a wiser man," he said, "I'd send you, Miss Corsa!"

CHAPTER X

THE SPARTAN BOY

THE CARLOAD OF men pursuing Kenneth Nicolls arrived at Jamison's Red Cross station eight hours later than he had anticipated. Their inquiries throughout the earthquake zone had been hampered by bad roads, lack of co-operation, and an insouciance as to the exact number or affiliation of field station personnel which shocked the Greeks to the core.

"But these Americans are impossible," wailed a small rat-like man who labored under the name Archimedes. "They have no order, no method!"

The thick-shouldered, bovine man at the wheel avoided a pot-hole before replying. "What is more, they do not seem to have this Kenneth Nicolls. So now, we do the Canadians. And then, I suppose, Australians and South Africans and God knows who else! I spit on these Anglo-Saxons!"

He lowered the window and did so.

The quiet voice from the back seat remained unprovoked. "There are no Australians or South Africans on the list of relief stations. And the Canadians only have this one we are going to now. Nicolls may very well be there. He would have no trouble pretending to be Canadian. I understand that they are the same as Americans."

"Surely they would ask to see his papers," said Archimedes. "His passport, his identity card."

"Did the Quakers ask for his papers?"

"But, Yanni," the driver protested, "if these Canadians are the same, they won't know whether he is there or not."

"All the better for us," Yanni replied calmly. "If they do not notice one man extra, they will never notice one man missing."

Everybody in the car brightened.

Once arrived at Jamison's, the three men almost failed due to the precision of their inquiries. Their description of the famous Swarthmore sweat shirt evoked no recollection. The sleepy men in the back of the truck at the Larissa hospital had seen only a dim hulk hurtling over the tailboard.

"No," they said politely, "we have no one of that description in the camp."

Yanni persisted.

"He was a large, blond man. And he was in Larissa the night before last."

"Oh, him!" they chorused disapprovingly.

They remembered him very well. He was an eccentric hitchhiker who did not know his own mind. First, he hopped on their truck, then he hopped off without a word of explanation. They were well rid of him.

"Where?" Yanni demanded eagerly. "Where did he leave you?"

But at this point, Kenneth Nicolls' luck came into its own. The men in the truck had been tired, they had slept until awakened on arrival. He could have debarked at any point on the road north.

The Greeks withdrew with apologies and thanks, leaving a chatter of speculation behind them. Only one man was silent. Jamison had arrived half way through the interrogation. He had many things to think about, but now he paused to think about this.

"Did those men show any identification?" he asked at last.

"No," a helper replied. "But what the hell! This Nicolls is a kook!"

Jamison remained thoughtful.

"Something odd going on," he decided. "Probably none of our business, but it won't do any harm if the next driver into town gives a ring to the American Embassy."

In the car they were thoughtful too.

"Why did they all have to sleep?" Archimedes complained. "Is that any way to run a relief station?"

The driver was more reasonable. "They could do nothing in the truck. It was right that they should recover their strength before returning to work. In fact, it would have been wrong of them not to seize the opportunity to rest."

Yanni broke in on this interesting discussion.

"Never mind that now. What I want to know is what Nicolls is up to. If he is trying to get to Athens, why did he join the truck in the first place? If he wants to hide in a relief station, why did he leave the truck? There is no reason for his behavior."

There was a depressed silence which was broken by the driver.

"You don't think that the others can have communicated with him?" he suggested hesitantly.

Archimedes almost bounced in his excitement. "That's it! They have arranged a contact with this Nicolls. He is going to meet them!"

The others were not so swift to adopt disastrous conclusions.

"Let us hope not," said Yanni grimly. "But if this is the case, we must find them quickly. Both of them. Neither must reach Athens."

But it is not easy to hurry when you do not know where you are going. As they sped southward they debated probabilities. If Nicolls were being directed by Greeks, then he would have been instructed to leave the truck at some small, unfrequented place and proceed cautiously overland to his rendezvous. If he were acting independently, then he would probably head for a large town where he could change his appearance and pick up public transport, but this independence was becoming less and less predictable.

"He is a deep one," the driver said judiciously. "Far more cunning than they told us."

Yanni bit back a sympathetic retort. The others must continue to have faith in their leaders—a faith he himself was rapidly losing. The leaders had told him to go forth and pluck this Kenneth Nicolls from the countryside. He would be waiting helplessly and harmlessly, as incongruous as a millionaire's yacht in the midst of a village fishing fleet. And what, instead, did they find? A man who skimmed over the landscape, ducking in and out of relief stations, diving into cities, heading first south, then north; a man who was one minute a respectable banker, the next minute a college boy. He was certainly not helpless. Of more immediate concern, he might not be harmless either. There were several hours unaccounted for in Larissa. Nicolls could be a walking arsenal by now.

The trip south did nothing to restore Yanni's confidence. In the small villages, their tale of a lanky American in a sweat shirt was met with blank incomprehension or, more disturbingly, concealed amusement. This could mean anything, from the immemorial contempt of the villager for the city rube to a gigantic conspiracy. At this point, Yanni was discounting neither possibility. In Verroia things were better. Busy townsfolk met brusque questions with brusque answers and went about their business. If the citizens of Verroia were to be believed, their town was a cosmopolitan center drawing visitors from all over the world. Lanky Americans were a dime a dozen, relief workers littered every corner. The sweat shirt? No, they did not remember the garment described. But it was warm at midday, many of the young foreigners strolled about in shirt sleeves, carrying sweaters.

"We will leave you here, Archimedes," Yanni announced. "It is a waste of time for all three of us to scour this town. Pavlos and I will continue. When you are through, take the bus and join us at Elasson."

And so, through scores of little villages, they made their way to Elasson. When they pulled up in the main square, they headed straight for their first objective, the bus station and the central telephone office. They were tired, thirsty, and exasperated. But they were professionals. As they asked their questions, their eyes roved over the crowds, alert for the first sign of a tall, blond American.

It was therefore not surprising that they failed to notice a short, buxom woman with raven black hair. She strode out of a telephone booth and walked directly in front of them as they questioned the girl at the switchboard. Head averted, shifting the string bag with protruding leeks from one hand to the other, she marched out of the building at the same steady pace, marched across the square, down a street and into an alleyway. Not until she was within the second-hand clothes shop did she throw discretion to the winds, flying behind the counter to rush up the stairs, fling open the door of the living quarters and cry out:

"They are here! They have come for you!"

Greek shopkeepers can be all smiling charm so long as a cash sale is in sight. But they lack any talent for being amused by tales of lost wallets and temporary lack of funds. When Kenneth Nicolls explained his plight, the woman who five minutes earlier had gracefully bowed out a customer, turned instantly into a raging virago.

"It is because I am a widow you think to rob me? It is because you are an American! Oh, shame, that a rich man should stoop to steal from a poor woman!" Here she seized on his coat sleeve like a limpet. "But you shall not succeed! I will call for the police, I will scream for the neighbors! Everyone shall know that you are a thief. You shall not steal my clothes!"

Ken, appalled at the hornets' nest he had roused, tried vainly to explain. He had no intention of stealing her clothes, he repeated over and over again. Timidly he plucked at her fingers. If she would only release him, he would remove and return her clothes.

Appeasement got him nowhere. Then he started to bellow. Dammit, his own clothes, now lying on the counter, were worth just as much as this shoddy suit of hers! She could have either set she wanted.

The shopkeeper was not diverted. What she wanted was the profit she would have made on the sale. Nothing less would satisfy her. It was a matter for the police, she declaimed.

By the grace of God no other customer had entered yet. Ken, who wanted to slip through Elasson like a shadow, now seemed destined to march through its streets pursued by this screaming fury, with all the publicity of several accompanying brass bands. Stung by the injustice of it all, infuriated by her accusations and frightened of the future, Ken resorted to the truth.

"Then call the police, you old harridan!" he threatened. "They're already looking for me, and they'll want to know what you're doing with public enemy number one."

He had half-hoped that his threat would have some effect. Not many Greeks these days wished to involve themselves in the political troubles of the new regime. But he had scarcely expected immediate paralysis to grip the woman.

Unmoving, she stared at him, her fingers still clutching his arm. Slowly her eyes moved to the counter taking in the sweat shirt and chinos. Then she let out her breath in a long sigh.

"A friend of Georgi's," she said bitterly. "I might have known."

To Kenneth, it seemed as if he had suddenly put out a thousand antennae, each one testing the currents very cautiously. He did not trust himself to say a word.

"It is always the same," the shopkeeper continued, heavily ironical. "A mother is no use until trouble comes. Will Georgi listen to me, will he do his duty and stay here to help me? No, he has to go off to the University, be a great thinker, an important radical. But now? Now you students are in trouble. And who does Georgi turn to? He turns to his mother!"

Transcendent satisfaction illuminated her face. It was obvious that this twist in events accorded with some ancient pattern deeply pleasing to her.

Audacity, Ken told himself, then more audacity.

"I have to hide until I can find a way to go to Athens."

Seer-like, the shopkeeper nodded. "Naturally."

"But they're after me."

The woman seemed to understand more than he did. She unbent indulgently.

"I will take care of you. But you students are all little boys.

Playing at being dangerous men. And when somebody takes you seriously you become frightened."

She clucked maternally. Then with a switch to practicality, she hustled Ken back of the counter. "Quickly. We must get you out of sight. You were wise not to tell me anything until my customer left."

Her tone indicated that wisdom, of the most elementary nature, would always come as a surprise from one of Georgi's friends.

Incredibly, that was all there was to it. His hostess was busy in the shop all day while Kenneth lurked in her living quarters upstairs. That night he had to fend off questions about Georgi, which he did by saying that their contacts had been limited because of political necessity. During his hours of leisure he had worried about the complexion of Georgi's political views. Was he a communist, an anarchist, a socialist? Presumably, whatever he was, Kenneth's safety lay in being his political twin. Years ago, when he was lying in the paddy wagon, he had hoped to avoid a firing squad by pretending to be a bloated capitalist. Now salvation might lie in the opposite corner.

Which part of the corner did not really matter. It developed that his hostess was a monarchist of the old school. Georgi, affectionately described as a dangerous leftist, might aim at nothing more alarming than a constitutional monarchy. And Mrs. Andreades, God bless her, was a born conspirator. She entered freely into plans for Ken's escape, agreeing to house him until these could be effected. One thing puzzled her.

"You Americans! Don't you have enough troubles at home? I suppose it's this Papandreou." She shook her head. "At least I can be grateful that, if Georgi has to go to a university, it was Athens. California must be a terrible place."

Kenneth resisted the temptation to come to the defense of California. Instead he urged the necessity of a phone call to Bill Riemer. To his home, not to the Embassy! There should be no danger of arousing suspicion, if the call were placed by a native Greek with a son in Athens.

"There is nothing to worry about. The girl at the exchange knows me. I call Athens many times. Not just Georgi, I have business with the tourist shops there."

Kenneth was therefore awaiting Mrs. Andreades' return the next day impatiently. If she succeeded in getting through to Riemer, many of his troubles would be over. But when she burst in with her alarming tidings, all thoughts of the call vanished.

"Blessed Virgin! How merciful that I saw them. They will be here in a matter of hours."

"You actually saw them? What are they like?"

"Two of them. Evil men. But there is no time for that. We must prepare for their coming."

Kenneth was slower than his hostess. "But what makes you think they'll come here?"

Mrs. Andreades raised fine dark eyes to heaven. "All this education! What does it teach you?" she asked, paraphrasing a question Kenneth had heard often enough from his own parents. "You walked through the center of town yesterday morning asking directions, did you not? The man at the kiosk told you about my shop, did he not? Then the man at the grocery told you how to find the alley. Do you think your pursuers will not find this out? It is only a matter of time."

She was right, of course. Nervously Kenneth surveyed his surroundings. Should he just lie low and rely on Mrs. Andreades to mislead the opposition?

No, said Mrs. Andreades firmly. Already he had lurked aloft for a full day. It would be a miracle if the neighbors had not already noticed. He must be in plain sight, obviously innocuous, a normal part of the background of any Greek store.

So, when a car finally nosed its way into the alley that was almost too small for it, Ken had a front-row seat. He was dressed in the faded, gray suit. A beret covered hair which was now mud-coloured, and shabby stubble once more adorned his jaw. He was unloading a cart in a side yard, carrying boxes to a shed in the back. Mrs. Andreades actually did employ a handy man, now out on his collection rounds. Any neighbor, asked about the shabby man in the yard, would testify that he had been part of the landscape for years.

Ken was happy to see that Mrs. Andreades' psychology had been sound. The two men who emerged from the sedan spared not a glance for the scene by the cart. They were intent on their errand. Even the length of time they remained in the shop did not disturb him. Mrs. Andreades would not let such an opportunity pass without making the most of it. They had agreed she should tell the men that Ken had bought clothing, describing some feasible but misleading attire. She would then add that he had left in a hurry, saying he had to catch the bus north. With luck this should send the pursuit streaming up to Verroia. Being Mrs. Andreades, however, she was no doubt telling them how he had trembled, looking furtively to the right and to the left. Even if they did not believe her, it would do no harm. The instinct to dramatize is well known in Greece.

It was a full forty-five minutes before the car drew off and another five before Mrs. Andreades circumspectly joined him.

"I was magnificent!" she announced.

Ken believed her.

"Not for a moment do they doubt me. Even when I tell them that you are now limping, as if from some bad fall. Have no fear. They will go to the north, looking for a man in a black jacket with a bad limp."

"Did you tell them I was going to Verroia?" Ken asked anxiously.

She looked at him with Olympian scorn. "Is it for me to make their task easy? I said that you were going *toward* Verroia. Let them look in every little hamlet on the way."

Ken relaxed. For the first time since Mrs. Andreades' tumultuous return from the post office that morning, he felt safe. The immediate future seemed free of pitfalls. Idly he watched the handy man returning from his rounds and bringing in the day's latest collection of merchandise.

"It's a pity Riemer wasn't home when you called," he said reflectively. "Did the maid understand your message?"

"I made her repeat it. And she said that she would call Mr. Riemer at the office right away. The word *embassy* was never used. But this Mr. Riemer, can you trust him to take action?"

"Oh, I think so. After all, they must be looking for me, by now." Hastily Kenneth pulled himself up. He had almost forgotten his role as student activist and revealed himself as a responsible businessman who does not simply drop out of sight with no questions asked.

Mrs. Andreades did not notice the slip. She was staring out at the street in horror. Then she found her tongue.

"They are coming back! And Marcos is in plain sight! They must not see you together."

Kenneth was almost immobilized when he saw that the car blocked their return to the shop and the sanctuary of the second floor. But Mrs. Andreades was made of sterner stuff. Grabbing both his arms she drew them into the shelter of the tiny shed, as the two men advanced on Marcos.

Huddled together they could hear every word of the exchange through the gaps in the battered board door. Mrs. Andreades hissed a running translation.

"You there!" the leader called. "Where is the owner? She was here a minute ago."

Marcos' surliness was a byword in Elasson. Without any idea of what was going on, he was instinctively unhelpful.

"Is it her business to wait for you? She's gone out. She'll be back."

There was a hasty consultation between the two men. They wished to set off for the north immediately.

"How long?" they pressed.

This time Marcos did not bother to reply. He shrugged, indicating the futility of predicting a woman's absence.

"It's no use," said Pavlos.

Yanni made one last attempt.

"Did you see the American yesterday morning?"

Marcos peered at him suspiciously.

"American?"

"Yes, yes. The American who was here yesterday morning and bought clothes."

Marcos, for all his rheumy eyes and misogynous age, did not miss much. He knew perfectly well that there had been an American resident for the better part of two days. And what business was that of these two?

"There are always Americans. But me, I go on my rounds. It is for her to be a fine lady and sit in the shop. I am out and about, I drive the cart, in rain, in winter, at my age I drive the cart. I am not one of the fine ones..."

As he spoke, Yanni and Pavlos were in full retreat. They knew this litany could go on forever. Even as Marcos reached for the further privations of his life, they were in the car, starting the motor.

As it pulled away, Mrs. Andreades and Kenneth subsided on each other in a surge of relief. Kenneth should have been more careful. As Mrs. Andreades clutched him, she made a great discovery.

Her dark, almond-shaped eyes slid upwards.

"But," she exclaimed, "you are not such a young boy, after all."

Kenneth had also made a discovery.

Mrs. Andreades was by no means an old woman.

CHAPTER XI

PROMETHEUS BOUND

DICTATORSHIP ENCOURAGES CIVIC myopia. In a few short weeks, Athenians had learned to turn blind eyes on tank deployments, on padlocked schools, on royal appearances designed to demonstrate the love of the people for their monarch, and on non-royal disappearances.

But there are limits to the tactful blindness that can be expected from any Mediterranean people. It is one thing for booted men to swoop down on unsuspecting victims in the small hours of the morning and prod them, barefoot and dazed, to prison cells or firing squads; recent history has presented Greece with too many instances of this. But to snatch an American tourist in broad daylight from Omonia Square, possibly the busiest spot in Athens—well, that was too much. As the small Fiat sped away with Everett Gabler (perilously negotiating a corner and narrowly missing a vendor of chestnuts), there was a moment of unbelieving silence. Then, as if summoned by a choirmaster, there came a tremendous release of Greek indignation.

"Po! Po! Po!"

"Did you see that!"

"Panos, I feel sick!"

The important personage overseeing the chaotic stream of traffic was drawn by the crowd. With tremendous dignity he halted all cars, then advanced slowly, demanding instant enlightenment. Inevitably, a rich cacaphony of claxons, bells, and automotive curses was added to the forceful, if conflicting, accounts which rained down upon him. Within minutes, the din was insupportable.

Peter Chiros had briefly reverted to type by shouting furiously at his nearest neighbor. But almost immediately, he came to his senses. Unnoticed amidst the mounting maelstrom—and the chestnut vendor had joined the group, claiming bodily injuries as well as property loss—he disengaged himself from what was, by now, a gathering of private citizens far in excess of the number currently allowed in Greece.

Chiros pushed through the mob, courteously murmuring *signome* but scowling hideously in thought. Like any Greek, Chiros first responded to drama, then accepted the inscrutable workings of fate with an expressive shrug, acknowledging both the capriciousness of life and man's frailty under forces bigger than he was.

But Peter Chiros was an employee of Makris & Son as well as a Greek; he knew that fatalism would not wrap this one up. Not when the man so unceremoniously bundled off was Everett Gabler of the Sloan Guaranty Trust.

"*Signome,*" he said again, elbowing his way to the entrance to his office. If he had affected worry beads, he would have been clicking them at a staccato clip by now. There were too many questions, too many perils, there was too much at stake.

Chiros pushed his way indoors and, ignoring the elevator which tended to be chancy, took the stairs two at a time. His first goal was the telephone. Others might be misled by the New York office's assurance that, in Athens, Chiros had full authority to act; Peter Chiros was not.

"I'm calling Makris," he declared, abruptly gesturing a colleague to follow him into his office. He relayed a terse but colorful description of what had just happened on the street below their windows.

The colleague was less well-tailored than Chiros. But he too was a Greek and an old Makris hand. He fingered a jowly jaw.

"Not so good," he decided. "A little overdone, don't you think?"

"That is not for us to say!" Chiros said harshly.

"Well, someone will!" Jowl-jaw riposted. "Or do you think that the Sloan will take the position that this was a one-way trip to Giaura Island?"

Chiros thought of that filthy, overcrowded prison island used by the colonels. Then he shook his head.

"Two of them? One right after the other? I do not think anyone will be offering simple explanations."

"And the explanations will really have to be complicated when Nicolls and Gabler reappear."

"Reappear!" Chiros snorted. "Only if they're lucky!"

The colleague, startled, sent up a ritual call to the Holy Virgin.

Chiros snarled several epithets at the Athens Exchange, then looked up:

"What I'm afraid is that, sooner or later, two bodies will be washed ashore someplace!"

Jowl-jaw whistled soundlessly. "Oho! It's like that, is it? Well, that's what comes of playing with fire."

Chiros shrugged. "I don't know what's going on. Maybe we'll understand more after we speak to Makris. But I'd give a lot to know what he's up to!"

Twenty-four hours passed. Everett Gabler was not washed ashore on one of Greece's rocky promontories. But he was not in evidence on dry land, either. He had disappeared as completely as Kenneth Nicolls.

As the softly plump Army officer across the desk repeated this refrain, Bill Riemer undiplomatically interrupted:

"Captain Cotronis! You, and your superiors, must recognize the very grave implications of this situation! Mr. Gabler was forcibly abducted in broad daylight..."

Cotronis arched pudgy fingers and said: "Crimes occur, my dear Mr. Riemer. Even in your own great country, I understand. Do not think that we underestimate the seriousness of the whole affair. Colonel Patakos himself said to me: '*Cotronis, this is serious!*'"

Riemer had orders to throw his weight around. It was a pleasure. He was developing a deep dislike for the representatives of the new, purified Greece with whom he was forced to deal; in addition, Cotronis' thin dark curls glistened with pomade.

"Captain, I am instructed to remind you that your campaign to encourage American tourism..."

Touched on a sore point, Cotronis quickly pointed out that the tourist season was progressing very nicely, despite lies and calumnies spread by Italy, France, Spain, and other tourist centers.

"Not enough to fill those new hotels on Mykonos," Riemer contradicted him. He had just noticed that Cotronis let the nail of his little finger grow long. "You have to increase dollar tourism by twenty per cent each season in order to justify the capital expenses you have been undertaking. We have made studies that I would be glad to lend to you."

Cotronis was baffled by percentage numbers and capital expenditures, but he was shrewd enough to know an insult when he heard one.

"Mr. Riemer, you forget—"

"And it's not going to do any good to your plans for encouraging U.S. investments if important businessmen disappear into thin air! You know that it is your government's policy to encourage U.S. investment, don't you!"

Cotronis' simulation of friendliness was betrayed by the vicious glitter in his eyes. Yet his voice remained ingratiating. He even managed a small smile.

"Ah, you Americans! How you like your jokes! Please, Mr. Riemer, remember that Colonel Patakos himself asks me to reaffirm the profound friendship of Greece—"

"What kind of friendship is this?" Riemer asked grandly. "Friendship that allows Americans to be snatched from the streets of Athens!"

Cotronis controlled himself with visible effort.

"Now, to get down to brass tacks," said Riemer in another tone of voice. "The Ambassador, and the highest sources in Washington, want to know what steps are being taken."

"Steps?" Cotronis trembled with rage. "Steps? What steps can we take, Mr. Riemer? We know no more than you! The police, the militia, they are searching for Mr. Nicolls and for Mr. Gabler. But we have no clues..."

"What about the car?"

"It was stolen!" Cotronis wailed.

"And the eyewitnesses?"

Cotronis wiped his brow and explained that there had been twenty-seven eyewitnesses and hence twenty-seven different versions.

So it went for some time. But there was nothing more to be learned from Cotronis. Riemer, although outranked, rose to indicate that the interview was terminated. He was a thin, pale man with a prominent Adam's apple, personally insignificant compared to Captain Cotronis, who was magnificent with ribbons, medals and epaulettes. It gave Riemer considerable pleasure to reflect that behind him stood two hundred million people, the Sixth Fleet and other support factors.

"Captain Cotronis, I am afraid that I must report to my government that your government is not cooperating fully..."

An hour later, Riemer was describing the scene to the Ambassador. Like Riemer, the Ambassador was bone-tired. He was as fed up with colonels as Riemer was with captains. And, if the whole truth were told, he was also tired of urgent high-level telephone calls, cipher messages and other communications concerning the Sloan Guaranty Trust and its wandering personnel.

"I pushed him pretty hard, sir," said Riemer.

"Good," said His Excellency absently. He himself had been struggling with an impulse to go further. "And you're convinced that the government didn't have a hand in any of this?"

Wearily, Riemer summoned his thoughts. "I wouldn't say I'm convinced, sir, since this bunch is absolutely outside the limit of anything I've ever encountered!" Riemer's previous post had been the Congo. "But on the whole, I don't think so. Cotronis would like to assassinate me, I know. But I think he was really sincere—or as sincere as anything so unsavoury can be. But Cotronis may not know everything that's going on. I do know that they are making inquiries about Nicolls and Gabler. Of course, that could be window dressing—but they're so simple-minded—well, frankly, I don't think they're clever enough to think of it."

The Ambassador growled but he did not deprecate these intemperate utterances. "That gibes with the line they're feeding me." He took a turn around the room. "But then, what the hell! I'm not convinced that the *colonels* know everything their supporters are up to! They might not even approve. First Nicolls, then Gabler! What do you think..."

Riemer brooded darkly. Then: "Frankly, I think Nicolls must be dead."

"And Gabler?"

Riemer closed his eyes against reality. "I think he's either dead—or damned near!"

Everett Gabler was not dead. He was, however, far from well. A very disagreeable nervous headache was pounding relentlessly at his temples. Moreover his stomach, always delicate, was in a state of outright mutiny. Yet, despite vile personal discomfort, in danger as in safety, Everett Gabler retained a strong sense of the dignity due him, both as an individual and as a representative of the Sloan Guaranty Trust.

Therefore, instead of sinking back in comfort, he sat bolt upright on the modern Danish sofa.

He had no idea where he was. Presumably, it was still Greece. Yesterday's wild automobile ride, while seeming endless, had taken an hour at the most. Since then he had been imprisoned—yes, imprisoned!—in what appeared to be a small country house. Certainly, sounds heard at dawn suggested that the house was in the country. And a small window revealed a sparkling sea with islands stretching to the horizon. Otherwise, for all that Everett could tell, he might have been in an apartment in New York. A rather expensive apartment, at that. There was a grand piano in the corner of this room; in the hall that led to the bedroom where he had been immured—immured!—were shelves of books, including many English titles.

A beautiful plant filled a large terra cotta vase now glowing in the lengthening sun rays. It was tastefully luxurious. Everett was infuriated.

"No, thank you," he said icily to the elderly woman mutely urging tea upon him. "No, thank you!"

The dark young man slouched against the open door to the balcony responded to the flow of speech this elicited.

"Eleni, she says it is the camomile! It will make your stomach feel better!" He then relapsed into silence.

Everett Gabler merely glared at him frostily, shook his head at the old lady and remained silent.

Eleni looked from one to the other, then, with a shrug of the shoulders, left the room.

The bald-headed man sitting opposite Gabler exchanged a few words with the young man at the window. From the kitchen, the old woman's complaints wafted back, interpolated with low masculine rumbles.

Gabler, whose suffering stomach cried aloud for tea, felt his resolve stiffen. Out there, in the kitchen, were two of the three gorillas who had had the effrontery to bundle him into a car, drive him around for an hour—with a blanket over his head! —then frogmarch him up the stairs into this very room. No doubt other toughs were patrolling the grounds! Well, let them! He would show these people the stuff that bankers are made of!

The bald man sighed.

"Mr. Gabler, why can you not cooperate?" he asked plaintively, echoing, although he did not know it, many of Everett's colleagues at the Sloan. "We are reasonable people..."

This was too much for Everett.

"Reasonable?" he exploded. "Well, that is certainly a very strange way to put it! You're a band of cut-throats, that's what you are! Reasonable? Hah! Kidnapping people from city streets may pass for reason in Greece, but I have another word for it!" Since he was speaking, he felt it incumbent upon him to add: "I demand that you release me immediately!"

There ensued a vigorous Greek exchange. Inwardly, Everett

Gabler smiled. Demands for reasonableness had been continuing ever since he had been delivered to this room. The only interruptions had been a few hours sleep, with two mustachioed villains watchfully stationed inside the bedroom, and a dinner composed of egg-lemon soup and fish with garlic sauce. Delicious, Everett had to admit that it had been. But poison to a man with his stomach. Yet Everett Gabler had held out; his own indignation was undiminished. The Greeks were beginning to sound disheartened.

The young man at the window left off his moody fingernail chewing and came over to station himself near Gabler. His dark, rather handsome face, glistened with earnestness.

"Mr. Gabler," he said hoarsely, "you must understand that this is serious for us, very serious. Already, you have driven us to action that we deplore—no!" His voice rose above Everett's expostulations. "No! We did not wish to abduct you. Do not force us to take other action that we—and you—would regret! But do not doubt that we will do—what you force us to do!"

A quivering silence fell. Both interrogators fixed their eyes hypnotically on Gabler. From the kitchen there was the clatter of pans punctuating the flow of conversation.

"We are serious," said the young man after an enigmatic look at his companion. "We are deadly serious. You must believe us, Mr. Gabler."

He had misjudged his man. Everett Gabler was already so ruffled that neither cajolery nor threats of bodily harm could get through to him.

"Disgraceful," he announced firmly. "This whole performance is disgraceful, and I demand..."

As he continued, the young man threw his arms into the air and exploded into profanity. Gabler settled back and mulishly confronted his tormentors. Curiously enough, his stomach felt better. Possibly it was the diversion. Because Everett Gabler, to do him justice, was not an egoist; he thought of self only when it was right and proper. At the moment, his attention was centered elsewhere—namely, on these two men.

Once Gabler had assimilated the fact that the younger man was a student of architecture and the bald man was owner of an importing firm—somewhere—his sense of affront had known no bounds.

This is not to say that for several hours Everett Gabler had not resigned himself to being in the hands of desperadoes. He had tried to compose himself to meet his Maker. But the villa, together with an architect student and an importer (and the two brigands in the kitchen were identified as an ex-seminarian and a professional photographer, although Gabler did not believe it) informed him that he was involved in something more complex than simple villainy.

The young man wheeled. "Enough! We must know where this Kenneth Nicolls is!"

Everett Gabler had one tone for students, Greek or American, hostile or friendly.

"I have already pointed out," he said with offensive precision, "that I do not know where Kenneth Nicolls is! That indeed is why I have come to Athens—to my regret!"

"I do not believe you," said the young man savagely.

Gabler merely pursed his lips but the bald man leaned forward and with patent cunning said:

"You have told us many times that you do not know where he is, this Nicolls. All right—no, no, Theo, do not excite yourself! Let us simply drop this point and move on, if we can. We wish to know where Mr. Nicolls is, that is true. But we have other concerns also. We must know what Mr. Nicolls' business in Greece really is. What is he doing here? What is his concern with Greece? This bank, that you represent, how is it involved?"

These were new questions.

Gabler searched his mind and could see no objection to a reasonably responsive reply. Carefully he outlined the Hellenus project.

The bald man nodded. "Ah, yes, the big power project in the north. I have heard of it. Go on!"

As the phrases fell from Gabler's lips almost automatically, his thoughts were racing. Insofar as he had assigned a motive to his abduction, he had assumed it was all a piece of the ruthlessness of the new regime. The Greek Army had descended on Nicolls in Salonika. Now, less official agents of the regime had descended on him in Athens. But surely no government agent, however unofficial, had to be told of the Sloan's interest in Hellenus? Hastily Everett rearranged his ideas.

"And so you see," he concluded, "Mr. Nicolls was preparing for the official conference opening in two weeks. Now that he has disappeared, I am carrying on his work. As well as conducting a search for him, of course. That is the sum of the Sloan's involvement in Greece."

"No. That is not so." The bald man raised a hand to stem Gabler's protest. "Perhaps you are telling the truth as you see it, but we know better. Let me tell you more of what passed in Salonika."

He began to tell the tale now so familiar to Gabler. The arrests, the death of Dr. Elias Ziros, the disappearance of the army truck...

Everett stirred restively. "I know all this," he said resentfully.

"Wait! Do you know this? The police have at last released Dr. Ziros' body to his family for burial. And his family, in going through his pockets, found this!"

Like a conjurer, the bald man whipped his hand through the air and suddenly flourished under his captive's nose the standard professional card supplied by the Sloan to its executives. Ken Nicolls' name was in the center.

"Very theatrical," said Gabler disapprovingly. "But no surprise to me. The police have already questioned me about that, and I will tell you the same—"

"The police!"

The bald man sank back, his pallor deepening. Then he spoke rapidly to the student and called in the ex-seminarian. Excited discussion followed with wide-armed semaphoring.

Gabler's patience came to an end. He cleared his throat authoritatively.

"If you could defer your discussion," he said, testiness in every syllable, "the explanation is quite simple."

He could not complain of lack of attention. His audience hung on his words as he explained the army surveillance of Dr. Ziros, the arrest of his most casual contacts in the railway station.

"There," he said, leaning back in satisfaction. "You see, Nicolls had nothing really to do with Dr. Ziros. Like the others, he was arrested simply because of a few polite words."

But his audience's reaction to this innocent statement left him plenty to complain about.

"That settles it!" cried the bald man, slapping a knee. "We must find Nicolls!"

The ex-seminarian bayed something menacing in Greek.

"But why an American?" the student exclaimed. "Elias must have been out of his mind."

"Or he had no choice," barked the others.

Baffled, Everett stared at his captors. Then he averted his eyes to the small, untidy heap beneath the piano. Here were Kenneth Nicoll's belongings, including the new two-suiter, stolen from the Hotel Britannia. Much was becoming clear.

The bald man seemed to recollect Gabler's presence with surprise. Visibly he strove for a more placatory manner. When he spoke it was with a grave courtesy that, oddly enough, made him seem older and more dangerous.

"Mr. Gabler, our interests are the same. You wish to find Mr. Nicolls for your own purposes. So do we. I assure you we mean him no harm. But it is essential that we have access to him. Surely, we can cooperate."

There was almost a siren call of allurement in his closing sentence.

If there is one thing to be said for a lifetime on Wall Street, it is the armor acquired against siren songs. In this respect, Everett Gabler was tone deaf.

"If we are to speak of cooperation," he said with impressive command, emanating as it did from a frail, no-longer-young man totally helpless in an alien land, "then the first step is to restore my liberty. You say that you intend no harm to Nicolls? On the record, your first act would be to incarcerate him."

"Incarceration!" fumed Theo. "Who are you to talk to us of incarceration?"

The bald man shook his head sadly. "I am sorry you take that attitude. There can be no question of releasing you. You say that you and this bank of yours think only of the Hellenus negotiations. Very well then! Here you stay! And there will be no Sloan representative at the negotiations. If it is so important to the Sloan, there are things that are important to us, too. Perhaps your Mr. Nicolls will now come out of his hiding. Perhaps your bank will find him. While we hold you, we have something to bargain with!"

Gabler was almost beyond speech. This threat to the negotiations touched him where he lived. It was beyond belief! Everett was not by nature an imaginative man. Hours spent contemplating the future had not prepared him for this. Although he knew full well that men who could snatch him off an Athens street were, presumably, capable of more and worse.

With an effort, he regained control. "Now this has gone far enough," he said, rising. "I am leaving!"

An iron hand grasped his elbow painfully and pushed him back down onto the sofa. The ex-seminarian had padded up from the rear.

"Listen," Theo snarled. "We are not joking, and you are going nowhere!"

Gabler was about to protest when the older man forestalled him. "You must wait. You do not realize what is at stake, what we are risking. This is the only thing we can do."

This might have made the blood of a lesser man run cold. Gabler rubbed a bruised arm and said:

"You realize that the police, too, are looking for Nicolls?"

The bald man nodded wearily.

"I realize that."

"And now they will be looking for me as well. Have you thought of the consequences if they find me?"

This time the silence was really dangerous. The young student, eyes blazing, took a step toward Gabler. Gabler did not flinch, but the older man intervened, pulling Theo away, speaking in a low persuasive voice. When he had pushed him with rough affection back in the direction of the window, he turned to Gabler.

"That was not a wise thing to say, Mr. Gabler. Not wise at all. It would be so easy for you to disappear permanently if the police pick up your trail." He nodded significantly toward the sea which could be heard far below. "Do not try us too much. We are already risking our lives."

Gabler could be astute. He did not reply. For a full twenty-five minutes, silence obtained in the room. The ex-seminarian retired. After a disgusted look at Gabler, Theo went out into the hallway and shouted something to someone else. The bald man settled himself at the desk, switched on the lamp, and turned his attention to a pile of papers which he marked with red pencil.

Gabler tried to sort the various impressions that had assaulted him like blows, but a sudden pang reminded him of his suffering digestive system. He sniffed delicately. A faint unrecognizable aroma was beginning to seep into the room, an aroma both appealing and somehow alarming.

"Ahem," said Gabler politely.

The Greek looked up.

"Would you tell me what we are having for dinner?"

The Greek was cold. "Octopus, Mr. Gabler. From the sea!"

"Thank you," said Everett mildly.

But it was at this point that he came to a decision. No matter how problematical his captors' intentions, one thing was certain: more meals like this and he would certainly not survive.

CHAPTER XII

ZEUS DESCENDING

MISS CORSA WAS as good as her word. Accordingly, John Putnam Thatcher was on the six o'clock plane to Athens despite the spirited attempts of his colleagues and subordinates at the Sloan Guaranty Trust to divert him.

"Listen, John, it may be dangerous!" Walter Bowman sputtered.

George C. Lancer chose a loftier approach. "Of course, I realize you want to be where your men are, but the press of business here..."

From Caracas, Charlie Trinkam fairly boiled over:

ATHTRIP UNWISE STOP WILPROSELF STOP GREEKS KNOW STOP REPLY PROMPTEST

Thatcher dismissed these qualms and continued obeying Miss Corsa's serene instructions. These got him aboard the six o'clock jet to Paris–Rome–Athens where not even *boeuf bourguignon* as prepared by Chef Maxim of Manhattan's chic El Rotundo weakened his resolution. By dawn, he was in fighting trim for Athens, after having beaten off lively attempts to route his luggage to Copenhagen without him.

"I have only what I am carrying," he said.

"But, M'sieur..."

"And I intend to continue carrying it!"

Thus, when he landed at Athens airport, to be passed through customs with flattering alacrity, he was well rested and raring to go.

"Despite the singing."

"Singing, sir?" inquired the courier from the Embassy deputed to greet Thatcher.

"In Paris we picked up some Greeks who had been working in France. They sang most of the way home."

The courier escorted Thatcher to the waiting limousine and glanced at the heavily armed soldiers lounging near the cab stand.

"Well, now that they're back in Greece," he said, "they won't feel like singing for long."

Thatcher heard but did not comment. After twenty minutes of dust, heat and extraordinary traffic, he was delivered, as had been others before him, to the Hotel Britannia.

The manager seemed strangely unwelcoming, but dutifully produced a sheaf of messages, appointments, and telephone numbers.

In short, with the arrival of John Thatcher, conferences between subordinates had ceased and the principals were moving into the arena.

The readiness with which American Ambassadors and Greek Cabinet Ministers made themselves available was only to be expected—it was a response both to Thatcher's seniority and to the increasing gravity of the Sloan's presence in Greece. But Thatcher suspected that more than a regard for punctilio was operating. Ambassadors and Ministers are, after all, only human. Like everyone else, they wish to be present at the passing season's more dramatic moments.

And they thought they saw one coming. After all Kenneth Nicolls, a very junior trust officer, had disappeared with becoming modesty as part of a random bag by the Greek Army. Everett Gabler, a senior trust officer, had been snatched in broad daylight from Athens' busiest thoroughfare. It was only natural to expect that John Putnam Thatcher, senior vice-president of the Sloan Guaranty Trust, should go to glory in an even more spectacular fashion. By now, the Ambassador and the Minister would not have been surprised to see a hovering helicopter scoop him up from the amphitheater during the first act of *Medea*.

Thatcher was not offended by this ghoulish interest in his manifest destiny. He had come to terms with human nature a long time ago. No, what disturbed him were the signs of ebbing faith in the Sloan's political purity. The Ambassador, naturally enough, was diplomatic.

"You'll find the Minister of the Interior a little edgy," he predicted. "Can't blame him, really. He doesn't like the way things look."

Thatcher said that he didn't either. The Ambassador nodded vaguely and pursued his oblique approach.

"Not as if this were a stable government—or even a coherent one. The military junta has the support of the old-line conservatives, as of now. But you know how these things go. And a lot of these conservatives aren't enthusiastic about American investment. Afraid of it. Money means political leverage. The Minister doesn't want anything to go sour."

Thatcher said firmly that the Sloan was not involved in back-stage politics.

"Of course not. But you can see how things shape up for the Minister. The Army has given him its story about Nicolls. As far as he's concerned, either they're lying or the Sloan is." The Ambassador did not sound happy.

"Other elements might be involved."

They had canvassed that possibility for a while. The Ambassador's final words were no comfort.

"The Hellenus project is important to a lot of people," he pointed out. "I suppose you're sure of your own men."

As Thatcher was driven to the Ministry, he passed the time trying to visualize Everett Gabler as lone wolf of international espionage. Upon being introduced to the Minister of the Interior and Undersecretary Stavros Bacharias his first impression was that they made more suitable candidates for the role. This was not, he hoped, simply chauvinism.

"The Army has been entirely frank with us," the Minister told him earnestly.

"Splendid!"

Thatcher immediately wrote off the Minister. If he believed what he was saying, he had no political future. If he didn't believe it, he should be preserving his flexibility until the danger of refutation was past.

Gravely the Minister reproduced the authorized version. The Army's excellent intelligence had learned that the notorious revolutionary, Dr. Elias Ziros, possessed documents "inimical to the welfare of the Greek Government." At the Salonika railroad station he was going to pass the papers to a courier en route to Athens. Accordingly the Army had arrested Dr. Ziros and all his contacts. The contacts had been loaded into a truck bound for headquarters. Had the truck arrived safely, of course, Mr. Nicolls would have been cleared at once and released with apologies. Unfortunately the earthquake had intervened. The Army had searched the immediate area and established that Mr. Nicolls had not returned to the Hellenus site. With profound regret it could only suppose that Mr. Nicolls had fallen victim to the natural cataclysm. It remained only to convey to the Sloan Guaranty Trust and the American Government its heartfelt sense of loss . . .

"Naturally," said the Minister, "we assume that, had such an innocent man as Mr. Nicolls survived, he would instantly have communicated with the proper authorities."

"Oh, naturally."

The Minister did not volunteer one word about the murder of Dr. Ziros, the abduction of Everett Gabler, or the persistent intrusions into the Hotel Britannia.

"This leaves a good many events unexplained," Thatcher said mildly.

The Minister replied with condolences for the disappearance of Everett Gabler. No doubt a man of many excellences. Unfortunately his stay among mortal men in Greece had been so transitory that the Minister had not had the opportunity to make his personal acquaintance.

Stavros Bacharias immediately informed his superior that Mr. Gabler's ability and diligence struck the beholder on first glance.

"But alas," the Minister continued, figuratively draping himself in black, "the Greek Government is at a loss. Only those with a more detailed knowledge of the activities of your great bank can explain the mysterious events overtaking its personnel."

Thatcher's composure remained unruffled as he made his adieux and accepted the offer of Stavros Bacharias' escort back to his hotel. The Ambassador had been right. The Greek Army said the Sloan was lying. And, for the Minister, that was more than enough.

His Undersecretary, Stavros Bacharias, seemed to share this view with modifications. After describing the latest progress at Hellenus and the complexities of the forthcoming round of negotiations, he was forced back to less congenial topics as they were brought to a full halt by Athens' lunch-time traffic jam. As they sat in a limitless sea of cars, with the cacophony of blaring horns, shrieking pedestrians and incensed traffic police ringing in their ears, Thatcher seized his opportunity. Pointblank he demanded his companion's opinion:

"I understand your grounds for suspicion," he said bluntly. "But these suspicions are not in fact consistent. Kenneth Nicolls' disappearance in Salonika, even if he were involved in some skulduggery, does not explain what is going on in Athens."

Stavros Bacharias threw up his hands.

"I am not unprejudiced," he admitted. "You must realize that I feel responsible for Mr. Nicolls' troubles. I must be honest. It would be a relief for me if he were something more than an innocent victim, set down in that railroad station by my stupidity."

Thatcher nodded thoughtfully. Bacharias' point of view was comprehensible. Thatcher did not pay much attention to over-refined feelings of personal guilt. He did understand that a civil servant's career could be damaged by embroiling prominent foreign visitors in local troubles. Bacharias predictably enough was searching for some other explanation.

Thatcher intended to show him that this particular explanation would not solve his problems.

"Let us be frank with each other for one moment," he suggested smoothly. "Allow me to point out something which you may have overlooked in the confusion of recent events. You have worked with the Sloan for many months and with Mr. Nicolls for several weeks. I leave it to you to decide whether either was likely to be party to Dr. Ziros' activities. But if you assume that Mr. Nicolls went to that railroad station to meet Dr. Ziros, then there can be no question of your having set him down there. He manipulated the entire sequence of events. It was *he* who arranged that you should both arrive when you did. In a sense, Nicolls made you party to the transfer of documents."

Stavros Bacharias didn't like it. Not one single bit. John Thatcher felt his first unqualified satisfaction for a long time. Visibly Bacharias recoiled from this picture of himself as a man who, however innocently, was guilty of insurrectionist activity. He was still struggling with this horrifying vision when the traffic clot suddenly dissolved and they were swept up to the doors of the Hotel Britannia. Thatcher got out and watched the car pull away.

Thatcher felt something had been accomplished at last. There was now one man in the Ministry of the Interior with a lot to gain by maintaining the Sloan's innocence. If the Sloan were guilty, then Stavros Bacharias had been its dupe. And happily, he seemed to be the Minister's chief source of information on the Hellenus project.

Good, that was the first step. The next step, and it must be carefully timed, had been broached in his discussion with the Ambassador. There were, as they had both agreed, other elements involved. To be precise, there was a third party present at the Hellenus site. Soon, Stavros Bacharias might be reminded that both he and Kenneth Nicolls might have been manipulated by Paul Makris & Son, the group that had been so peculiarly neglected throughout his interview with the Minister, the group that was always on the spot when something happened, whether in Salonika or in Athens.

His ruminations were interrupted by the porter.

"A Mr. Riemer awaits you in the Café Taxos across the street. He wishes to speak with you, Mr. Thatcher."

Thatcher turned in his tracks with his hopes high. Perhaps something new had come up in the short time since he had left the Embassy. It could not be disaster. After all, the next scheduled disaster was his own disappearance. Maybe they had touched bottom and were on the way up.

His hopes were not dashed. Bill Riemer, rising from a corner table where he had been nursing a milky *ouzo*, did not waste time on preliminaries.

"It looks as if Nicolls may be alive. We've just gotten a phone call from the north."

Thatcher went straight to essentials.

"Alive when?" he demanded.

"Three days ago."

Well, that took care of the swallowed-up-by-the-earth theory, once and for all. It had seemed just as unlikely in Athens as it had in New York.

"Tell me the details."

"The call wasn't from Nicolls. It was from some people at a Red Cross camp in the disaster area. They had a very peculiar story to tell."

Slowly Riemer went on to outline events as seen from the vantage point of Jamison's Red Cross field station—Nicolls' sudden appearance on the truck in Larissa, his unexplained departure from the truck along the road, the descent of three unidentified men tracking him.

"You're sure it was Nicolls?" Thatcher asked.

"There doesn't seem to be any reasonable doubt. A big blond American, Jamison said. But it certainly was Nicolls the three men were looking for. They not only had his name, they had a complete description." Riemer raised his eyes from the table. "What do you think it means, Mr. Thatcher?"

Thatcher fairly barked his reply.

"Nicolls is on the run. Somebody who isn't the Greek Army is looking for him, and he knows it. What's more to the point, he seems to be taking very effective evasive action."

"Yes. I suppose so." Riemer sounded surprised. Kenneth

Nicolls had not seemed the type to take to the hills successfully.

A slow smile was beginning to break on Thatcher's face. He could not quell his optimism. The men of the Sloan were beginning to come into their own. Kenneth Nicolls—thank God!—was not only alive, he was giving the opposition a run for its money. Was it too much to hope that, somewhere in the south of Greece, Everett Gabler was doing the same? Of course, Everett hadn't had an earthquake to help him. But then Everett was more than capable of manufacturing his own earthquakes.

"You say this man Jamison thought that this car was making the rounds of all the relief stations?"

"Yes. He said they had a list. He could see other camps had been crossed off."

"A big effort then." Thatcher reflected for a moment. "It must be important for them to stop Nicolls. And they haven't done very well so far, have they?"

Bill Riemer looked across at his companion with mounting unease. No one in the Foreign Service likes to see businessmen suddenly taking the bit between their teeth and stampeding off through a foreign countryside. He spoke hesitantly:

"The best thing, Mr. Thatcher, would be to find Ken Nicolls, and Mr. Gabler too, of course, and get them safely back to Athens. Then we can decide whether it's a question that can openly be put to the authorities, or whether the two of them should be gotten out of the country."

This pedestrian course of action had no appeal whatsoever for Thatcher. The smile grew broader.

"My boy, you're right about one thing. We have to ensure their safety and find out what's going on. But after that, I think it's time to rethink our policy."

Riemer's heart plummeted.

"How?" he asked cautiously.

"We've been on the defensive too long. These people, whoever they are, are probably already rattled at losing Nicolls. It's time we took the offensive!"

CHAPTER XIII

ACHILLES' HEEL

SUCH SENTIMENTS, OF course, were very American. They were what won the West, delivered the mail and, in an earlier era, created U.S. Steel. Yet, even as he made his way back to the Britannia pondering (and dismissing) various means by which he and the Sloan could take the offensive, John Putnam Thatcher forgot that he was in a land where ancient gods let puppets strut their brief moment, then step down from Olympus to take a hand. Greece was about to produce a Homeric case in point. Oddly enough, it came in the form of a chartered bus, filled with German tourists, just pulling up to the curb as Thatcher neared the hotel.

The imposition of dictatorship had discouraged American tourists; a Middle Eastern crisis had deflected cruise passengers; currency restrictions were limiting the English to Blackpool and worse.

But no power on earth can keep Germans in Germany. Primal forces as powerful as those impelling lemmings to the sea put bibulous Bavarians into lederhosen and deliver them to the Côte d'Azur, Port 'Ercole, and the Kingdom of the Hellenes. This particular contingent, complete with motherly wives in flowered print dresses, was occupying a small stunned hotel around the corner. But they assembled, debouched, checked cameras and drank *Fix* in Syntagma Square. They were not noticeably noisier than the surrounding Greeks—nobody could be. But they were fair-haired, blocky, rumpled, and energetic. As a result, each of their foregatherings conjured up the bivouacking of some Nordic tribe.

Now the bus door opened and the occupants thundered out.

Thatcher, like everybody else in the immediate vicinity, instinctively drew out of the path of the juggernaut.

And there, ringed by chunky burghers, was a business-suited Wall Street executive, clutching his brief case.

"Everett!"

Thatcher was not really conscious of having called out.

Gabler looked around. His clothes were not as meticulous as usual and he certainly looked out of sympathy with his surroundings. But he seemed to be in sound shape.

"Everett! Here!" This time Thatcher began to cleave through the crush.

"Well, John! What are you doing here... Just a minute, will you?"

Fascinated, Thatcher watched Everett punctiliously tip the guide and shake hands with three bellowing Germans. He then posed for two photographs and finally worked his way to Thatcher's side.

"Remarkable people, the Germans," he said. "I know they feel the heat dreadfully, but they don't let it stop them..."

"Everett," said Thatcher awfully, "where have you been?"

Gabler expelled a small sigh of fatigue.

"It's a long story. Perhaps tea..."

Thatcher knew that nothing would be forthcoming until the tea was provided. Ruthlessly he propelled Gabler past the sidewalk tables, into the hotel. When an incredulous waiter was refused the opportunity to serve *ouzo*, ices or similar exotica and told to bring tea, Everett again sighed.

Then he said crisply:

"John, the sooner we extricate ourselves from Greece, the better!"

"My feelings exactly," said Thatcher. "But I'd like to take young Nicolls with us when we go. Everett, what have you been up to?"

Everett bent his lips in a smile. "First I was kidnapped. Then I was systematically poisoned. Then I escaped."

Thatcher controlled himself. "Ye-es. Yes, I see. Of course,

I had heard about the kidnapping. But, Everett, could you bring yourself to fill in some of the subsequent details?"

"Ah!" The tea had arrived. After peering into the pot, Everett indicated satisfaction. "Well, I was standing on the sidewalk..."

Invigorated by his favourite brew, Everett began his tale. As was to be feared, in this version he left out nothing, at all.

The bald-headed man had not been exaggerating. Everett's first day of imprisonment, baffling and alarming, had indeed ended with a solitary meal in his bedroom cell. As promised, it was octopus, thinly sliced and served in a garlic and walnut sauce. Naturally Gabler paid the price. Acute gastric distress, compounded by unavoidable mental anxiety, kept him awake for a second night in a row. Fortunately, during this second night he was not further exacerbated by two alien presences at his comfortless bedside. The door to his bedroom was locked, to be sure. Outside, he had no doubt, the ex-seminarian waited, brutish and menacing. Everett had already ascertained that in the garden beneath his small balcony other enemies lurked. Indeed, certain snuffling sounds suggested dogs as well.

"This," he said to himself, between painful turnings, "is too much!"

Everett Gabler's captors might have been surprised to learn that he was industriously mulling over possible escapes.

Or then again, they might not have been. Certainly the bald man had begun to take Everett Gabler's stubborn measure.

This may have explained the dogs.

But dogs were, in the last analysis, an error. A career in banking had done nothing to develop Everett Gabler's feeble penchant for derring-do. It was not that thoughts of dramatic assaults on young, muscular toughs unnerved him; it was simply that Everett Gabler did not think along these lines. Nor of clambering up the vines to the roof and skulking around chimneys, abstracting shawls and impersonating aged Greek ladies, nor of burning down the entire edifice.

Everett turned, emitting a grunt of discomfort. Swashbuckling was out.

What about creating some sort of disturbance to bring the authorities to the scene?

Everett contemplated this for a moment. He knew that his abduction from the streets of Athens must have been reported. The police must be seeking him out.

But Everett's realism obtruded at this point. From what he had seen of Greek authorities—in all forms—he knew that they were a far cry from New York's Finest. In fact, they made the Turks look good. He, personally, would not trust the Greek police to locate the Mediterranean Sea.

Then too there was his present location. Everett had been hustled from car to villa without much opportunity to scan the countryside. Since then, he had been confined to bedroom and living room. But he was obviously in a building with some pretensions to elegance; there was a flower garden beneath his window, perfuming the night air. The sea spread a sequined carpet from the rocks below.

All of this told Everett not that Greece was a land of incredible loveliness, as the tourist bureaus insist, but that he was in a rich man's country place. It was either secluded or, more possibly, in a resort area. What the local authorities would run to, Everett preferred not to think. Upstate New York, after all, was bad enough. It would be folly to rely on aid from locals, whoever they were.

Everett took a deep breath. Just as he had foreseen, the only way to get out of this mess—and he made a note to have a frank talk with Charlie Trinkam on his return—was by his own, unaided efforts. Presumably in Greece, as on Wall Street, the game goes to the quickest wits. Tired, shaken and generally unwell he might be, but Everett Gabler had no doubt that he was an abler man than those louts outside. It was unfortunate that he spoke no Greek, that he did not know where he was, and that he lacked perfect comprehension of whatever was exercising his captors. But all of this was beside the point; a keener mind, trained to be analytical and dispassionate, must triumph.

Reassured in the broad sense, if still vague about particulars, Everett fell into an uneasy sleep.

The next morning, not much refreshed, Everett awoke determined to put his analytical and dispassionate intelligence to work. The problem was to find material worthy of it. Proceedings, when they resumed, suggested a duplication of the previous day. And breakfast, an inky black liquid, two slices of bread and honey, did little for a man with Everett Gabler's high regard for wheat germ.

When Everett finished the breakfast that the aged Eleni served him, he was again ushered into the living room, still cool and shaded against the sun that was beginning to sear the sea and distant islands.

The bald-headed man was again behind the desk.

"I hope you slept well," he said.

"As a matter of fact," said Everett coldly, "I had a very disturbed night."

"That is too bad," said his opponent. "Now, Mr. Gabler, surely you must realize that we are in deadly earnest. We must get in touch with Nicolls..."

For over an hour the tiresome dialogue continued. As an experienced negotiator, Everett managed to reply, deny and protest, while at the same time storing and registering facts for later utilization.

Unless he was mistaken—and Everett discounted this instantly—the tempo had been relaxed. The bald-headed man was beginning to sound weary. Theo, the younger man, was nowhere in evidence. And the two thugs were not skulking nearby.

"I thought so!" said Everett to himself in triumph. He knew what had happened. These villains had nerved themselves for one dramatic confrontation; when it was protracted, they lost their fighting edge.

As he so frequently remarked at the Sloan, nobody seemed to have staying power these days!

Everett took heart, while outwardly continuing to expostulate. Of course, his captors' impatience might portend fast strangulation followed by disposal of his corpse. But Everett firmly put such spectres behind him and concentrated on the possibilities offered.

As he did so, he was provided with a suddenly expanded view of his prospects.

In the midst of a series of threats centering upon Everett's obduracy, the bald-headed man was interrupted. The telephone at his elbow rang three times.

Swiftly he picked it up, snarled a few words. Then, as swiftly, he looked at Everett:

"All right! Get out!"

He was enraged.

Rising with dignity, Everett said: "Does this mean I am free to go?"

The bald-headed man clapped a meaty hand over the receiver.

"One step out of this house and you are dead," he said brutally. "Get out of this room! I have business!"

Without unseemly haste, Everett stepped into the hall, closing the door behind him. With his customary precision, he docketed one precious fact; he had the freedom of the house. He proposed to make use of it.

The corridor was long, shadowy, tiled and cool. It was also quite empty.

Unhesitatingly, Everett proceeded past the door to his own bedroom, to the stairs leading to the ground floor. He was trying to fix the physical layout of his prison and to estimate the task before him.

No doubt about it, he decided, descending, they were letting down. Telephone calls—important, if appearances were correct—and unless he was in error, fewer people around. According to the bald-headed man, guards were posted outside...

At the frosted glass front door, Everett determinedly grasped the ornate handle and shoved. It was not an easy task, but the heavy door finally yielded, admitting a blast of quite incredible heat and a fusillade of hoarse Greek. Firmly, Everett pulled the door shut. He was not the man to take anything on faith, but now he knew; there were guards outside.

He continued down the tiled hallway to the rear of the house. Little though he realized it, his fundamental nature was shaping the course of his reconaissance. Everett was heading for the kitchen.

First he passed through a gloomy Victorian dining room filled with heavy, carved furniture. The kitchen, just beyond, was large, with a huge stove and strange aromatic objects strung from low rafters. The windows were shuttered but the back door stood open.

There, under a canopy of grape leaves, sat Eleni, a shapeless black heap. Her gnarled hands were automatically peeling vegetables. Lounging beside her was the ex-seminarian.

They both looked at Everett with hostility, then the crone said something that ended in a cackle. The ex-seminarian, his eyes squinted at Everett, made a mildly offensive gesture. Everett retreated to the stove where a huge cauldron, gently bubbling, emitted more of the strange and wonderful odors that permeated Greece.

Momentarily forgetting his immediate preoccupations, Everett inspected it. A pale grey-yellow mess with unidentifiable objects simmered and steamed.

Eleni let out a brief screech. As Everett turned to look at her, she tapped her forehead.

Seeing that Everett did not grasp her meaning, the ex-seminarian weighed in.

"Head," he said with an unpleasing gargle of gutturals.

"Head?" asked Everett, deciding that the kitchen offered him no useful means of egress.

The ex-seminarian tapped his brow meaningfully, then he too, like Eleni, gave a roar of what must have been amusement.

Everett looked at the doorway then back at the stove. Suddenly, his stomach heaving, he grasped the message causing their laughter.

That stew boiling so gently on the stove was another Greek culinary speciality: brain soup.

With uncontrollable revulsion, Everett jammed his hands into his pockets. And there his fingers encountered something.

At this point, Everett sipped his tea, snapped for a passing waiter and communicated the need for more hot water and dry toast.

"For God's sake!" Thatcher said.

With care, Everett adjusted his glasses.

"As you may recall, John," he said, "I am a martyr to sea and air sickness."

"You're going to be a martyr to something else if you don't get on with this," Thatcher told him grimly. "How did you . . . ?"

Everett resumed his narrative. He had discovered a bottle of pills, prescribed by his medical man in the event that his overseas flight to Turkey proved uncomfortable. While not believing in unnecessary medication, Everett had suffered enough in jet planes and heaving ships to yield to the temptation of precautionary measures. Now, while Eleni and the ex-seminarian were doubled up with mirth, Everett emptied the whole ample supply into the day's lunch.

"Without qualms, eh, Everett?" Thatcher asked.

Everett pursed his lips. "I only wished it were something stronger!"

It had been clear from the quantities being prepared by Eleni that she was feeding the whole household, although Everett ate alone in his room. It was also clear that Greek cookery could mask any quantity of soporifics. With a last horrified glance, Everett sped from the kitchen, reaching the upstairs hallway just in time to find the bald man emerging in search of him.

Their fruitless dialogue was resumed.

Until lunchtime. Everett was escorted back to his room; Eleni climbed the stairs with a tray in her hands. Everett waited until she had left then hurried over to check the menu.

Bread, cold lamb, salad, a carafe of wine—and a steaming bowl of soup.

Congratulating himself, Everett lunched delicately but adequately upon bread, lamb and salad.

"Greeks put something into their wine," he reported austerely. "Something very strange."

Then, after disposing of the brain soup in his bathroom, he settled down to wait. If his calculations were correct, the household was now settling down to the large dining room table. How long would it take Dr. Rubin's pills to work? He did not know. In the meantime, supremely confident, Everett dozed briefly.

When he awoke, he went to his door. There was utter silence. Taking a deep breath, he turned the handle. Unlocked.

"Splendid," said Everett. He picked up his dispatch case, looked around vainly for the hat he had misplaced, and set off.

"Were they slumped over the dining room table?" Thatcher asked, enthralled by this emergence of the Scarlet Pimpernel.

With his customary disapproval of inessentials, Everett replied that he had not stopped to find out. Instead, he hurried downstairs, opened the door, waited for a moment, then, when no restraint appeared, walked out.

"Dogs," suggested Thatcher weakly.

He had forgotten that Everett was a stalwart of the American Kennel Club.

"Two unprepossessing animals," said Gabler. "Certainly not trained guard dogs. It was only necessary to speak firmly to them. One did bark. But since nothing happened, I continued. Fortunately, the garden gates were not locked. I found myself on a dirt road. In about a mile, I came to a paved highway, which turns out to be the road from Athens to Sounion..."

"And that was when the bus went by?"

"Precisely," said Everett.

Thatcher was quite truthful. "Everett, I find all of this impressive." He did not add that Everett among the Teutons was a picture he was going to cherish. "Now then, can you tell me anything else?"

Everett searched his memory and came up with nothing he had not already recounted.

"Hmm," said Thatcher. A determined, and rather desperate, search for Kenneth Nicolls was in its way heartening; the men who had kidnapped Everett Gabler at least thought that Nicolls was still very much alive.

These men at Sounion, like the police, knew that Kenneth Nicolls' business card had been found on the murdered Dr. Elias Ziros. But why should that make them assume that Ziros had passed his subversive documents to a stray American?

"You don't have any doubt that these people are opponents of the current regime?" Thatcher asked thoughtfully.

Gabler considered this. "Not unless the whole thing was an elaborate hoax," he decided. "They certainly sounded as if they thought they were in danger. And there is no doubt they were connected with Ziros, who was killed."

"Which suggests that they are leftists, too," said Thatcher.

Everett greeted the arrival of tea and toast with enthusiasm. "John," he said, "I do not want to see the Sloan getting involved in the political maneuverings of this country!"

Thatcher made a gesture of impatience. "But, Everett, Nicolls is still missing! We're still committed to these damned Hellenus negotiations! And for all we know, you may be a mass murderer!"

Everett Gabler, for once, was thunderstruck. "Mass mur— good heavens! That never occurred to me!"

It did not dismay him unduly.

Thatcher forged on. "Once you've finished that tea—"

"And had some sleep," Everett interposed firmly. "Regular hours are the most important health requirement and I haven't..."

Thatcher cut in. "We're going to have to report your return to the government. And they're going to want to know..."

Everett Gabler had clearly decided that all Greeks, whatever their political persuasion, were his enemies.

"I was on the main road to Sounion," he pointed out. "I gather the whole area is honeycombed with vacation homes, so that it would be difficult to specify exactly where I was."

"Could you?" Thatcher asked.

"Of course!" said Everett Gabler. "Then, after I was kidnapped, I was asked meaningless questions about Kenneth Nicolls..."

"I suppose we'll have to say that much," Thatcher muttered.

"By people whom I understood only imperfectly. What their motives, their politics or their goals were, I did not understand!"

Everett, the very model of Protestant rectitude, lofted a cup triumphantly. Thatcher grinned. The Sloan Guaranty Trust was about to take a very strict reading of the letter of the law. At the moment, Kenneth Nicolls was still missing. And Sloan investments might be in jeopardy.

John Putnam Thatcher and Everett Gabler were not putting their faith in anybody.

Particularly not the current Greek Government.

CHAPTER XIV

STRANGER, GO TELL THE LACEDAEMONIANS...

A POACHED EGG, A few hours' sleep and a change of dress completed the restoration of Everett Gabler. When he and Thatcher met for breakfast the next morning, Everett was ready for action. This did not surprise Thatcher, who had never been misled by soy beans, herbal infusions and other healthful messes; Everett had always been as tough as old boots.

"I only hope," Thatcher remarked when they sat down, "that Nicolls comes through his adventures as well as you have come through yours."

Everett had been brought up to date the night before. "He seems to have been able to keep one step ahead," he said. "All things considered, he's doing very well—for a young man."

Thatcher saw that the chips were down; Everett Gabler was now defending the Sloan against all comers, particularly Greeks. Presumably this included Captain Philopoulos and the police. He could only hope that Everett would not run across a colonel.

"Now, Everett, when you report to the police this morning—"

"The Embassy insists on being present, for some reason or other," Everett interrupted to say.

"Yes. Now about what you're going to tell them..."

Everett detached himself from an orange and cast a cold eye upon his chief. He was perfectly prepared to mislead the police; he refused to put it in quite those terms.

"I shall, of course, cooperate fully," he proclaimed, with a return to his pre-solidarity censure. "Everything which I know, for a fact, I shall report to the proper authorities. Naturally, I would not convey theories or speculations. That would be grossly irresponsible."

He returned to the orange and, not for the first time, Thatcher wished that he could live up to Everett Gabler's militant propriety. It was his own lamentable propensity for calling a spade a spade that distressed so many of his subordinates. Not that any such distress had precluded a full, frank exchange of views. Despite differences in personal style, Everett Gabler and John Putnam Thatcher were currently as one on fundamentals: until Kenneth Nicolls turned up, until certain ambiguities concerning Hellenus were resolved, nothing—and nobody—in Greece was to be trusted.

Thatcher was reminded of this after seeing Everett off in the direction of Kotzia Square, the luckless Mr. Riemer in tow. Everett was warming up.

"I hope that the strongest representations will be made," he had crisply told Riemer, cutting into congratulations upon his happy escape. "Certainly if this regime cannot keep the streets free of violence..."

Gabler's spirited paraphrase of an American political dialectic was still ringing in Thatcher's ears when a depressed youth materialized at his elbow, whispered something incomprehensible, then resorted to pantomime to indicate a waiting telephone call. As he approached the desk, Thatcher caught sight of Mr. Tsaras, the Britannia's manager. He was gazing bleakly and unhopefully after the departing Gabler.

Well, whatever the rest of Greece felt, one thing was certain. The Hotel Britannia looked on the Sloan as an enemy.

The telephone was Peter Chiros of Makris & Son suggesting a business lunch.

"What business?" Thatcher asked tartly.

But Chiros glided on to warm felicitations about the safe return of Everett Gabler. So happy did it make him, it seemed, that he was repeating his pleasure two hours later when he and Thatcher met in the carefully Hellenic bar of the Athens Hilton.

"Ah, Mr. Thatcher! Here, let me recommend the martinis. They are excellent!"

They were. Nevertheless, Thatcher projected impatience. The morning's review of the Hellenus file had been punctuated by fuming telephone calls from Everett Gabler, still closeted at the Ministry. The calls reported no progress; the files were uninformative; Thatcher's irritation mounted.

"How extremely fortunate that no harm has befallen Mr. Gabler," said Chiros. "In these troubled times, with so much confusion, it is perhaps natural for us to fear the worst."

Repressively, Thatcher agreed. He was not tempted to relax his caution when it came to Makris & Son, or its local agent, Peter Chiros.

With the appearance of genuine interest, Chiros asked if Gabler had returned with any new information.

Thatcher obliged with a liberally abridged version of Everett's misadventures.

"Ah, yes," said Chiros, politely mournful. "Yes, I can understand that a foreigner not speaking Greek might find it difficult to know who his captors were. Or where they were."

"With a blanket over your head," Thatcher pointed out, "it doesn't really make much difference what language you speak."

"He did not form any opinion, then, of the political complexion of the... er... criminals who were holding him?"

Just how genuine was this, Thatcher wondered. The Makris interests had learned of Everett's escape with unusual promptness. Was it possible they did not know that leftists had kidnapped Everett?

If so, this was the first gap in Makris' intelligence. And the Makrises of this world do not get where they are with flawed intelligence systems.

Aloud, Thatcher said, "I gather that Everett had no extended discussions with them. They asked where Nicolls was—and that was all."

"Ah yes." Chiros was too polite to sound skeptical. Instead

he sounded remote. "Tell me, Mr. Thatcher, how did Mr. Gabler manage to escape?"

Thatcher was tiring of Byzantine cunning. He gave way to his baser self. "He overpowered them," he said unhesitatingly. "Everett happens to be one of New York's crack karate specialists!"

"I see," said Chiros. Still, he could not keep from growing even more remote. "Perhaps we can have our second drink at the table."

Mercifully, lunch was Hilton-International with a view to the traveling American. This enabled Thatcher to eat a very adequate steak and a baked potato. He was still waiting for Chiros to come to the point. Unless he was mistaken, Peter Chiros, for all his dapper tailoring and showy cuff links, was a high level messenger boy. And, Thatcher fulminated, Makris & Son had better not be wasting his time at this juncture.

Particularly since he strongly suspected that Makris & Son already knew more about Everett's experiences than Everett did.

On the other hand, was there any reason why Makris & Son should worry about what the Sloan knew—or did not know?

Absently chewing, Thatcher thought how little cerulean skies and alien tongues alter fundamentals; the stakes were high. Thirty-six million dollars. Hellenus was large enough to cause a lot of trouble.

But here Thatcher checked himself. It is one thing to behave with prudent circumspection. It is another to assume that one's partner is double-dealing.

In the absence of proof, that is.

But something was most assuredly in the wind. Thatcher waited.

It came with the thick syrupy coffee and baclava which was the Hilton's gesture to local color.

"I have asked you to join me, Mr. Thatcher, because certain

facts have come to our attention. So often . . . er . . . informal contacts are more informative than official channels. Particularly during days of change and confusion."

"Official channels have been more than useless," said Thatcher, suppressing an insane desire to shake Chiros until his teeth rattled.

"About Mr. Nicolls," Chiros continued. "We have asked our representatives in the north to make inquiries. And now, reports are coming in. Not, you understand, that they are very clear . . ."

"Do you know where he is?" Thatcher demanded with Anglo-Saxon directness.

Chiros shook his head. "No indeed. We would have reported that to you immediately. We have learned that he has been seen in the north . . ."

The urge to shake was being supplanted by an urge to strangle.

"And we are fairly certain," Chiros continued, "that he is still there. More coffee? Ah, *paidi*!"

After the waiter ambled away, Chiros presented Thatcher with a detailed description of Kenneth Nicolls' movements. Thatcher, a good listener, did not interrupt as Chiros repeated what was already known to him. First came a description of Nicolls in the Salonika railroad station. Then the fleeting encounter with Ziros.

"Who was," Chiros said precisely, "a prominent member of ASPIDA, which is the leftist opposition to the current government. Ziros was probably carrying something of interest—possibly something subversive, or worse. Somehow"—here Chiros delicately applied napkin to lips—"somehow the government was informed. It would be interesting to know how. But, at any rate, that was why your Mr. Nicolls was arrested."

He then proceeded to an elliptical account of the Ziros murder. Thatcher registered the fact that the word used was murder, not execution, but again made no comment. Chiros went on to the earthquake and the sudden liberation of the Greek Army's prisoners.

"Until this point, you see, we know what happened to Mr. Nicolls."

Thatcher, unsmiling, was quite deliberate. "It almost sounds as if you had sources among the men who were arrested with Nicolls."

A flash of dark eyes informed him that he had scored a hit, but Chiros continued:

"After Mr. Nicolls broke away from the Army van, his track is not so easy to follow. However, we know he is moving steadily southward."

Chiros recited his evidence: Nicolls' stay at an American Friends Service camp, his departure from the camp in an ambulance bound for Larissa, his failure to return.

But Nicolls was not coming steadily southward, Thatcher knew. There had been that call from Jamison, the Canadian—up north. Thatcher decided to keep the call to himself.

"And now?" he asked. "Where is Nicolls now?"

Chiros unbent enough to shrug. "We cannot say. There have been people searching for him. Perhaps they are the same people who kidnapped Mr. Gabler. Or perhaps others. Perhaps Mr. Nicolls has found some place of safety. But then, we cannot be sure."

Thatcher's voice was level. "I appreciate this information, Mr. Chiros. Not that it seems immediately helpful..."

"Then perhaps this may be," said Chiros in a silky voice. He leaned over to fumble in the briefcase at his feet. "It was found in Larissa. Fortunately, it came into our hands. No doubt there was once money in it... but still..."

He laid an object before Thatcher.

"Yes, it is the wallet of Mr. Nicolls."

Clearly it was his revenge for karate.

"And I can't really blame him," Thatcher was saying two hours later. "No doubt this Mexican stand-off is as infuriating to him as it is to us. But he obviously had instructions to be careful."

Everett Gabler was industriously poring over the contents of Kenneth Nicolls' wallet. Credit cards, in a quantity that would not have escaped comment if the derelict wallet had not been so ominous. Two snapshots of Jane Nicolls; six snapshots of the Nicolls infant (and, naturally enough, none of the newborn). A library card. An appointment with a Brooklyn Heights dentist. Many scraps of paper with cabalistic notations that were totally meaningless to Thatcher and Gabler, and probably to Kenneth Nicolls as well. Two receipts, one for a snow tire, one for a portable television set.

A thick wad of business cards.

There was not one cent, one dollar or one drachma.

"I don't suppose that should surprise us," said Everett, carefully checking every single business card again. At each pencilled note, he squinted with cold appraisal. "These poor people need every penny they can get. I suppose we can consider ourselves fortunate that the wallet has turned up."

Thatcher saw that the tables were turned. Here was a veteran naysayer and pessimist embarked on espousing the power of positive thinking.

Everett Gabler stubbornly reiterated an earlier cause for cheer.

"And we know that this wasn't picked from Nicolls' pocket in Salonika or at Hellenus earlier—because of *this*!"

This was a business card, segregated from the rest by virtue of its size and importance.

Elias Ziros, Docteur ès lettres
Senior Archivist and Ephor of Antiquities
University Museum
University of Thessaloniki

"God knows," said Thatcher wrathfully examining it, "it seems inhuman to say so now that this poor wretch has been gunned down, but I wish it had happened before Nicolls came onto the scene! And remind me to tell Nicolls—if and when we get the chance—that he should be careful about these casual conversations of his!"

Everett Gabler, who had spent the day turning away questions from the police and certain representatives of the Army, had one of his own.

"And just where Makris fits into this, I'd like to know!"

CHAPTER XV

...WE LIE HERE AT THEIR COMMAND

THE QUESTIONS THAT can be asked about a limp fold of pigskin are limited. As for answers, they are in even shorter supply. Everett Gabler's query had been rhetorical, as he was the first to admit.

"Pah!" he said, pushing aside the small pile of documents. "This is nonsense, John. The only important thing about this wallet is how it came into Peter Chiros' hands. It's suspicious, very suspicious."

There was no reply.

"Well, isn't it?" he pressed.

"What? Oh, yes, there's no doubt he knows more than he's telling." Thatcher brushed Peter Chiros aside. "But I was thinking of something else. Has it occurred to you, Everett, how unlikely it is that Nicolls has the papers these leftists are looking for?"

Gabler snorted. "It always has been unlikely. Anyone who wasn't demented would have realized that."

"I don't think you can assume these leftists of yours are demented. They must have some reason for going to all this trouble. And, remember, the Army's story is that a whole wagonload of prisoners escaped. Suppose that the genuine courier who went to the Salonika station to meet Ziros spotted the trap. He might have planted the papers on Nicolls. Then, after his escape, he reported to his superiors and they started the hue and cry."

"Possibly," Gabler conceded, "but it doesn't really matter to us, does it?"

Thatcher persisted. "I think it does. What do we know so

far? The people at that Red Cross station say that Nicolls was masquerading as a college boy. When he realized the pursuit was being extended to relief stations he decamped, probably assuming another disguise. He seems to be shedding clothes all along his route. Somehow he lost his wallet, because we have it. The Army still has his passport and the suitcase that they seized in Salonika. The leftists have everything from his hotel room. Is it likely that having lost everything else, Nicolls is somewhere in the Greek countryside clutching a manila folder of papers that don't belong to him?"

"Certainly not!" Gabler's eyes brightened combatively. "These people *are* demented. Nicolls is under no obligation to safeguard their possessions. If he acquired these papers involuntarily—"

The telephone rang, cutting off what promised to be an extensive review of the rights and duties of the involuntary bailee. Thatcher eyed it with misgiving. Nowadays the phone seemed a conduit for only the most bizarre communications. Bracing himself, he lifted the receiver.

The hotel switchboard, which inclined toward magniloquence, announced: "For Mr. Thatcher, it is the Dr. Jenkins calling from the American Academy."

Thatcher had time to wonder briefly what this outpost of American scholarship wanted of him when an exuberant woman's voice took charge.

"Mr. Thatcher? Cardy told us you were coming!"

Cardy? Classicists? It took a minute for the penny to drop. Professor Cardwell Carlson, Laura's father-in-law, obviously abandoned formality among his colleagues in the field.

"How lucky that I caught you," the voice continued. "We're having some people in for drinks this evening. I hope you can come."

Thatcher began a polite refusal. Then, before Everett Gabler's reproving eyes he changed his mind. He had a colleague with him, he said. Would it be an imposition if they both came?

"Not at all," the voice reassured him. "There will be one

or two photographers here. Cardy told us you were interested in taking color slides."

Thatcher murmured his thanks and as he rang off reminded himself to have a word or two with Professor Carlson. His attention was immediately claimed by the voice of outrage.

"John! I am shocked! Is now the time for us to go to cocktail parties?"

"It is precisely the right time!" Thatcher countered briskly. "The more people we meet in the American community, the better. Everett, have you stopped to think what we're going to do with young Nicolls if he manages to get through to Athens?"

Gabler did not hesitate. In spite of his budding career as a mass murderer, he still thought along conventional lines.

"Complain to the authorities!" he said roundly. "Their behavior has been disgraceful. Throughout! They allow Nicolls to be hounded over the length and breadth of Greece through no fault of his own." In his heat Everett was abandoning the axiomatic culpability of the young. "They permit me to be kidnapped in broad daylight. They start the whole deplorable situation by arresting Nicolls in the first place..."

His voice died away into a thoughtful silence. Then he resumed, more slowly: "Perhaps, on the whole, it would be wiser to ship Nicolls off to New York, and *then* complain to the authorities."

"The Army still has his passport. We couldn't simply bundle him aboard the first plane out. At worst, he might be arrested. At best, there would be delay." Thatcher shook his head. "Tell me, Everett, did those leftists seem to be at all interested in the other men the Army arrested? Or were they simply making a dead set at Nicolls?"

"They mentioned only Nicolls to me. And they seemed certain he had something of theirs. But I have no idea of how much they really knew. They may have put undue emphasis on the fact that Ziros was carrying Nicolls' business card. After all, the police questioned that, too."

"They may not know anything. We certainly don't." Thatcher drummed his fingers in irritation. "These leftists may simply be covering the field. They may be breaking into homes and slitting up clothing all over Athens. But I don't want Nicolls sitting around this hotel for days, at the mercy of the first comer. Our task this evening is to meet as many Americans as possible—resident Americans with apartments and houses. And remember, Everett, we're out to make friends!"

Everett said that he would.

"What an attractive apartment you have," Gabler said stolidly. "And spacious as well!"

Lorna Jenkins looked at her surroundings as if seeing them for the first time. "Do you like it?" she asked doubtfully. "Kate and I are subletting it from a movie producer."

Everett relaxed slightly. Presumably he was required to produce no further paeans to the chromed steel and glass against which he was barking his shins. The apartment lay high up in one of Athens' deluxe modern apartment buildings in Kolonaki. International contemporary, it could have been found in any major capital of the world. Although *contemporary* was becoming something of a misnomer. The living room might have been lifted bodily from the Barcelona Exhibition of 1929. Gabler had hated it on sight. Apparently his hostess did too. He looked at her with dawning approval.

Lorna Jenkins was worth looking at. Although she was well over fifty-five, there was distinction in every line of her body. She was a tall, exceptionally slight woman, fine-boned from head to toe. Her white hair was cut into a sleek crop that followed the delicate moulding of the skull. A black dress set off her alert blue eyes and long elegant legs.

Gabler was notoriously uninterested in legs. But he did recognize a lady when he saw one. Before leaving the hotel he had been prepared for bohemian academics. Upon sighting the building he had shifted to international riff-raff. Instead he was getting a whiff of an older, statelier past.

"This is very unlike our home in Princeton," Dr. Jenkins continued in a kindly attempt to follow her guest's interest, "but Kate says it does us good to have a change."

She nodded across the room where Kate—otherwise Dr. Mary Katherine Murphy, Fellow of the Royal Archaeological Society, Fellow of the American Academy, Reith Lecturer—was propelling a reluctant John Thatcher into conversational amenities with two enthusiastic photographers of the Greek landscape.

"Yes, I can see how you would like to get out into the country when you can find the time, but it must be a relief to get back to your apartment in Athens, or your house," he said, keeping an eye on business.

"Find the time!" Kate Murphy exploded indignantly. "We have nothing but time these days. Do you realize these colonels won't let us dig on our island? I suppose they're using it for another one of their prisons!"

There was a short interval for abuse of the current government, very specialized abuse relating to interference with archaeological sites.

"Not just archaeological sites. Archaeologists too! Do you know they have arrested the finest erasure man in Greece?" an untidy zealot called Ingraham demanded scornfully.

"Erasure man?" Thatcher asked although it was against his policy to let the conversation stray into unrewarding side-channels.

"When you have a blank tablet, he tells you if an inscription has been erased," Ingraham explained with primer simplicity.

"And we promised steady work to the diggers," Kate Murphy continued her lament. "Now it looks as if we won't be able to get to work all summer."

She was not a woman made for lamentation. Plump and cheerful, with a bird's-nest of short black curls, she faced the world with an expression of pleased expectancy. She had dignified the occasion by donning a hit-or-miss collection of garments.

"Well, it's all terrible," said the photographer, "but there's no point in wasting free time. I'm leaving for Sparta tomorrow.

I'm going to try movies this time. Nobody has really *done* Sparta. Not that there's much of Sparta to do."

"Movies!" Ingraham was disdainful. "No composition, no definition. That's for amateurs, Mr. Thatcher. What you should do is come and see some of my slides."

"I'd like to," said Thatcher perjuring his immortal soul.

Kate Murphy looked up from a stain that had unaccountably appeared on the sleeve of her velvet jacket. "You really should," she said as if detecting some underlying insincerity. "Carl has the largest set-up I've ever seen. An enormous room with an enormous screen. It's like an auditorium."

Carl Ingraham was abashed. "I suppose it is over-done," he confessed. "But I planned it as an antidote to my work. You spend the day microfilming and you don't want to spend your nights with anything pint-sized."

"Miniaturization!" the other photographer scoffed. "That's the cry nowadays. Have you seen some of the cameras the Germans are putting out? I don't say it isn't a technical achievement, but who wants a camera that'll go through the eye of a needle?"

"But microfilm is different." Kate Murphy spoke with the authority of a scholar. "Every library is running short of storage space."

"Because they're not selective. That's what's wrong with the entire intellectual community." This familiar war-cry drew a chorus of response.

Thatcher was grateful when his hostess led him off. They left as somebody was mourning the present-day academic's reliance on technical gadgets.

An hour later, Thatcher, circulating clock-wise, met Everett Gabler coming from the opposite direction.

"Not bad," he summed up. "I've collected eight names and addresses of residents, plus two specific invitations."

Gabler produced his own modest haul. He had fallen in with a nest of epigraphists. "And Dr. Jenkins. She wants us to come and have dinner next week."

Thatcher surveyed his subordinate admiringly. Really, there

was no limit to Everett's capabilities once he was on his mettle. First, he overpowered whole congregations of leftists; now he was fascinating the rather rarefied Dr. Jenkins.

Thatcher would not have been so pleased if he could have overheard the exchange between the two ladies as they emptied ashtrays later that evening.

"Kate! I told Mr. Gabler we'd like to have them to dinner."

"Gabler? That was the skinny one with John Thatcher, wasn't it?"

Lorna Jenkins nodded. An ashtray remained in mid-air as she continued thoughtfully:

"They're up to something. Why on earth were they stalking everybody in sight? Even poor Huttlemayer. Most people run when they see Huttlemayer."

Kate Murphy continued to look pleased. "I thought there was something fishy about them too. Did you hear all those innocent questions about apartments?"

The lady-like Dr. Jenkins suddenly snickered.

"I bet I can find out what it is."

"Yes." A low chuckle. "You usually can. But it'll have to wait till next week, Lorna. Remember, we're going north tomorrow."

John Thatcher and Everett Gabler returned to the Britannia pleased with their undercover work.

"That was not a bad idea," Everett said handsomely as they stepped out of the elevator. It took more than a Huttlemayer to deflect Everett Gabler.

"And no one suspects a thing," said Thatcher. "We may never need these contacts, but if we do, we can probably arrange a bolt-hole for Nicolls on several hours' notice."

Gabler shared this assurance. "I shall be relieved when we can get young Nicolls under cover. Your point about his not having the papers any longer—if he ever did have them—eluded me at first. But I can see that these leftists might be very difficult to convince on that point."

"Particularly as they must know that the Government doesn't have them."

Everett Gabler frowned as they stopped outside Thatcher's door.

"How do they know that?"

Fumbling for his key, Thatcher expanded. "To judge by the stir everybody is making, these papers are important, some action hinges on them. If the Government got them, then presumably there would be arrests or seizures or... Good heavens, get down Everett!"

The next few seconds were a confused medley of cries and thuds. A dull shape, dimly outlined against the window, had risen from one of the chairs. Thatcher threw himself sharply to the right. Gabler, with no choice, had thrown himself to the left, colliding with an end table and lamp. Only when a familiar voice was heard did Thatcher flip the light switch.

"I'm terribly sorry, Mr. Thatcher," said Bill Riemer advancing to disentangle Gabler from the extension cord. "I guess I must have startled you."

"You did," Thatcher snapped. He was letting the atmosphere of the Hellenus project go to his head. But after abductions in Omonia Square, was it too much to expect assassins in the hotel room?

Having helped Gabler to a chair, Bill Riemer was embarrassed, in his turn. "I suppose it was an unnecessary precaution. But I was hoping nobody would see me with you. So I got one of the maids to bring me up the service stairs and let me into your room."

Thatcher raised his eyebrows aggressively. "Have we become suspicious associates?"

"No, no! But I think I may know where Nicolls is. I was afraid to send a written message and I didn't want to use the phone. And I thought it might be a good idea if no one realized you'd gotten sudden news from the Embassy."

Bill Riemer was surrendering something to diplomacy. Ever since yesterday's declaration about seizing the offensive, Riemer had been expecting to hear that Thatcher was caught up in some situation unworthy of an American businessman abroad, perfectly without fault, of course. The Sloan seemed to specialize in innocent dramatics and, after Everett Gabler's performance, Riemer wouldn't put anything past them.

Thatcher had things on his mind other than his public image.

"Do you seriously think the phones are tapped?"

Riemer shrugged. "I don't know. But Nicolls seems to think so."

"Ah! You were going to tell us about Nicolls."

"It's another of these mysterious phone calls. I didn't take it myself. It was made to my home by a woman speaking Greek. My cook took the message, and she's very reliable."

Thatcher and Gabler leaned forward eagerly, silently indicating their willingness to trust the cook.

"The woman said that Nicolls was afraid to try to phone in English, or to reach the Embassy directly, because the exchange might be watched. But he wanted me to know that he was staying in Elasson over the store that this woman owns. The buses and roads are being watched to prevent his reaching Athens. He doesn't know why. She said he intends to stay where he is, if he can, until we get to him." Riemer came to the close of his message and looked at his audience hopefully. It was not approval that he wanted; it was explanation.

He received neither. Thatcher and Gabler looked at each other, one thought in common.

"Elasson." Gabler let the word fall suggestively. "I don't know where it is, but it's not Larissa, where Peter Chiros said the wallet was found."

"Let's be fair, Everett. Nicolls seems to have been wandering around a good deal."

"I suppose the thing to do is go and get him," Riemer said disapprovingly. Paul Makris & Son was also an American business entitled to the protection of the Embassy and, what's more, an American business that seemed to eschew the sensational approach favored by the Sloan.

"I'm sure we can manage that end of it, Mr. Riemer,"

Thatcher said. "We do want to thank you for all you've done. Not only relaying the message, but the care you've taken to do so discreetly."

Riemer knew when he was being dismissed. And he was not sorry to go. He had liked Ken Nicolls and he would be happy to have him back in the land of the living. But if these two desperadoes were going to the rescue with shotguns blazing, then the less he knew about it, the better.

"You were rather short with him, John," Everett Gabler commented. "He's done all he can."

"Never mind that now," said Thatcher. "I daresay he was glad to be rid of us. While he was here, I remembered something I heard at that party. We have been gigantic fools, imagining Nicolls, or Dr. Ziros, for that matter, wandering around with a great swatch of papers. Dr. Ziros, Everett, was an archivist!"

Gabler looked up from caressing his maltreated knee.

"And what does that mean?"

"That he worked in a library where every bit of paper they get their hands on is microfilmed!"

"Microfilm!" Gabler straightened. "Microfilm! But that means only a tiny strip of celluloid. It could be anywhere."

"I'll make you a bet, Everett," Thatcher said with heavy pleasantry. "I'll bet it's where it's been all along. Right under our noses!"

CHAPTER XVI

THE TROJAN WOMEN

GABLER FOLLOWED THE direction of Thatcher's forefinger. It was pointing to the desk drawer in which they had nominally secured Kenneth Nicolls' wallet. Nominally, because a flimsy desk lock was scarcely proof against the marauders who made free with the Hotel Britannia. On the evidence of past form, if balked by the lock they would simply cart off the desk.

"Nicolls' wallet?" Gabler asked. "Oh, come now, John. You don't believe that a total stranger could march up to him and say: 'Here, please let me put this microfilm in your wallet for safe-keeping.' "

"Not exactly, no. He got Nicolls to put it in there for him."

While he was speaking, Thatcher had opened the drawer and removed the wallet. Now he flipped onto the table a single square of thick pasteboard—very thick pasteboard.

"It's Dr. Ziros' calling card. Feel it, Everett. With the resources of a modern pressing machine, how many thicknesses do you think could be there?"

Dutifully Gabler picked it up and felt it. Like many such cards, it was paneled, with a relatively thin outer frame enclosing a heavy central section where the engraving appeared.

"Good heavens! There could be a dozen layers here in the middle," he said, rubbing the rectangle. "It would be child's play to sandwich a strip of microfilm between two thin sheets of cardboard."

"And it explains a good deal about the certainty of the leftists, doesn't it?"

"You mean it tells us why they were so sure that Nicolls was the man who had their papers? Of course! They knew because Nicolls' card was found on Ziros' body."

"Yes. If this is how Dr. Ziros customarily relayed documents, he would probably arrange to meet his courier in a public place and exchange business cards with him. It would be a perfectly innocuous transaction, the kind of thing you see a dozen times a day in any continental hotel or cafe."

Gabler, slow but sure, was coming up the home stretch.

"Wait a minute! If Nicolls and Dr. Ziros exchanged cards, I admit that explains the leftists' certainty. At the same time, it explodes your theory about a courier afraid of the police who planted the incriminating documents on Nicolls."

Patiently Thatcher argued that that theory had been developed only to explain the behavior of the left. They now had a better rationale.

"But, John, why did Dr. Ziros give the papers to Nicolls?"

Thatcher frowned. "I don't suppose we'll ever know, Everett. I can only guess that Nicolls quite accidentally gave the password or whatever it is that modern undergrounds use as a recognition device. Obviously, Ziros didn't know his courier by sight."

"Not by sight. But surely he expected a Greek, didn't he? No one could mistake Nicolls for a Greek. Dr. Ziros must have known he was American."

"Why should Ziros be so fussy?" Thatcher demanded. "Neither the Army nor these leftists of yours have the slightest difficulty believing Americans are involved. And, from the way they're acting, the American Embassy and Paul Makris & Son think so, too."

"I wish you'd stop calling them my leftists," Gabler was provoked into retorting.

"They will always be your leftists to me," said Thatcher straightfaced. Gabler was always reduced to petulance when events took a promising turn. Success was not the air in which he flowered. "But, Everett, you've overlooked one difficulty, you know."

This was rubbing salt into the wound. No difficulty was so small as to escape Everett's attention.

"Possibly," he said stiffly.

"Nicolls' room was searched twice. And those two searches represented a progression in outrage."

"Yes. The first time the room was left a mess, with curtains torn down and clothing strewn about, but there was no actual destruction or theft. The second time the room was gutted... oh! Yes, I see what you mean." As Gabler plunged into the problem, he lost his sense of personal affront. "The first time someone was searching for papers. The second time, someone was looking for microfilm. When I saw Nicolls' belongings in that villa, I simply assumed the leftists were responsible for both searches. Do you think they didn't know about the microfilm in their first attempt?"

"No." Thatcher paused to organize his argument. "On their own admission, the leftists don't seem to have gone into action until the police released Dr. Ziros' body and they found out about Nicolls' calling card. That didn't occur until after the first search. Furthermore, I'd be willing to bet that Dr. Ziros was chosen for this job precisely because of his ability to reduce documents to microfilm. Can you think of anything more desirable for an underground movement than a man who has all the facilities of a modern library at his disposal? After all, we're going to need one ourselves as soon as we get this microfilm out."

"The location of the microfilm is still a matter of surmise," Gabler rejoined with professional acuteness. "How do you propose to find it?"

Thatcher looked at the card appraisingly.

"Soak it?" he suggested tentatively.

Gabler saw objections on principle. "That seems very cavalier," he protested. "Surely it's more complicated than that."

"Be reasonable, Everett. These people intended the documents to be accessible. And if we're wrong, a little water isn't going to hurt modern film."

Displaying a good deal more confidence than he felt, Thatcher strode into the bathroom, plugged the washstand and filled it with cold water. He had some dim recollection that hot water had an unfortunate effect on film emulsion. Immersing the card, he reflected that this must be the only time in his life when he could have used the expert support of Professor Cardwell Carlson.

Everett Gabler peered over his shoulder. "Nothing's happening," he remarked.

"Give it time, Ev."

Rather than face the unspoken accusation from the rear, Thatcher busied himself removing wristwatch and rolling up sleeves.

"Still nothing!" The accusation was no longer unspoken.

"We'll probably have to peel it apart," Thatcher improvised.

In the event, he failed to allow enough time. Twice he removed the card and held it sideways, squinting for signs of a tell-tale crack. Twice he returned the card to its bath and resisted the temptation to add a little—just a little—hot water.

On the third attempt, the crack was there.

Thatcher's thumbnail slipped neatly into the slit. Then, with an ease that mocked earlier difficulties, two cards peeled cleanly apart. On the bottom half reposed a small strip of film.

Both men let out the breaths they had been holding.

"It was really there." Gabler sounded surprised.

"Certainly," said Thatcher, making hay while he could. "You really should try a little optimism, every now and then."

Gabler disregarded non-essentials. "Do you think we can read it?"

"We can try. But everybody's been talking about papers as if several sheets were involved. The reduction must be substantial."

Nevertheless they turned on the room's brightest light bulb. As Thatcher prepared to raise the film, he cocked an eyebrow.

"You know, we're reading someone else's mail, Everett," he said.

Gabler was beyond such bait. He cleared his throat severely.

"Hand it over!" he ordered. "These people have been remarkably free with our belongings, not to mention our persons.

They certainly have earned no extraordinary degree of civility from me."

Meekly Thatcher handed over the microfilm. It was obvious that the blanket still rankled. Manhandling had roused the tiger in Everett Gabler. There was going to be no nonsense about Marquis of Queensberry rules for any Greek unfortunate enough to stray into his path.

After a moment's fruitless activity, Gabler threw down the film. "Tcha!" he grumbled. "All this delicacy about nothing. It's perfectly illegible."

"Which brings us back to what I was saying. We need an archivist of our own."

"They'd have a microfilm reader at the Embassy—as well as at some of the banks," Gabler offered. "But I suppose that's out of the question."

"It certainly is! I hate to think of the storm we could brew up if these papers are as explosive as a large number of people seem to think. No, we need two things." Thatcher held two fingers aloft for his enumeration. "We need a nice private reading of this microfilm. And we need to get Kenneth Nicolls into a place of safety."

There was a moment's silence. Then, with unusual moderation, Gabler spoke:

"Don't you think you have your priorities reversed, John?" he asked quietly. "Important as these papers may be, I would willingly flush them down the drain in order to assure Nicolls' safety."

Thatcher was astonished.

"Of course! I had no intention of suggesting anything else. But these papers may give us leverage. At the very least we ought to be able to persuade the left to abandon its interest in Nicolls. We can always go out to that villa and negotiate with them. But we might do better than that. We can't tell until we've read this thing."

He waved the film strip under Gabler's eyes.

"And how do you propose to accomplish all this? If we go out and buy a microfilm reader, we may as well tell the world we have the papers." The objection was pro forma. The word *negotiation* to Everett Gabler was like a trumpet call.

Thatcher was thinking.

"What about that man Ingraham we met? He does the microfilm work at the American Academy. If we approach him about a hide-out for Nicolls, we'll have to take him into our confidence to a certain extent anyway. We may as well kill two birds with one stone."

Gabler didn't like it, but even he had to admit that they would be forced to confide in someone if they were to achieve their goals.

"Do you think he can be trusted to be discreet?"

"Better than discreet. Uninterested. These classicists seem to be indifferent to political upheavals except insofar as they affect archaeological excavations. Unless our papers shed light on the new Atlantis, we should be fairly safe."

Surprisingly this remark moved Gabler to the long view.

"I suppose, to a classicist, the history of Greece is simply one political upheaval after another," he said thoughtfully. "Probably this coup is very pedestrian compared to the troubles of Alcibiades."

Thatcher looked at his subordinate with alarm. The long view was all very well, but they didn't want to let Ken Nicolls sink into being just one more atom of humanity in the countless eons of history.

"Very well, then," he said bracingly. "We'll get in touch with Ingraham right away." Then he glanced regretfully at the clock. It registered two-thirty a.m.

"First thing in the morning," he amended.

Saboteurs, revolutionaries, and spies pursue their vocations largely independent of mundane considerations like the eight-hour day and the working week. Not so, the rest of the world.

Promptly on rising, Thatcher made a number of discoveries. Carl Ingraham had no telephone listed in his name. His address remained a mystery. Dr. Jenkins and Dr. Murphy were apparently not at home.

And the American Academy, resorted to in desperation, finally answered something like twenty rings in the shape of a sleepy caretaker.

"But monsieur," said that worthy in tones of horror, "today is Sunday!"

Thatcher grounded the receiver savagely and reported this frustrating turn of events.

"We have no alternative but to camp on the ladies' doorstep," he decided. "We can't get any information on Ingraham from the Academy until tomorrow. And time is critical. We need every hour we can save."

Wordlessly, Gabler reached for his hat and prepared to accompany his chief. He was not discouraged by the news. While ready to work a seven-day week himself, he valued an orderly world in which timetables were decently predictable, a world in which people were to be found at their desks Monday through Friday and occupied with appropriate recreation on the weekends.

When they reached the apartment house in Kolonaki, Everett said encouragingly, "Perhaps the ladies have only gone out for a short time."

"With our luck, we'll probably have to wait all day!" Thatcher tried, unavailingly, to gain relief for his feelings by slamming the door. A gentle pneumatic hiss was no help at all.

Gabler heroically refrained from counseling small dosages of optimism, now and then.

The elevator operator remember them from yesterday's festivities and greeted them like old friends. Garrulously he made them a present of his knowledge about the ladies' comings and goings.

"But yes, yes. The American ladies were up at first dawn. They plan to go away, you understand. Dr. Murphy was out for six o'clock Mass."

Gabler nodded approvingly. Things were as they should be. People were out on Sunday morning going to church. True, he would have liked it even better if Kate Murphy had been attending eleven o'clock service at the First Congregational Church of Athens, but you can't have everything.

The gentlemen must dispatch themselves, the elevator operator urged. The ladies were busy with their truck at the lock-up garage. Even now, they would be on the very brink of departure. It was simplicity itself to find them. It was only to take the first right at the herb shop, and then right again into the alley. But quickly, quickly. Haste was of the essence.

He whisked them toward the door with the native Athenian's inborn love of drama, and the two bankers rounded the corner at a dog trot. At the mouth of the alley, they spotted their prey and paused, partly for breath and partly for sheer astonishment.

Gone were the ladylike figures who bloomed amidst linear furniture and abstract paintings. There was no sign of the svelte elegant Dr. Jenkins or the grandmotherly, untidy Dr. Murphy. Instead two disheveled street urchins swarmed over a disreputable pick-up truck.

With legs straddled Lorna Jenkins stood atop the load in the back of the truck, silhouetted against the sky. Today her thin rakish form had an air of piratical practicality. Her faded blue jeans were tucked into old, lace-up hunting boots. As she heaved sacks of plaster about, shirt tails flapped in the breeze.

On ground level Kate Murphy was more circular than ever in chinos and a pair of gaiters reminiscent of the First World War. Effortlessly she tossed picks and spades over the tailboard. Her black hair was thrust back by the gaudy scarf she had wrapped around her forehead as a sweatband. It was she who spotted the visitors and halloed a welcome.

"Mr. Thatcher! Mr. Gabler! Over here!" She beamed at them. "Have you come to see us off?"

Briefly Thatcher explained their errand. They were very anxious to communicate with Mr. Ingraham. Did they know where he was to be found?

Apparently nothing could have pleased Dr. Murphy more than an opportunity to be of assistance. She rattled off Carl Ingraham's address and phone number.

Thatcher's thanks and adieux were interrupted by Lorna Jenkins. She had been silently listening to the exchange from her perch on high. Now she dropped lightly to the ground and said:

"But you won't be able to get him today, Mr. Thatcher. He told us he was going out with a fishing party."

Kate Murphy's face fell. "So he did. And they'll have left hours ago. But there," she added comfortably, "you'll only have to wait until tomorrow."

Thatcher could have cursed. Tomorrow was too late! They needed the microfilm to help with Nicolls' rescue. But they could not leave Nicolls hanging, day after day. Already a night had gone by with no action on their part. God alone knew how hard Nicolls was being pressed! And they still had no plan for effecting that rescue. Bleakly, Thatcher stared ahead, searching for some inspiration. And then, as he took in the scene before him, it came!

The whole dusty ensemble, truck and women, was eminently ready to sink into the background of the parched Greek countryside—Lorna Jenkins' boots, so scuffed and scarred that the identity of the original leather was lost forever; the half-ton pick-up with rusty side-panels, so decrepit it creaked with every weight shift; tools all bearing the signs of many years' usage. Greece, more than any other country in the world, is familiar with the sight of working archaeologists. Scarcely a road or hamlet has not seen them pass hundreds of times, going back and forth to their scattered diggings.

Cautiously Thatcher broached the scheme that the gods had suddenly vouchsafed him.

"Are you by any chance going to the north?"

Lorna Jenkins and Kate Murphy looked first at him, then at each other.

"Yes, we're going north," said Kate at last.

"North?" Gabler saw light.

"North," Lorna Jenkins repeated impatiently. "The direction which is due opposite from south."

The cautions Gabler had been formulating died stillborn as

he too looked at the little cavalcade with sudden appreciation.

"If you can spare the time, we would like to explain a problem of ours," said Thatcher.

The ladies were silent.

Thatcher spoke of Ken Nicolls and the Nicolls family. The picture he conjured up of the newborn baby with the pink halo was truly touching.

The ladies' silence, while unbroken, somehow became tinged with skepticism.

Desperately Thatcher began to speak of the Salonika railroad station and a man's body lying in the dust as a truck roared off into the night. Somehow, little by little, his version became less expurgated and more truthful.

The silence became slightly more receptive.

Thatcher shored up his crumbling morale by reminding himself that these two women were professionally adept at wrenching testimony from stones and pots over five thousand years old. A living breathing witness was necessarily a piece of cake.

"I suppose you want us to winkle Nicolls out of Elasson for you," Kate Murphy said before Thatcher could reach his request.

"Yes," he agreed. "We're afraid that we are being followed. We would be most grateful—"

Lorna Jenkins cut in on his expressions of gratitude. "But that isn't all you want," she interrupted. "You want Carl Ingraham for something too. Let me see, what could it be?"

Thatcher did not believe that the ladies would have any trouble remembering Ingraham's remarks of yesterday about his work with microfilm. Bowing to the inevitable, he capitulated completely and told the whole story—disappearance, abduction, microfilm, everything.

When the ladies were sure that they had shaken the very last bit of information out of him, they paused in their relentless interrogation and eyed each other.

This time the silence became positively congenial.

Thatcher was not surprised when, at the end of their wordless communication, they suddenly smiled at him.

"We'll do it," Lorna announced. "What's more, we'll give you a note for Carl, telling him what to do. If you meet the fishing boat at the dock, he can get it done for you tonight, or at latest tomorrow morning. That way you should have your papers before we're back."

Gabler knew his limitations in the field of woman well enough to have remained aloof from the hard sell. Now he joined Thatcher in profuse acknowledgements of indebtedness. Unfortunately he felt the necessity to temper gratitude with advice.

"You won't drive through the night, will you?" he asked in concern. "It might draw attention to you. You want to look as normal as possible. There may be more than one faction involved. These Greek political questions can become quite complex."

Lorna Jenkins' lip quivered.

"So I understand," she said, gravely.

"We suspected as much during the Civil War," said Kate Murphy brightly.

Was that a glint of amusement in Lorna Jenkins' eyes?

"You mean you were here during the Civil War?" Gabler asked, astounded.

It developed that the ladies had been digging throughout that time of turmoil. Indeed they had been right in the path of the retreating Communist force, with its immense detachment of hostages, during its final withdrawal over the border. The communists had made spirited attempts to add the ladies to that detachment. Not quite so spirited, however, as the ladies' resistance. They had no wish to go to Bulgaria, a country singularly without interest for the classicist.

"Everything was very confused then," Kate Murphy recalled nostalgically. "But not as confused as during the war."

"Were you here then, too?" Gabler asked weakly. Thatcher had enough sense to keep his mouth shut.

Oh, yes, they replied. They had been digging so assiduously that the events of 1941 had overtaken them. They had ended up on the beaches of the Peloponnesus with the ill-fated

British Expeditionary Force and been evacuated with them to Cairo.

Thatcher now had a question. Why had they not stayed as guerillas? Aloud, he asked: "And what did you do then?"

The ladies were nothing if not adaptable. They had, perforce, turned themselves into Egyptologists for the duration.

"A very unrewarding field," Lorna Jenkins summed up.

"Difficult, too," Kate contributed. "Particularly with all those armies trampling back and forth."

To give him his due, Everett Gabler knew when he was beaten. He did not venture any further counsel on what to do when in Greece. The two bankers contented themselves with standing to one side and waving as the rackety truck finally swung out of the alley and turned to the north.

"I am glad you did not probe further into their Egyptian experiences," Thatcher observed. "They probably turned back the Afrika Korps single-handed."

Everett Gabler had always reserved his highest approval for people who go on with the job. He was beginning to rank Lorna Jenkins as one of the world's few entirely satisfactory human beings.

"This is no time for witticism, John," he said sternly. "We should be deeply thankful. There is no doubt that we are delivering Nicolls into trustworthy hands."

CHAPTER XVII

PANDORA'S BOX

THE LADIES WHO were setting out to rescue Kenneth Nicolls inspired Everett Gabler's confidence. Once converted, they did not need extensive briefing. Not so, Carl Ingraham. Finally tracked down amidst smelly boats, untidy tackle and foul-weather gear, he was willing but confused. With exasperating care, he read the note Kate Murphy had scrawled and examined Thatcher's microfilm. He agreed to do what he could.

"Right away?" Gabler pressed.

Ingraham did not see anything to get excited about.

"Well, sure, if you think it's important."

He did not sound convinced by their assurances, but a midnight telephone call testified that his doubts had been dispelled.

"Listen, no names!" he whispered hoarsely. "Just follow these instructions..."

Accordingly, at six o'clock the following morning John Putnam Thatcher and Everett Gabler, both impeccable in business suits, were perched on dusty rocks by the Parthenon. From this historic height, they were watching the sun's first golden fingers touch the ancient marble of Athens with the daily miracle of light. Six Swiss school-teachers from Zug, studying the maidens of the Erechtheum and commemorating their timeless beauty with expensive cameras, were puzzled at their inactivity.

"Look, Xavier," one of them adjured another. "That hill, over there! How beautiful in this light of early morning. Do you know what it is?"

Xavier exchanged guide book for camera, riffled through it,

then shook his head. Agilely stepping down a ruined step he approached the silent and immobile Gabler.

"Please," he said. "Do you know what it is—that beautiful hill there, almost as high as is here the Acropolis?"

Everett, never at his best before breakfast, did.

"That," he said firmly, "is the municipal gas works of the city of Athens."

The Swiss retreated to relay this information to his companions who gave loud cries of disbelief. Casting reproachful looks behind them, they scrambled away.

"And is it?" Thatcher inquired.

"I believe so," said Gabler. "However, that is neither here nor there. I still wish I knew why it was necessary for us to hurtle up here at this unearthly hour."

Thatcher sighed. Everett had his difficult moments. He was not protesting at the early hour, being an adherent of the early-to-bed school of mental and physical health. But midnight phone calls and surreptitious trysts—even in a good cause—were not Everett's way of doing business. Fortunately his further strictures were forestalled.

Carl Ingraham came huffing up the path.

"Sorry to be so mysterious," he said dropping down beside them. "But I thought it would be better to meet where we couldn't be overheard." He glanced at a large party of Dutch nuns who were chirping merrily as they followed in his wake. "Amazing how many people come up here early, isn't it?"

Before Everett could explode, Ingraham, in the best tradition of his new calling, handed Thatcher a brightly coloured guide book.

"Page seventy-three," he hissed.

Thatcher opened the book. There, interleaved in a description of the Cyclades, were three pages of microfilm enlargements. He had to turn to the Ionian Islands for the handwritten English translation.

"Sixty-three Plateia Eugenia," Thatcher read softly. "Garage near the Church of the Annunciation. Taverna Nauplia... This is a list of locations, isn't it, Ingraham?"

Furtively Ingraham looked around. "There's more further on. Each of these locations is numbered. Go on!"

Thatcher obeyed him. Then, without haste, he shut the book and slipped it into a pocket.

"Light machine guns, carbines, grenades," he repeated aloud.

The three men sat in silence amidst the growing splendor of the sun flooding the Attic plain. More and more sightseers were trudging up the dusty path to look at the great marble remnants of the glory that had been Greece.

Ingraham shifted. "That microfilm looks to me like a list of arms dumps in the Athens area," he said, sounding rather thrilled. "Do you want to tell me more?"

Thatcher thought briefly. "I appreciate what you've done already, but on the whole, I think it would be wiser—and possibly safer—if we don't involve you any further, Ingraham."

Ingraham arose and brushed himself off. "Okay," he said. without rancor. "But remember, I'm here if you should need help. I've lived in Greece for a long time and I know my way around. Not that it's any of my business, you understand, but arms dumps can spell trouble. Well, you two must be hungry. Come on. I know a pretty good little restaurant down here in the Turkish quarter..."

Only after Ingraham had regretfully left adventure for the humdrum of replicating fourth-century inscriptions could Thatcher and Gabler chew over this latest discovery. They watched him pile into his car, sketch a mock military salute and shoot into the maelstrom of traffic winding through the alley-wide streets. Then they removed to a nearby sidewalk cafe.

"A list of arms caches," said Thatcher ruminatively. "Either the left is planning an uprising..."

"Or," said Gabler, "the Army caught them offguard with their master plan up in Salonika."

Thatcher looked at him. Normally he would expect Gablerian denunciations of the left. But no. If anything, Everett was being more than scrupulously fair; he was leaning slightly in favor of his erstwhile captors. Thatcher remarked as much.

Everett gave his spectacles a good going over. "That is true, John," he admitted. "But don't forget, I have had several extended sessions with representatives of the current government. And besides, I have never met a military man—in any country—who could understand anything as simple as a balance sheet."

This was deep condemnation in Gabler's lexicon.

"At any rate," Thatcher continued, "for some reason or other, Ziros passed this list of arms dumps to Nicolls. Since then a lot of people have been trying to get their hands on it."

Everett was inclined to spell things out. "Yes, that's clear enough. But why should Ziros give it to Nicolls in the first place?"

"That's one question we can't answer until Nicolls gets back," said Thatcher. "Let's hope the ladies don't run into any difficulties. I'm not sure I would have enlisted their aid if I had realized it was a question of arms dumps."

"I am quite sure they can surmount any obstacle," said Everett. "And for that matter, Ingraham was sound as well."

Somewhat surprised, Thatcher concurred in this general approval.

"I have come to the conclusion," said Everett implacably, "that this Ugly American business is another piece of journalistic incompetence. On the whole, the Americans we have met compare very favorably with most other nationals."

Travel, after all, can broaden only so many minds.

In any event, Everett Gabler's assessment of the capabilities of Dr. Lorna Jenkins and Dr. Mary Katherine Murphy was dead right.

Thatcher, Gabler, Peter Chiros, two representatives of the Ministry of Economic Development, Mr. Riemer from the Embassy, and various associates spent the afternoon reviewing a proposed change in Hellenus tax liabilities presented to the gathering by Stavros Bacharias. Since Greeks were included in the gathering, the discussion grew animated and lively. It could not however camouflage the essential futility of the meeting. This did not surprise the representatives of the Sloan Guaranty Trust. Everett Gabler currently distrusted all other parties to the Hellenus venture, specifically the Greek Government and Paul Makris & Son. Thatcher disliked conferences on principle.

Not that Stavros Bacharias suggested anything but tempered eagerness on the part of his Minister and the entire Greek Government in regard to the progress and health of Hellenus.

"Onward and upward," muttered Thatcher disrespectfully under his breath as the meeting finally broke up.

Dinner, however, was simply a prolongation of the conference in the guise of conviviality.

By the time Gabler and Thatcher finally returned to the Britannia, it was late in the evening. In a way, this was fortunate since it presented them with the only genuinely welcoming Greek face on the hotel staff.

Lycurgos Diamantis, Assistant Night Manager, looked upon John Putnam Thatcher as a feather in his cap. His own persuasiveness had lured Mr. Thatchos to beautiful Greece. This made him very, very happy. The only fly in his ointment was that Mr. Thatchos was spending so little time on beauty.

"Ah, the Acropolis! Good! It is very, very beautiful, no! Perhaps tomorrow you drive to Delphi? My cousin, he is an excellent guide. No? But before you leave... no, no letter, Mr. Thatchos. But here"—he made a ballet dancer's gesture—"here, a message! Perhaps you are waiting? Good. Please to call Dr. Murphy! But what beautiful Greek the lady doctor speaks..."

Dr. Murphy sounded beautiful to Thatcher as well. Her splendidly timbred voice held laughter in its corners.

"Oh, good, Mr. Thatcher. You know Lorna and I took a little trip? Well, we've picked up some marvellous trophies. I know you'll want to see them. Why don't you and Mr. Gabler drop by for a nightcap?"

"We're on our way," said Thatcher happily.

Lycurgos Diamantis watched them hurry out to the taxi-stand. He valued Americans and the dollars they represented but there was no doubt that they were, culturally, barbarians. Rushing here and there at all hours—and not interested in Delphi, in Epidaurus, in Mistra...

"Po! Po! Po!"

Thatcher looked upon Kenneth Nicolls with profound satisfaction. This was a tribute to his deep determination that none of his subordinates was going to be a pawn or victim, so long as he had any say about it, rather than to Nicolls' overall appearance. Begrimed, unshaven, and red-eyed, Nicolls struggled to make the transition from footsore fugitive in the Greek bush to correct young banker.

"Er . . . good evening, Mr. Thatcher," he said self-consciously.

"You're a sight for sore eyes," said Everett Gabler excitedly, pumping Nicolls' hand up and down.

The younger man swayed slightly.

"Here," said Kate Murphy, proffering a steaming cup. "Coffee should help. The boy is asleep on his feet."

This signalled the end of the preliminaries. Kenneth Nicolls was no longer the missing young hero but again a junior, unseasoned staff member of the Sloan Guaranty Trust.

"Dr. Murphy and Dr. Jenkins," said Everett Gabler. "You have been marvelous!"

Somewhat deflated, Kenneth Nicolls sank onto the luxuriant sofa. Both Dr. Jenkins and Dr. Murphy, on the other hand, still sporting exuberantly functional clothing, looked bright-eyed as squirrels.

"Oh, it was easy enough," said Kate Murphy puffing deeply on a cigarette. "No difficulties at all. Just zipped up to Elasson and went to the store. Of course Mrs. Andreades didn't really want to hand him over to us."

She cocked on eyebrow at Nicolls.

He flushed slightly. "She thought you might be part of that gang."

"Young man," said Dr. Mary Katherine Murphy, PhD, FRS and, during her teaching days, a notable disciplinarian, "I know exactly what Mrs. Andreades was thinking—and you should be ashamed of yourself!"

Thatcher thought it best not to follow this exchange. But by a natural process of thought, he recalled an item that should be of interest.

"Nicolls," he said, accepting coffee and a glass of brandy from Dr. Jenkins who appeared with the bottle tucked under her arm, "in your absence, you've had a baby. A daughter. Both Jane and the little girl are fine..."

"Good God!" Nicolls exclaimed, letting coffee cup crash to the table. "Oh, I'm sorry..."

With immense good humor, Dr. Murphy produced a large red bandana, performed cursory mopping up, then stuffed the cloth back into her hip pocket. "Men!"

"Now, Kate!" said Dr. Jenkins. "Congratulations, Mr. Nicolls."

Thatcher began to regret introducing the subject; young Nicolls now looked shellshocked.

"I've got to call," he mumbled, getting to his feet unsteadily. "Jane..."

Thatcher waved him back. "No, I'm afraid you can't. We don't want people to know where you are, Nicolls. You're safe here, but we can't be sure how safe. Don't worry, I'll get a message through to Miss Corsa."

Dr. Murphy broke in to say that the apartment was quite secure. Old Mattina wouldn't talk.

Everett tore himself away from a conversation with Dr. Jenkins. "Perhaps," he suggested, "we should get down to your story, Nicolls."

Thatcher was glad to see the young man make a visible effort to pull himself together.

"To be honest," Nicolls said, "I've been hoping that somebody could explain things to me. Ever since I got to the railroad station in Salonika, I've been in a world without rhyme or reason."

Thatcher took the guide book from his pocket. "I think I can make a start, if I can't explain everything. In the railroad station, you fell into conversation with a Dr. Ziros..."

"Elias?" Kate Murphy exclaimed. "How does he...oh, sorry!"

"You exchanged business cards," Thatcher continued, ignoring this tempting bypath.

"How did you know that?" Nicolls asked.

Dr. Jenkins poured ample second dollops of brandy, then observed that, unless everybody refrained from interrupting, the story would never get told. Everett Gabler radiated approval.

"He gave you his card. And that card, in fact, contained a microfilm," Thatcher continued. "That microfilm listed arms dumps in the Athens area."

"So that was it," Nicolls said. "I never knew..."

"Presumably that list of arms dumps was the reason why the Army arrested you, Ziros and everybody who had spoken to him. They thought they had uncovered a plot to overthrow the Government. That's clear. But I don't understand why they then shot Ziros out of hand..."

Both ladies gave exclamations of horror and distress.

"They shot him?" Kate Murphy demanded fiercely. "By God, what brutes! Elias was a dedicated idealist. Just a mild-mannered intellectual filled with theories about bringing Greece into the modern world." Her dark eyes sparkled wrathfully.

Lorna Jenkins frowned unhappily. "Elias was the last man in the world to have anything to do with arms dumps. That's the trouble with these colonels. They're driving men like Elias to extremism. And that's the kind of man this Government executes! What's going to happen to Greece?"

"The military mind," said Everett. "What you can't understand, you shoot!"

If they didn't get him out of Greece soon, Thatcher thought, Everett would be taking to the hills with a band of guerillas.

Ken Nicolls, ignoring this outpouring, shook his head. "No,

I don't think the Army did shoot Ziros. And I don't think it's the Army who's been bird-dogging me!"

"What's that?"

"But surely..."

"But why were you arrested..."

Thatcher quelled the ejaculations with a terse: "Explain!"

Nicolls tried to order his thoughts. "I've had some time to think in the past day or two..."

This had the happy effect of diverting Dr. Murphy. She gave an eloquent snort.

"Kate!"

Speaking more quickly, Ken said: "First of all, when we were herded together—the shot came from someplace beyond the shed. I got the impression, and the others in that paddy wagon did too, I'll bet—that those soldiers were just as surprised and scared as we were."

"Hmm," said Gabler, preparing a scathing indictment of the military mentality which has been famed through history for unerringly training artillery, and indeed long bows, on its own men.

"Go on!" said Thatcher. Nicolls' words were encouraging a train of thought he had begun to follow during the afternoon's interminable—and useless—meeting.

"Then, when I set off cross-country, I was trying to avoid officials. I guess you know about my zig-zagging..."

"In broad outline," said Thatcher. "Sometime you must tell me why you got so involved with Quakers, but go on."

Nicolls frowned in thought. "Well, pretty soon it developed that somebody was after me, sure enough. But it wasn't the Army. Or any police officials. At least there certainly wasn't a general alarm out for me. Hell, I got a lift from one bunch of soldiers."

Everett Gabler, foregoing his customary displeasure at profanity in the presence of ladies, leaned forward and presented a brief description of his own treatment at the hands of Dr. Ziros' leftist associates.

"So you see, Nicolls, the Government is not the only group

eager to get their hands on that microfilm. The left is just as anxious. Good heavens, they kidnapped me. They ransacked your hotel room and stole all your belongings."

Nicolls groaned and looked down at Elasson's idea of sartorial splendor.

"Obviously, the left is desperate to get that list of arms dumps. And God knows what they're planning to do with tons of ammunition."

Pugnaciously, Kate Murphy declared that whoever Elias Ziros had been associated with, it was not a bunch of irresponsible terrorists.

"And remember," said Thatcher. "Somebody else searched Ken's room, as well, Everett."

Eager to defend his interpretation, Nicolls said: "That's it. This gang of thugs was openly going from town to town. They had a car and could move freely. They asked questions and used the phone. I don't know what's been happening down here, but I can tell you that up at Hellenus—and all over the north—anybody who isn't enthusiastic about the colonels is lying low."

Again Kate Murphy waded in. "If they're not lying low, they're in prison."

Thatcher began to feel he was getting her measure. First, a passion for digging up primitive sites, under conditions of extreme difficulty; then a robust disapproval of injustice, violence, cruelty and pain. Dr. Jenkins, cooler and more objective, had a tenacity of mind and purpose that recalled the various high-minded New England ladies of Thatcher's youth.

"Oh, there's no doubt that this bunch is thoroughly second-rate," Lorna said. "But the question is, if it wasn't the Army *or* the left tracking you down, Ken, who was it?"

"If we knew the answer to that," said Thatcher slowly, "we might know exactly why Dr. Ziros gave that microfilm to him."

He looked at Ken's startled expression. "Oh, hasn't that occurred to you? That you were set up—by force or forces unknown?"

"You mean by Dr. Ziros?" Ken virtually stuttered.

Dr. Murphy took the point instantly. "More likely," she said, "he was a patsy too!"

Thatcher felt enormously cheered. "Here's a pretty mess," he said. "A strange government, revolutionary threats, unknown enemies gunning for Nicolls, dangerous microfilm..."

"And," said Everett Gabler portentously, "some very dubious allies."

Kate Murphy projected indignation. "Well, I like that. Lorna, did you hear the man?"

While Everett floundered in a morass of explanations and apologies (and young Nicolls sank into a stupor), Thatcher thought hard. On the plus side, the Sloan's human bodies were warm and accounted for. This being so, he could consider with equanimity the very considerable minuses.

A nasty Greek political cauldron was boiling, and perhaps boiling over. Willy nilly, the Sloan had been thrust into a precarious situation. And, with all the experience behind him, Thatcher did not believe that this was sheer fluke. No, he would be willing to bet that there was reason, however perverted, behind it. More to the point, he was willing to bet that that reason had dollar-and-cents dimensions.

He woke to find Dr. Murphy regarding him with indulgent outrage, hands on hips.

"I said," she repeated, "don't worry about your young man. We'll take good care of him. And Mr. Thatcher..."

"Dr. Murphy?"

"Remember, you have friends here, if you need us. You'd better give me that microfilm. I have a feeling it will be safer here."

Obediently, Thatcher handed over the guide book. Dr. Murphy, completely serious now, formidably intelligent, with great strength of character and a commanding presence, although she just came up to his shoulder, turned and slipped it into a book case that was full to overflowing. "There, now. Between Milonas and Finley. Don't forget. Now, just one more thing, Mr. Thatcher. I don't know much about banks and big business, and I don't want to. But I know about people." She looked at him severely. "Young men should be kept very close to home."

Thatcher glanced over to Gabler, taking elaborate farewells of Dr. Jenkins who, despite her attire, managed to look indefinably regal.

"And old men, Dr. Murphy?" he inquired politely.

"Old men?" She gave a rich chortle. "Oh, nothing much can hurt them—short of a shotgun!"

The Sloan Guaranty Trust had indeed acquired redoubtable allies.

"Remarkable woman," said Everett Gabler sleepily as they neared the Britannia once again.

Although Thatcher agreed sincerely, Everett felt that his enthusiasm was insufficient.

"Dr. Jenkins, and Dr. Murphy too, of course, have done very valuable work. I don't know if you're familiar with the finds at Philogrylla. Well, they've unearthed tablets..."

A wave of archaeological lore broke over Thatcher, reinforcing his already high opinion of Dr. Jenkins. In a very short time, she had added fourth-century vases to dogs, sun-dried figs and the few other items Gabler considered worthy of men whose great concerns centered on Rails and Industrials. Gabler was, in fact, in the midst of an extended disquisition when he broke off sharply. Gone, in a second, was the extra-curricular Everett Gabler. In his place was the man the Sloan knew very well.

"What's *he* doing here?" The voice was all suspicion.

Lycurgos Diamantis, beaming with pleasure, was registering a late-night arrival at the desk.

The slight figure turned as they approached.

"Ah, Mr. Thatcher. What a happy coincidence. Just the man I have come to see!"

Lycurgos Diamantis was dizzy with joy. Two hotel guests, meeting here, who wanted to meet here.

"Mr. Makris," said Thatcher pleasantly. "I didn't know we could expect you in Athens."

For the first time, an unguarded expression crossed that impassive, almost Oriental face.

"I didn't know it myself," said Paul Makris. He paused for effect. "But I think the time has come for us to talk."

"Certainly," said Thatcher with unruffled courtesy. "I am at your disposal."

Makris looked at a wrist watch, made a vexed noise, and said: "It is too late now, and I have some calls to make. Perhaps if you are free for breakfast tomorrow?"

The appointment was arranged, then Everett Gabler and Thatcher watched Makris stride away.

"A very, very nice man," chirped Mr. Diamantis.

"And," as Thatcher said later to Gabler, "a worried and irritated man."

Gabler expected the worst.

"What do you think he wants to talk to you about, John?"

Thatcher was feeling better and better. "Oh, any number of things, Everett. But I think I'll just wait and see."

CHAPTER XVIII

THE SQUARE OF THE HYPOTENUSE...

JOHN THATCHER ENJOYED a good night's sleep, untroubled by curiosity about Paul Makris and the Athenian din penetrating the Hotel Britannia. These undisturbed slumbers were testimony to his revived sense of well-being. True, the Sloan Guaranty Trust was not yet out of the woods, but Kenneth Nicolls was safe.

As for charges of arms running, well just let those bloody colonels try, Thatcher had thought defiantly as he penned a night cable to Miss Corsa. His expression distressed Lycurgos Diamantis.

"Yes, yes," he said nervously. "We send it on the instant..."

The message was not calculated to enlighten him:

TRINKAMS CHESTNUTS EXFIRE STOP SUGGEST LIGHTS BROOKHEIGHTS WINDOWS STOP RETURNS UPCOMING

With Olympian benevolence, Thatcher contemplated Charlie Trinkam's relief when he learned that he did not have to shoulder Ken Nicolls' domestic responsibilities; then Thatcher considered the other deeper emotions at the brownstone on Brooklyn Heights once it was known that husband and father would be restored. Then he retired, virtuously conscious that the humanitarian had triumphed over the banker.

But this, as Miss Corsa could have told him with a wealth of supporting detail, was self-deception. As kindhearted as the next man, John Putnam Thatcher was understandably pleased that young Nicolls was alive and destined to return to Brooklyn Heights, if the Greek Army could be circumvented. Yet, as Miss Corsa had occasion to know, relief from anxiety rarely left Thatcher exhilarated. Normally his high spirits required more positive support. It was not Kenneth Nicolls' deliverance alone which had put Thatcher into fine fettle, but something else. He was beginning, insensibly, to discern purpose behind the shadows of current reality; the mad charade was beginning to hint at method, of a sort. Then too, the tide of misfortune had definitely ebbed. The last twenty-four hours had turned up lucky hits, for Thatcher, the Sloan and Nicolls. The ladies alone, Thatcher thought sleepily just before he dropped off. They were a stroke of luck. And when luck turns . . .

Like Napoleon, John Putnam Thatcher wanted his generals —and captains and NCOs as well—to be lucky.

In a word, as Miss Corsa knew so well, Thatcher was a hunch player. And it had come to him in the last hours: *The timing's about right! Something's going to break!*

Morning was a rebuke to Thatcher's wellspring of optimism. Nor did Everett Gabler help.

He materialized, leading a beslippered cleaning woman, before Thatcher had finished knotting his tie.

"But, Everett, we're breakfasting with Makris." Thatcher protested mildly as the old woman deposited a tray with coffee, fruit and slices of bread on the dresser, bobbed gratefully when Everett produced a tip, then ducked out into the corridor.

"Lorna says that she finds Greece a tremendously comfortable country to live in because you can arrange things the way you want," said Everett, making New York sound like one of the less emancipated portions of the Bible Belt. "Before I turned in last night, I ordered breakfast. We're not seeing Makris for a half hour. And the longer I stay in this country, the more I feel that if we take care of our digestions, the rest will take care of itself."

Everett deftly spread honey on a slice of bread. Thatcher accepted a tiny cup of coffee and reflected that Dr. Jenkins was effecting as great a revolution as Colonel Patakos. But it was speedily borne in on him that Everett Gabler remained, at heart, a Wall Street professional. Despite qualms, disclaimers, demurs, despite small habits and favorite techniques, he too, in the last analysis, relied on a sense of smell.

". . . was worried last night, don't you agree?"

With an effort Thatcher recalled his attention. "Makris? Yes, there's no doubt about it. He wasn't himself."

Everett smiled grimly and, heedless of the delicate stomach of which the entire Sloan stood in awe, munched energetically.

"Now, John, just remember what we decided yesterday. If it isn't the government tracking Nicolls down, and it isn't the left—then it has to be some other group. Now before I went to bed last night"—Thatcher, who had suspended all thought on nearing his bed, was reminded that many of his subordinates were better men than he—"I realized that Makris might well represent that third force!"

Thatcher had seen this coming some time ago. He did not evince shock, and Everett, pouring more coffee, continued: "It sounds insane, I grant you. But think, John! Naturally, we've concentrated on getting Nicolls back—that's only right and proper. But he's safe now and, if we have to, we can smuggle him out as a rolled-up rug!" Momentarily, Everett looked like a rum-runner. Then: "But we've got to get to the bottom of this whole situation and, John, it must involve Hellenus. Let's not forget it. I was opposed to Hellenus from the beginning, but now it's a multi-million dollar investment. There's got to be an explanation for all of this—and where it's a matter of dollars and cents—well, I personally am not surprised to see Makris' fine Italian hand."

Thatcher knew it was folly to dismiss Everett's interpretations (and useless to reproach his metaphors).

"I'll go along with the possibility that there may be a dollars-and-cents reason for everything that's been going on," he said slowly. "But, Everett, just stop to think about the rest of it. There's been a cold-blooded killing. There's been a ludicrous—but dead serious—chase through Salonika. The Army has been coopted. For all we know, local assassins have been hired. Now, Everett, in all seriousness—does this sound like Paul Makris & Son to you?"

Thatcher had scored a point. On Wall Street, Everett probably was a leading supporter of the "Balkan" reading of Paul

Makris. But here, to do him justice, he adapted to reality. When abduction, chase, murder and arms dumps became something more than idle words, Everett Gabler revised his thinking.

"No," he said regretfully. "Now that you put it that way, it doesn't sound like Makris. He'd cut our throats if he could, but in a perfectly legal fashion."

With Everett, this was a matter of the propriety expected from occupants of high-rental floors at Rockefeller Center. With Thatcher it was something else. He felt, without, he hoped having succumbed to propaganda, that Paul Makris was efficient. Had he been the enemy, Kenneth Nicolls would not be alive to tell his tale.

"Come on, Ev," he said rising. "We're going to be late."

"Be careful!" said Everett Gabler.

Thatcher fully intended to be.

Paul Makris, awaiting them in the large, nearly empty dining-room, gave no evidence of having slept well. Dismissing a waiter, he rose to greet his guests with a constraint suggesting pressures and passions behind his mask.

"Ah, Mr. Thatcher and Mr. Gabler. Shall we order?"

His comments to the unfortunate staff sounded like a whipsaw.

Fortunately, before Everett was seized with a paroxysm of renewed distrust, Makris got down to cases.

"I think this is the time for a little frankness, Mr. Thatcher."

"And the place?" Thatcher asked blandly. Indirection and eastern subtlety in Manhattan, and blunt forthrightness in Athens? He wouldn't put it past Paul Makris.

"Greece, Greece, Greece!" said Makris in a breathy explosion, half-amused, half-exasperated. "As you know, I do considerable business here in Greece. I started in a small way and now I am a partner with the Sloan Guaranty Trust in the biggest development Greece has ever seen."

Thatcher waited.

"Then too, I myself am Greek," said Paul Makris. "So I understand."

"I'm sure you do," said Thatcher when the silence became mildly embarrassing.

Makris shot him an ambiguous look. "The thing to remember is that Greece is a very poor country. Hellenus may help economic development in the north, but otherwise prospects are always very hard. Greeks have learned to scramble for work, for money, for a chance to get ahead..."

Thatcher could scarcely believe that Paul Makris had arranged this early morning meeting to deliver an elementary lecture. Everett, stirring restively, was heroically refraining from an acid reminder that the Sloan was well equipped with economic surveys of Greece which left no doubt that Greece was, as Paul Makris said, very poor.

Makris evaded their eyes.

"So, I was not surprised, six months ago, when I was approached—oh, quite informally, you understand. By one of my wife's cousins, as a matter of fact. He pointed out that there would be more money for me—if the Sloan Guaranty Trust were forced out of Hellenus. It would be better for Greece, if American institutions were kept out..."

"Do you mean to sit there and say you were being asked to..." Words failed Everett.

"To double-cross the Sloan," said Makris. "To make difficulties. To drive you out. So that I—and these unknown allies of mine—we could control Hellenus on our own. I would make the money—and Greece would not have American banks meddling. This kind of suggestion is not—er—unknown in this part of the world."

Thatcher appreciated Paul Makris's reluctance to tell this tale. "Come on, Everett. It's not unknown in New York either." This was no time for Everett's views on commercial integrity, in theory and practice. Thatcher returned to Makris. "You turned down your wife's cousin, I believe you said?"

"I did," said Makris. "He is an agreeable nullity, you understand. He knows everybody in Athens and Paris, and runs messages from one place to another. Whoever used him chose well—I doubt if Myrto realized what he was saying. He just repeated his lesson—like a parrot. But I was emphatic—I was not interested."

"I am happy to hear it," said Thatcher dryly.

Makris raised an eyebrow. "This is not to say that I have not made little mistakes. On the contrary—I have made some serious mistakes. And now, now I wish to apologize for them."

What was up?

"I hope," said Paul Makris, "that this is not boring you."

"Far from it!" said Thatcher.

"I put this overture from my mind," said Paul Makris. "We continued the negotiations about Hellenus in good faith, assuming that Myrto had been representing some Greek businessmen. Then, when there was the military take-over—then, I began to think again."

"But the colonels aren't anti-American, whatever else you may say against them," Everett protested.

Makris indicated agreement. "No, what I meant was that I remembered this nonsense of Myrto's about taking over Hellenus. That sounded—confused to me. But things continued smoothly for a while. Then, your Mr. Nicolls disappeared. And I made a serious mistake..."

Everett was braced for some atrocity.

"No, no," Paul Makris said. "I did not arrange his arrest. Although, to be honest with you, one of my men was in the police car with him. You see, by then I was afraid that the Sloan had joined forces with someone—to elbow Paul Makris & Son out of Hellenus."

Everett was outraged, but Thatcher got in first. "I am flattered that you think we are capable of that, Mr. Makris, but I assure you we have done no such thing."

Makris said agreeably that he realized that now. Still, he felt that Thatcher should be apprised of his earlier suspicions, if only to explain why Peter Chiros, for example, had not been more forthcoming.

Which was, Thatcher thought, one way to put it.

"With the murder of Dr. Ziros, I should have revised my thinking," Makris said seriously. "Even in Greece, simple businessmen do not customarily indulge in murder. And, as described to me, that shooting seemed more than simply Army brutality. At this point, I should have wondered if the Sloan was being victimized. After all, we are in the midst of political maneuverings!"

Thatcher observed that after a military take-over which jails its opposition and suspends the constitution, some political unsettlement was perhaps to be expected.

"Ah, Greece, Greece!" said Makris again. "But the details, Mr. Thatcher, are even more interesting. You know, I take it, that Dr. Elias Ziros was a member of ASPIDA—the militant left? When the colonels took over, Ziros had emergency information that his confederates here in Athens needed. He made arrangements to meet a courier at Salonika—he could not risk coming to Athens himself, you understand—"

"Of course," said Everett impatiently. "And Nicolls was mistaken for the courier—"

"Exactly." Makris was sure of his facts. "According to my informants, somebody managed to learn ASPIDA's secret..."

"And informed the police?"

Makris said, without noticeable sarcasm, "No, here things get complicated."

Thatcher maintained a poker face. He was not sure if Paul Makris knew that the emergency information was a list of arms dumps and that it was, currently, at Thatcher's disposition. Well, if he did not, then it was going to be an ace in the hole.

Makris said: "I have reason to believe that somebody learned of ASPIDA's plans and reported to the Government authorities. That much is clear. Now, I think it was no accident that a man from the Sloan was arrested. This fits too well with the approaches made to me. Somebody, Mr. Thatcher, is out to discredit the Sloan."

Thatcher only wished he could refute this, but unfortunately it fitted. Above all it fitted with Nicolls' impression that he had been hunted down by somebody other than the Government or the left.

"But who?" he murmured aloud. "And why?"

Makris shrugged. "I have made inquiries—among my contacts here and there. Even that idiot, Myrto. So far, nothing has come to light. But it seems that whoever it is, he—or they—are both powerful and determined. I am worried—very worried—about the safety of your Mr. Nicolls."

Did he trust Paul Makris? Thatcher was not sure. He did, however, recognize horse sense when he encountered it. It was certainly not Paul Makris & Son currently bedeviling the Sloan, with corpses and violence.

"Nicolls was in serious difficulties," he said carefully. "But he has been extricated..."

Makris smiled faintly at this caution.

"Good," he murmured. "I am very glad to hear it. Now he must lie low until the uproar dies down. If you are very careful, the Hellenus negotiations may proceed as scheduled. Then, in time, Nicolls can be smuggled out of the country. This may all blow over."

Thatcher frowned. "And we go on as if nothing had happened? No, I don't like that."

Makris spread his hands and shrugged. "It is very unpleasant, granted. One does not like to be victimized in this fashion. But you must be reasonable. You do not know who your enemy is. You have no lever to use against him. It is no small accomplishment that you have saved Mr. Nicolls. If you have..."

"What's that?" Everett demanded sharply.

Makris became very Greek. "An enterprising opponent might not yet admit defeat in his attempts to incriminate the Sloan."

Thatcher digested these comments. What Makris said was true... an unknown enemy... no means of attack.

These musings were interrupted by a waiter announcing a call at the desk.

"Come right over!" Mary Katherine Murphy ordered crisply. "We've got something."

CHAPTER XIX

THE FOX AND THE GRAPES

DR. MURPHY WAS waiting at the door for them, her eyes sparkling with excitement.

"Wait until you hear. You won't believe it," she promised.

Thatcher replied that nothing in Greece would ever surprise him again. Gabler said nothing; he merely passed ahead of Thatcher, questing eagerly forward into the living room.

Thatcher paused in the hall to lay down his hat.

"I gather you found out something from Nicolls?"

"Yes, but we haven't really gone into it yet. Do come in," she urged him through the doorway. "We're bursting to figure out what it means."

In the living room, Lorna Jenkins was setting ash trays while Kenneth Nicolls protested ignorance to Gabler.

"There's no point in looking at me. I don't know what's going on," he maintained. "I was just describing how I got into this mess when, suddenly, everybody got excited and started phoning you."

Nicolls had made another of his lightning character changes. Gone was the oppressed Greek handy man. For a moment Thatcher was alarmed, fearing that the ladies had been busy collecting clothing from their acquaintances. Then, as he assimilated the glory of his junior's appearance, he realized that the dashing silk sports jacket and slacks must belong to the absent movie producer. Thatcher decided that comment would be unkind.

"Let's go back to the beginning. We want you to hear this yourselves," suggested Lorna Jenkins.

Patiently Ken obliged. "I was describing how I got from

the Quaker camp to Elasson. And Kate wanted to know how I found the Quakers in the first place."

"It was clever of him," Kate interposed. "To figure out that an earthquake would automatically mean an American Friends camp in the offing."

"More than clever," Thatcher acknowledged. "Almost inspired."

"It would have been, if I had anything to do with it," Ken said. "But I was wandering around with a Red Cross badge in my buttonhole. Some Greek soldiers who didn't speak English gave me a lift and drove me straight to the Friends."

Lorna Jenkins was tense with excitement.

"So we asked him why he emerged from an earthquake with a Red Cross badge."

Ken was now elaborately reasonable. "I got it at the Salonika station," he said in reply to looks of inquiry from Thatcher and Gabler. "At a newsstand. The man there had a collection can. When I dropped my change into it, he gave me the badge."

Kate Murphy could no longer restrain herself. "And it was after that," she exclaimed triumphantly, "that Elias Ziros came over and sat down beside Ken."

"Yes," Ken picked up his tale. "Ziros said something about being surprised to find an American involved in Greek difficulties. At the time I thought he was talking about the transportation difficulties. Now I realize he was surprised to find an American acting as courier for his organization. It must have been that. Because, when he was satisfied about me, he gave me a business card and then immediately made an excuse to leave. But I still don't see what there is to be excited about." He looked at the ladies with good-natured resentment. "As soon as you knew that card contained the microfilm, you could figure out most of it without my help."

"Except for one item." Lorna Jenkins paused to assure herself of the room's attention. Then she delivered her punch line. "There will be no Red Cross collecting in Greece for another five months!"

Thatcher expelled his breath softly. "A recognition device," he reminded Gabler. "We said there must be one."

"You mean it was that little tin badge that got me into all of this?" Nicolls exclaimed indignantly.

"Oh, I wouldn't blame it on the badge," said Lorna Jenkins in a voice of steel. "That lapel pin was no accident. Why don't you describe how you got it?"

Ken frowned in recollection. Slowly he recapitulated those distant events overtaking a respectable banker not yet on the run. His recital was interrupted again and again as his audience seized on a fresh point.

"The collection can wasn't on the counter in plain view, was it? He brought it out especially for you."

"So he told you to be sure to wear it, did he? He certainly wasn't taking any chances."

"I'm not surprised Elias Ziros was reassured by your reference to California. That's where Andreas Papandreou was teaching before he came back to Athens. Elias probably thought you were old buddies."

"Yes, but how did you get to the newsstand in the first place?"

Finally the spate of questions and observations came to a halt. There was no longer any need to belabor the obvious. But Thatcher allowed only a short breathing spell before hitching himself forward and saying grimly:

"We seem to have underestimated our friend from the Ministry, Stavros Bacharias. The question is, what are we going to do about it?"

"Certainly you're not going to let him get away with it?" demanded Lorna Jenkins, all moral outrage. Her posture conjured up a host of abolitionist and suffragette forbears. Those women didn't ask what you were going to do about temperance. They reached for the nearest axe.

Thatcher knew that he must inevitably fall short of standards such as these. "Not at all. But you see," he said apologetically, "while it is clear to me that Stavros Bacharias is the one person who could have stage-managed that scene in Salonika, I am still not sure why he did it."

"You know, sir," Kenneth Nicolls spoke diffidently, "I think the answer may be in Greek politics."

Thatcher suppressed the retort that that much was obvious. "Yes?" he invited.

Ken marshaled his argument. "I don't know if you've heard of Cliff Leonard, the engineer up at Hellenus?"

Thatcher nodded encouragingly.

"Well, the day after the coup, Stavros Bacharias was running around like mad. Leonard has had quite a lot of experience with revolutions. He said that Bacharias was at a level where it made a real difference to him what coup became successful. Then, when the situation had clarified twenty-four hours later, Leonard said that Bacharias had come out about the same. He was still in the Ministry, but he hadn't gone up. That's when Bacharias started to interest himself in my travel plans," Nicolls ended on a note of bitterness.

"Very interesting. You see what it means, Everett?"

Gabler had been making little bleats of satisfaction to himself.

"Of course," he said briskly. "Bacharias is an undersecretary —he's practically at the top of the Ministry now. If there was any possibility of his becoming Minister he must be a member of some group that has been contemplating a coup of its own. And Bacharias' group is either still contemplating a coup or intends to infiltrate the present government by peaceful means."

"The latter, I would say." Thatcher turned politely to the ladies. "Our people at the Embassy were outlining the position for me the other day. The rightists are now firmly in command. But there is a good deal of dissension among these rightists. The colonels are all for encouraging foreign investment and foreign tourism. You might call them anti-isolationists. There is however a strong conservative element in Greece that is rigidly isolationist."

"The Ottoman Empire," said Kate Murphy suddenly.

"What?" Momentarily Thatcher braked his well-oiled argument. Then, rejecting temptation, he continued.

"If we assume that Bacharias is one of these fanatic isolationists, it explains a lot. Imagine the situation if Kenneth had been arrested, searched, and found to be carrying a list of arms dumps to leftists in Athens! No one would have believed his disclaimers. More important, no one would have believed that he was not acting as a representative of the Sloan throughout. And with the Hellenus negotiations coming up in the near future? What do you think would have been the result?"

"There's no doubt about the result." Everett Gabler seemed to be deriving some obscure relish from the scope of the disaster they had avoided. "There would have been a public outcry for expropriation of the Sloan's interest in Hellenus, as well as a hardening policy against all other American investment."

"It explains a good deal," said Lorna Jenkins soberly. "One of the things that has been puzzling me all along is the pseudo-official quality of the men running after Ken. But if they were rightists who are not in the government, but very close to it, then no one would dare question their authority after the take-over—at least not for a week or two."

Thatcher nodded somewhat absently. He was pursuing his own line of thought. "It also explains how Bacharias learned of Dr. Ziros' rendezvous in Salonika. I suspect the real courier was arrested by the Army that first night—by an officer who was a member of Bacharias' group."

"But, John, aren't we letting this theory run away with us?" Everett, as usual, had come up with a difficulty. "If Ziros hadn't been shot, the whole story would have come out, sooner or later. At least enough to confirm Nicolls' denials."

Thatcher stared at him.

"Now, wait a minute, Ev. Just let me think." He held up a hand to impose silence as an idea labored to the surface. "That may be exactly why Ziros was shot! The Army has claimed all along that they didn't do it. But what if Bacharias did? He had a real motive. If only we knew exactly what happened."

Ken Nicolls turned to look at his superior reproachfully. "Have you forgotten, Mr. Thatcher? I was there."

Under prodding, Ken told the story. No, he said, none of the soldiers had been holding a gun. In fact, they had been as paralyzed by the occurrence as the prisoners.

"I didn't pay much attention," he confessed. "I was too busy getting under cover. If I thought anything, it was that some other Army detachment had started to snipe at us."

"That corroborates the post mortem findings," Gabler said. "The man was shot from a distance, by a rifle. And Bacharias knew, after all, that Ziros was going to be arrested at the station that evening. He was a sitting duck."

"Poor Elias," mourned Kate Murphy.

"Either Bacharias killed him or one of his followers did," Lorna Jenkins added. She straightened her shoulders. "That makes it a deliberate murder. I'd like to see the authorities try to wriggle out of that when you tell them this story."

Gabler shared her martial desire for action.

"They shan't be given the opportunity," he promised. "We'll bring the State Department into it, if necessary. Their own Ministry personnel, trying to incriminate the Sloan falsely! It passes anything in my experience."

And no one had to be told that Everett Gabler's experience was singularly rich in instances of unsatisfactory government liaisons.

Kate Murphy looked shrewdly across the table. Then:

"I don't think Mr. Thatcher agrees with you," she said quietly.

Thatcher shook his head. "No, I don't. Oh, I share your indignation. But I think you're being optimistic if you see the Greek Government reacting the way we would like. I have no doubt that we could make the present regime look askance at Bacharias—particularly the Minister whose job he wants—but a good deal of mud would stick to the Sloan. After charges and counter-charges, after Nicolls and Bacharias had each called the other a liar, everyone involved would be suspect.

And that would be the end of working cooperation on the Hellenus project."

It was impossible for Gabler to resist this reminder of the Sloan's purpose in Greece. But he was a man of standards.

"The situation is certainly not desirable. But what else can we do? It's intolerable that Nicolls should have to slink about like a criminal. It's unthinkable that Bacharias should feel he can blackmail the Sloan into silence."

Seeing that an impasse had been reached, Kate Murphy let her instincts take over.

"There's no point in worrying a problem like a dog with a bone. What we need is some coffee and sandwiches. Mr. Thatcher, why don't you help me put things together. We'll think of something, you'll see."

Thatcher was happy to leave the charged atmosphere. As he followed his hostess, the other three were already putting their heads together in a protest meeting. Gabler and Lorna Jenkins both had firm principles which demanded that Stavros Bacharias pay for his crimes; Kenneth Nicolls, usually more malleable, had a personal commitment to the problem.

In the kitchen, while Kate filled the electric percolator, Thatcher busily sliced Greek sausage and bread.

"You don't want to go to the authorities, do you?" she asked, spooning coffee.

Thatcher tried to be honest in his answer. "No, I don't. One way and another, I've had a good deal of experience with authorities all over the world, and their collective intelligence is always lower than that of their most stupid employee. I hate to think what they'd make of this story."

"There's more to it than that," Kate said with quiet assurance.

"Yes. I'm afraid I'd like to accomplish Bacharias' undoing personally. And I resent the thought of any mud sticking to the Sloan, not only as a matter of policy, but because that is precisely what he intended."

"You know how I feel? I think all this talk about authorities is too tame. You can't have murders and arrests and abductions and end it all with a conference at the Ministry." She plugged in the coffee pot savagely. "There, that will be about twenty minutes. Could you use a drink in the meantime?"

Thatcher admitted that he could and accepted a Scotch and water, hoping it would provide inspiration.

"By the way," he said reflectively, "what did you mean by the Ottoman Empire?"

"It conditioned the thinking of a good many Greeks about foreigners and foreign intervention. Of course, partly, it's harking back to the golden years."

"The golden years? I thought they had a miserable time of it."

"Oh, they did," she agreed, absently refuelling their glasses. "But it was a time of great emotional unity—you know, one people and one church united against the Turkish tyrant. You don't get that kind of unity unless a country's occupied. Greece tried to recapture the same wild fervor over Cyprus, but that turned out very unsatisfactorily from the emotional point of view. So now I'm afraid there's a group that will be happy to cast the Sloan in the role of the Ottoman Empire."

"That should please Everett. He seems to have become pro-Turk during his stay in Istanbul."

"I think the Turks are a different kettle of fish nowadays. Not so cunning you know." As she spoke, Kate took a bowl of Greek olives from the refrigerator and placed them on the table. "Here, try some of these. They're very good..."

Unhopefully, Thatcher obeyed. "Cunning," he mused. "That's what we need. Some low cunning to deal with Bacharias."

"Did you notice what Ken said about the Army just rushing away when Elias was shot, leaving him there on the ground?"

"I know it seems harsh," he said gently, "but they didn't know who was firing at them. They probably didn't want a scandal at the station either."

"A fine time to worry about that," said Kate with lavish contempt. "But that isn't what I meant. I meant that nobody knows that the microfilm wasn't still on Elias. There's no reason to admit that Ken ever had it. Your story could be that some leftist rifled the body."

Thatcher looked at her with dawning admiration. "Or someone else?" he anticipated her. "Someone like Stavros Bacharias? You could give lessons to any stray Ottoman."

"You do pick up a knack for these things living in the Mediterranean," she said modestly. "But I have an idea that there's a germ of something here."

She looked at their highballs in sudden dissatisfaction. Then dismissing such refinements as ice and water, she produced two utility glasses and recommenced operations on a more heroic basis. Serious thought was about to begin. Suddenly, in the background, the percolator started to thump musically.

"Paul Makris said I couldn't go on the offensive because I didn't know my enemy and I didn't have any weapons." Thatcher emptied his glass at a gulp. "One of those objections has just been shot to the ground, at least. We know our enemy and his name is Stavros Bacharias."

"I expect he was thinking of a different sort of offensive," his hostess mumbled, indifferent to the new name.

"He doesn't have as high an opinion of the Sloan's Italianate hand as you do. You're suggesting framing the framer or blackmailing the blackmailer, I take it."

Kate Murphy seemed to have fallen into a sybilline mood. Behind a handful of olives, she enunciated clearly: "To get something, you have to give something."

"Very true," said Thatcher sagely. Without conscious thought he replenished their glasses. The solution to their problem was around the corner, he could feel it in his bones. He could feel other things, too. A sudden clarity of mental vision, a conviction of their superiority to mere circumstances.

Kate, finding a full glass before her, took a sandwich to help it along. "And you're the last man to be described as without weapons," she pointed out. "You seem to have seven ammunition dumps right here in Athens. And nobody knows where they are, except you."

From his height of pellucidness, Thatcher corrected her. "And the leftists, don't forget them."

Kate Murphy shook her head stubbornly. "No, if they knew, they wouldn't be so anxious to get that microfilm. Nobody knows but you."

She liked the last sentence. She made a little tune with it, which she sang over several times. *Nobody knows but you.*

"I think it's been done before," she said doubtfully.

Thatcher was silent.

"Don't you think so?" she persisted.

Thatcher was beyond politeness. "Kate!" he exclaimed, throwing formality to the winds. "You've done it!"

She looked at him hopefully. "I have? Tell me how."

Slowly he began to tell her.

In the living room, the indignation meeting had covered a good deal of ground. Time had sped as they canvassed means of approaching the Greek Government, deplored the narrowness which could try to evade so clear a duty, promised to bring John Thatcher to his senses on the next round.

They examined the tale of Ken's arrest and subsequent wanderings in the desert, looking for tangible proof which could be used to force acceptance on a reluctant Army junta. They were still doing so when the door from the kitchen opened.

"I didn't see anybody after I got clear of the truck," Ken was saying. "I just pulled myself up the mountainside and hid out in that scrub throughout the next day."

"Ah," said Gabler appreciatively, showing signs of his new interest in a classical landscape. "The hills of Greece, covered by wild thyme."

"Oh, is that what it was?" Kenneth asked dully.

"Not that far north," Lorna Jenkins objected. "It was probably juniper."

"Never mind that now!" thundered a voice from the doorway.

John Thatcher stood there brandishing a bottle of Haig & Haig pinch which he had prudently retained. Beside him, Kate Murphy stood, her black curls tumbled as she ran a hand through them. They were not actually leaning against each other. Nonetheless they were inclined toward each other in an instinctive search for equilibrium. Their eyes gleamed with triumph.

"Dr. Murphy and I had a splendid idea," Thatcher proclaimed grandly. "We are going to hoist Bacharias with his own petard."

As he finished this Jovian pronouncement, he paused to take note of his surroundings. His troops, all cold sober, were staring back at him. Two of them were mercifully silent. The third spoke for all.

"Well!" said Lorna Jenkins.

CHAPTER XX

NEMESIS

CONTRARY TO POPULAR myth, great and complex undertakings do not emerge complete from the furrowed brows of their originators. All too frequently, the first Homeric insight must be supplemented by such anti-heroic activity as planning, coordinating, reviewing, and even rehearsing.

So, the moment John Putnam Thatcher and Dr. Mary Katherine Murphy looked on truth plain and saw the gods smiting *hubris*—as Thatcher interpreted anti-Sloan machinations—did not lead directly to thunderbolts, trembling mountains or any other immediate rebukes to the sin of pride.

Some of the preliminaries, of course, could be attributed to the twentieth century's (and Everett Gabler's) passion for terrestrial detail; others, however, would have met with the full approval of Zeus, himself.

Dr. Murphy and Mr. Thatcher had to be restored to complete sobriety.

Yet endless cups of syrupy coffee did nothing to dim the golden prospects.

"Of course, it will take careful preparation," said Thatcher with his customary guile.

"It certainly will," said Everett snappily, producing a notebook. "But nothing beyond us, I trust."

Moral lapses on the part of his confreres always had a happy effect on him. "Now then, *if* I could have your attention, John—*and* Dr. Murphy . . ."

Metaphorically speaking, everybody synchronized watches.

Quite early the next morning, Everett Gabler, together with Dr. Lorna Jenkins, undertook an important foray. Together, they were en route to a certain villa near Sounion. After consideration, it had been decided that the Academy truck, while undeniably the ideal transport to and from digs, did not quite answer the needs of the moment.

"Besides," said Kate Murphy, narrowing her eyes dramatically, "I may need it myself!"

Lorna Jenkins gave her a sharp look, but said nothing. From somewhere, an aged Buick was produced, with a driver who assaulted Athens traffic and the clogged artery to Sounion like a demented toreador.

"I agree that we do look more respectable," said Dr. Jenkins, herself to restored to urbanity in a black suit that set off her silver hair and sun-darkened skin. "Greeks do set great store on appearances."

"Ah, yes," said Everett, peering out the window. After several miles, he gave an exclamation. "Here! It must be about here—no, there! By that stone! That's where I flagged down the tourist bus."

Lorna Jenkins relayed rapid Greek instructions to the front seat and the driver, cutting smartly in front of an overloaded bus, immediately slowed to a crawl, supremely indifferent to the violent protests trailing him.

"I must have walked perhaps a mile or two," said Everett thoughtfully.

They inched forward. Maddened, the bus nosed out to pass in the teeth of an onrushing truck. Everett remained intent upon the slowly passing scenery while Dr. Jenkins, who did not have a nerve in her body, reflected that it was just as well that he knew no Greek. The suggestions and observations hurled their way might have distracted his attention. The driver whistled provocatively and shook a fist at the truck driver, who was fumbling to restart his engine.

"Here!" said Everett with pleasure. "Here it is! This is the path I took, I am sure of it."

When Lorna directed the chauffeur to turn off the highway onto the narrow, dirt road, he had a comment. "A cool one, the old American," he said, not without respect. "We must be slow here because of the ruts."

A great bouncing confirmed his words, but in minutes they had covered the winding path to the crest of the hill. A wall and gate blocked the way.

"Is this the house you seek? Not a bad place at all."

Every impoverished Greek slum dweller is a real estate tycoon when it comes to the property of others. The driver agilely jumped from the car before Everett remembered to warn him about the dogs. Flinging open the gate, he returned and they were soon driving up the gravel path to the front door.

"Yes, this is it," said Everett with profound satisfaction. He helped Lorna alight, and beneath his breath, added: "I see they got rid of the dogs. I suspected that they were so much window dressing. Yes, properly seen this is a nice little property."

This was mild praise for a classic Mediterranean villa perched atop a hill above an olive grove, commanding a superb view of seas famed for their beauty since Pindar.

The front door opened. Eleni, the aged housekeeper, shuffled out into the sunlight. For a moment, she squinted in surprise at the Buick and at Lorna Jenkins. Then her rheumy eyes found Everett Gabler. With lightning speed, she crossed herself three times, simultaneously emitting a high tremulous screech. Then, both arms outstretched, she backed through the doorway and disappeared into the gloom.

The driver's already high opinion of Gabler rose. Dr. Jenkins was amused. "Well, *she's* alive, at least, Mr. Gabler. By the way, she was warding off the Evil Eye as she left."

"In the light of what happened," Gabler began heatedly when another remembered figure appeared.

It was the bald man. No longer stocky and menacing, he sagged against the door jamb. His complexion was strangely yellowed.

"Gabler!" he croaked. "I didn't believe her... why have you come back?"

"I have a business proposition to discuss with you," said Everett, with calm. He then introduced his companion and suggested they remove indoors. As the bald man simply stood there, he added: "Have you been ill? You don't look at all fit. Of course, I myself found the diet very difficult..."

The bald man's lips drew into an involuntary snarl. Then, mastering himself with an effort, he gestured for Gabler and Dr. Jenkins to enter.

As he found himself again in the cool tiled shadow, Gabler took precautions.

"I hope I need not say," he said as he and Lorna followed their host upstairs, "that many people know of our whereabouts and will take action if we do not return on schedule."

"The police?" their host asked wearily. He turned to look down at them, an unfathomable expression in his dark eyes. "You have spoken to the Government?"

"Don't be silly," said Everett, who made no allowances for foreign ways. "If I had told the police or the Government what I know, do you think we'd be here? Use your head, man!"

The bald man sighed wearily. "You are right. I am not thinking clearly. But even apart from that, let me assure you, Mr. Gabler, you would be in no danger of my attempting to detain you. Rather than have you in my house again, I would invite vipers! Asps!" His English failed him and he rounded out the sentiment in his native tongue. Lorna Jenkins promptly translated with the smooth detached fluency of an interpreter.

"He says he would rather have Turkish pashas overrunning the place. That's an old peasant saying."

Their host brightened briefly. "You speak Greek? Remarkable."

Lorna, who saw nothing remarkable in it, did not respond, but for a fleeting moment they might have been figures out of the travel agency literature of so many countries. The illusion of people getting to know people was shattered, however, the moment they entered the room which had seen Everett's earlier interrogation. The sullen young man was not lounging moodily at the balcony window. He was prone on the sofa.

Upon their entry, he opened his eyes. Sighting Everett, he closed them again and commenced what seemed to be a long, deeply felt prayer. When the bald man hastily informed him that the lady spoke excellent Greek, he relapsed into smoldering silence.

"Will you sit down, Mr. Gabler and Dr. Jenkins?" The bald man was regaining something of his old manner. "You may be interested to know, Mr. Gabler, that Dr. Viarranghos thinks that Stylianos will probably recover—in time. I know you will be relieved, as I was. I hold myself responsible, you understand. It never occurred to me that American businessmen customarily travel equipped with quantities of poison on their persons."

"I have not come," said Everett coolly, "to enter into mutual recrimination. Although I trust that this has shown you the perils of indiscriminate kidnapping. And threats..."

From the sofa came an impassioned, if weakly voiced, imprecation.

"Shame on you!" said Dr. Jenkins disapprovingly.

The bald man, sagging back in his chair, was apathetic. "My country has been betrayed by military imbeciles. My friends are dead, in jail or in hiding—all of them in terrible danger. Enemies have betrayed our plans to restore decency and democracy to Greece." He paused, shook his head. "Yet, of all the catastrophes God had sent to rain upon us, I am inclined to think you may rank first!"

Everett Gabler was impervious to compliment and abuse alike. Moreover, he knew better than to enter into rhetorical contest with an emotional Greek.

"The proposition I wish to put to you concerns a microfilm," he said briefly. "The microfilm contains very detailed descriptions—and addresses—of seven arms dumps in and around the Athens area. Are you interested?"

The sofa emitted an incautious howl.

"What is your proposition?"

"I am prepared—and authorized—to return that microfilm to you, without prejudice, as it were. That is, without informing the police, the Government, or anybody. Indeed, I am prepared to forget its very existence—which I should be most pleased to do!"

An outburst from the sofa brought Lorna to her feet. "No, it is not a trap, you silly boy. Do try not to be so—excitable! I'm sure it isn't doing you any good."

Without seeking permission, she went to the doorway and raised her voice in a commanding bellow. Returning to the chair next to Everett, she commented: "I thought refreshments would be good for all of us, if we're going to talk business."

The bald man was in a trance. With an effort, he roused himself. "What... oh, no! Although I am afraid Eleni is too frightened to... never mind. Mr. Gabler, you say you will restore this microfilm to us? Why?"

"Because I want something in return," said Everett frankly. "I want your cooperation to trap the man who kept you from getting the microfilm in the first place. A man who has been playing a deep game of his own—and using you and the Sloan as cat's paws."

"And," Lorna Jenkins added, lighting a cigarette efficiently, "the man responsible for Elias Ziros' arrest."

From the couch, Theo anathematized the present Greek regime. "Army pigs!" he groaned weakly. "To butcher such a man as Dr. Ziros!"

Automatically, Everett bent a warning glance on Dr. Jenkins; they had already decided it might be dangerous to identify the real murderer of Dr. Ziros in this company.

Dr. Lorna Jenkins needed no reminders.

"Elias was a great loss," she said in formal condolence.

It had begun to dawn upon the bald man that this middle-aged American lady was not quite what she seemed.

"Did you know Elias?" he asked suspiciously.

"At Argyrocastro," said Lorna Jenkins, puffing furiously to get a kindle.

Everett was the only one at sea, but even he realized that

this placed Lorna and Elias Ziros on the same side—the gallant side—in a last great display of Greek courage.

The bald man shrugged again, this time indicating capitulation. "But this cooperation," he asked with open alarm. "What, Mr. Gabler, do you mean by cooperation?"

Clearly he was envisaging mass poisoning of some sort. Everett, too experienced to reveal triumph, drew out a fat notebook.

By the time the ex-seminarian entered with a sumptuously laden tray, the three men—including the late invalid—were hunched over the desk. The two Greeks were shouting furiously. Everett was saying:

"Now, if you two would simply listen for a moment!"

Looking up, Lorna saw bewilderment. In Greek, she directed the ex-seminarian to deliver the refreshments to the desk. Then, with an appraising look at his muscular bulk, she added:

"You'd better stay too. You look like the sort we can use."

Several thousand miles and many time zones away, Charles Trinkham, currently deputy chief of the trust department of the Sloan Guaranty Trust, was casting about for a suitable outlet for frustration.

He was reading yet another cable from John Putnam Thatcher:

INFOSEEK CARRUTHERS CRIMLAW ATHENS

Now what the hell, Charlie irately demanded of his empty office, would a staid Wall Street lawyer like Carruthers know about Greek ambulance chasers?

And what the hell was John up to?

Charlie took an unsatisfactory turn around his desk, reviewing the many things that were all wrong.

First, last and apparently always was this murky Hellenus mess. Nicolls disappears. Everett disappears. Everett returns. Nicolls returns.

Or does he?

Charlie Trinkam, stuck in New York, didn't really know.

All he knew was that Walter Bowman was beginning to get to him.

"Any news today?" boomed a cheerful voice from the doorway as Walter paused on his way to his own office.

"Sure!" Charlie exploded. "Sure! Read this!"

With real savagery, he thrust the offending radiogram at the chief of research, knowing that Walter would whistle.

Walter whistled. "Something must be up! Why should John want a criminal lawyer?"

"Sure something's up. The whole bunch will probably end up in the pokey..."

Infuriatingly, Walter rejected this reading. "No...no. Not John. And Everett can take pretty good care of himself."

Charlie Trinkam's cup of wrath overflowed. He launched into an intemperate tirade, embracing flaws seen and sensed in John Putnam Thatcher, Everett Gabler, Kenneth Nicolls and all Greeks. On the bird-in-hand principle he began zeroing in on Walter Bowman and the economic research unit. But before he could get there, Walter Bowman, no fool, simply waved a cheerful farewell and removed his large person from the line of fire.

Charlie ground his teeth audibly for the next hour. Humble secretaries walked with eyes meekly downcast. Even IBM programmers trembled.

"But he's usually so...so nice," wailed a youthful stenographer, before dissolving into tears in the ladies' room.

"I can't imagine what's got into him," said Miss Carew angrily. She was from Document Processing and an Old Sloan Hand.

This was not surprising. Reasons for Charlie's malaise were not, however, hard to find. In addition to the great Hellenus ordeal, Charlie had two additional burdens exacting a heavy toll on his normally good spirits. First, directing the trust department in John Thatcher's absence lost its salt, it developed, without Everett Gabler's abrasive presence. Administrative detail, without sidebattles and skirmishes, left Charlie bored beyond belief.

Then too, his keen and commendable sense of responsibility had led Charlie, upon his hurried return from Venezuela, to commence regular visits to the bereft Mrs. Kenneth Nicolls. This had exposed him to bravery in the face of adversity—not easy on a man of his habits. Fortunately, it had recently been replaced by incandescent radiance, following Thatcher's cryptic reassurances, which was more up Charlie's alley. But above all, in sadness and in happiness, Charlie had spent too many hours in a very nice house on Brooklyn Heights with: a young mother, *her* very nice mother, a three-year-old moppet and a newborn infant.

Aunts, cousins, brothers, neighbors and old college friends seemed to drop in, call up, or write with machine-gun repetitiveness.

At one point, Charlie had been mistaken by a nearsighted neighbor for the grandfather.

For a man of his temperament, this was slow poison.

"Well, we'll just see!" he growled, flinging himself out of his office to his secretary's undisguised relief. He launched himself down the hall on the double. "We'll just see!"

Miss Corsa, as was to be expected, did not recognize danger when it stormed into her office. Without a quaver, she interrupted her typing:

"Yes, Mr. Trinkam?"

"Miss Corsa!" he said awfully. "Do *you* have any news from Thatcher?"

Miss Corsa, who had her own notions of the proper modes of address for her employer, made an instant and iron decision.

"I have had several messages, Mr. Trinkam. They all concerned Mr. Thatcher's personal affairs."

Charlie opened his mouth to expostulate, then collapsed.

"Personal?" he asked blankly.

"Yes," said Miss Corsa firmly. (The messages, in toto, were: one, an imperative demand for all sizes of all Thatcher's female relatives. This rankled, since Miss Corsa normally provided a list when time permitted. Two, an equally imperative demand for all sizes of all Nicolls' offspring. This in turn had been followed by cabled instructions concerning a sizeable anonymous donation to the American School of Classical Studies' excavations at Mavromidion.)

"Mr. Thatcher," Miss Corsa reported without complete approval, "seems to be feeling fine."

"I'll bet!" said Charlie Trinkam. "I'll probably have to go over and get the whole lot out of jail, or worse. He's up to something! And he doesn't know those Greeks the way I do. Maybe I'd better get right on over. Talk some sense into them..."

Now, this was the sort of talk that Miss Corsa was not going to brook in her office. She struck, and she struck hard.

"Oh, I wouldn't bother, Mr. Trinkam," she said, returning to her typing. "I expect that by the time you got there, Mr. Thatcher will have taken care of everything."

Then, and only then, did Charlie Trinkam identify his real grievance: he was missing all the fun.

CHAPTER XXI

SEVEN AGAINST THEBES

IN ATHENS, THE fun was just beginning.

"You say you have heard from Mr. Nicolls?" Stavros Bacharias asked in astonishment.

Thatcher looked around the café and lowered his voice before replying. "Yes, he seems to be with some people who are bringing him to Athens. I don't understand it at all. But you can see why I didn't want to speak about it at the hotel. Until we know more, the fewer people who hear about this, the better."

"Ah!" Bacharias could not control the sudden leap of exultation in his voice. But immediately he turned it to good account. "What an unbelievable relief to know that he is alive and safe. You will go to him immediately, of course."

Sorrowfully Thatcher shook his head. "It's not that simple. Apparently these people are planning a furtive entry into the city some time tomorrow. They're going to leave a message for us, down by the docks, telling us where we can meet them."

"By the docks? Then they are coming by sea?"

"That was my conclusion."

Bacharias chewed his underlip as Thatcher watched appreciatively. The strategists at the apartment in Kolonaki had chosen a sea route after deliberation. Bacharias and his followers did not have the manpower to patrol every little fishing village. Nevertheless, considering the difficulties that awaited a foreigner attempting an escape over water, they must have dismissed this loophole as negligible.

Now Bacharias leaned forward tensely, delicately tapping the table to emphasize his points.

"These friends of Mr. Nicolls may well have reason to be secretive. You will forgive me if I undertake to advise you?"

"But of course! Mr. Gabler and I would appreciate advice."

"Then, under no circumstances must anyone discover your rendezvous. You have considered the possibility that you may be followed, I am sure. Would it not be wiser if I went for this message? As a Greek, I would attract no attention."

Thatcher permitted himself to be overcome. "You are more than generous," he murmured. "Mr. Gabler and I worried about this problem also. But we dare not send an emissary in case the message appoints an immediate meeting. On the other hand, you are perfectly right that we would look conspicuous at the docks. So we have decided to arrange a sightseeing party. It will look innocent, in itself. And it will make it easier for us to slip away if that should be necessary."

"A sightseeing party?" Bacharias frowned.

"Yes. A group of people cruising around the Piraeus. We have already found two American ladies willing to go."

Bacharias relaxed. "It should be all right. As long as they do not know the true purpose of your trip. Being followed is not your only problem. These people with Mr. Nicolls will not wish their affairs broadcast. Are they hostile, do you think?"

"No, surprisingly not." Thatcher picked his way with care. "Nicolls spoke in haste, you understand. And he sounded near collapse. But he insists that everything is all right now."

"Because he has succeeded in reaching you?"

"Possibly." The uncertainty in Thatcher's voice was masterful. "Nicolls muttered something about having helped these men to get back something they wanted desperately." Thus having raised Bacharias' hopes that the missing microfilm would arrive with Kenneth Nicolls tomorrow, Thatcher broke off artfully. "You know, we may have to ship Nicolls home right away. He didn't sound like himself. I'm sure he needs medical attention, and a long rest."

Bacharias could barely keep the impatience from his voice. "Poor man," he said perfunctorily.

"I may have done your excellent Army an injustice,"

Thatcher continued reflectively, as he tasted a morsel of the preserves served with his *ouzo*. "Nicolls may have been an earthquake victim after all. Fortunately not a fatality. But if he has been wandering around the hillside in a state of shock ever since the night of his arrest, I don't like to think of his condition."

Bacharias saw a chance to direct the conversation. "Surely, if he has been helping people to find something, he must be in full possession of his faculties."

"Let us hope so," Thatcher said piously.

As Bacharias dutifully echoed this sentiment, Thatcher noted that the time was five minutes to twelve. He had chosen this table after careful scrutiny. Not, as his companion thought, because of any superior defenses against eavesdropping, but because it provided a direct view of the wall clock. He had promised to have Stavros Bacharias at his side in Syntagma Square at noon precisely.

He signaled for the waiter. "I will not be happy until I have seen Nicolls with my own eyes," he said laying down bills and rising. "But there is nothing we can do until tomorrow."

As the two men emerged into the brilliant sunlight, Thatcher scanned the benches in the Square. He almost missed Carl Ingraham. That enterprising young man had taken advantage of his sudden involvement in melodrama by going into disguise. He had done such a good job that he almost defeated the entire exercise. But there he was, elegantly lolling on a bench encased in a white silk shirt and skin-tight pants. With dark wraparound sunglasses and a cigarette dangling from his lower lip, he was a picture of the complete spiv.

Thatcher carefully chose his position before extending his hand. Bacharias was forced to stand in unshadowed sunlight directly opposite Ingraham.

"I must get back to the hotel now, but we will expect you tomorrow morning," Thatcher said. "If anything develops, I'll let you know."

"Please do," Bacharias replied, shaking hands. "I shall be anxious to hear."

And that, thought Thatcher, is the first truthful word you've said.

In the meantime, somewhere on Carl Ingraham's person, a miniature German camera was rapidly clicking off exposures, one by one.

"Here are the pictures of Bacharias," said Kate Murphy later that afternoon. "Can you get them distributed this evening?"

Paul Makris' famous composure was badly shaken. Thatcher had promised the pictures before three, but he had not revealed the nature of the Sloan's messenger. Probably Makris would have been dismayed at the intrusion of any woman into his plans, but he could have fallen back on traditional precedent if he had been confronted with an *ingenue* or a sleek woman of the world. Kate Murphy definitely fell into neither category.

In fact Paul Makris—presently enjoying his third marriage, this time to a woman thirty years younger than himself—had not seen a woman like Kate in years. Dr. Murphy's standards required that a visit to a business office in Omonia Square be accomplished in a suit. Such occasions did not arise frequently; therefore the suit was correspondingly old. Its original lines had long since been lost. Now the beige linen fell in baggy amplitude around Kate's contours. On her feet she wore uncompromising lace-up oxfords, polished to a high gloss. A defeated hat, also linen, completed the ensemble. From beneath its turn-down brim errant wisps of hair protruded.

The last time Makris had seen anything like this was before the war, when he had visited friends in England with a nanny. That nanny, he recalled, had been retained, in spite of her manifest incompetence, because of her kindness to small children. The last quality in the world that they needed at the moment.

"All arrangements have been made," he answered mechanically.

"Good! It's essential that everybody be able to recognize

Bacharias." Kate beamed at him cheerfully. "And now, perhaps, we could review the route."

"You will be in the party going to the docks tomorrow?"

"Oh, yes!"

Makris closed his eyes briefly, his opinion of John Thatcher plummeting sharply. Then he opened them and looked cautiously across the desk. He supposed that Thatcher had found her in the hotel. He had to admit that, from one point of view, her appearance was perfect. She would cast a mantle of dithering innocence over any party she joined. But she was also likely to commit some incredible stupidity that would give the game away. Mentally he shrugged. Well, if so, the Sloan would pay the price. The only thing he could do was give her adequate coaching.

"Send in Karillides," he ordered his intercom. Turning to his visitor, he explained: "Mr. Karillides is in charge of the preparations. He will give you a map of the route. In addition, he will instruct your driver tonight."

Kate nodded happily, little knowing that her look of childish pleasure was rousing deep misgivings across the desk.

The man who came in silently would have been recognized on the spot by Kenneth Nicolls. His nut brown face was just as alert as when he had brightly predicted instant death in the paddy wagon, just as eager as when he had been wolfing his stew at the American Friends relief station.

But that was only until he saw the plump smiling woman in the chair. Then he became transfixed with joy. On her part, she rose and rushed forward.

"Katerini!"

"Demetri!"

They embraced.

Paul Makris stared. They paid no attention to him, but burst into frenzied exclamations, gesticulations, interruptions.

"But you are alive! When we left you on the beach, I never thought—"

"To think that you are here in Greece! Ah, we of Greece do not forget. There are many—"

"And One-Eye? Did he survive too? And Louis the Knife? You must tell me."

"And the beautiful Lorna? Is she here too?"

Not the least surprising feature for Paul Makris was the torrent of demotic Greek that fell from Kate Murphy's lips as she casually referred to people called Costa the Pimp.

Finally his subordinate remembered his presence and turned apologetically. "You must forgive us. But it is years since I have seen Katerini. Not since we fought the Germans together."

"You see, I never knew Demetrios' last name," Kate explained.

"Those were the days," said Karillides fondly. "And what a fighter was our Katerini. You should have seen her with an Enfield."

"I always have had an eye," Kate said modestly. "I expect it's all these years of croquet and ping-pong."

"Croquet! Ping-pong!" Makris strangled. "Enfield rifles!"

When Thatcher and Gabler returned to the hotel that evening the night manager, Lycurgos Diamantis, pirouetted gracefully toward them.

"Ah, you enjoy the beautiful evening of Athens! The floodlighted Acropolis! The Mediterranean sky!"

This was not precisely what they had been doing, but it was certainly the first evening in which the two men had felt some of the dark magic of midnight Athens.

"Very beautiful, indeed," said Gabler tolerantly.

"You enjoy yourself," said an ecstatic Diamantis. "Your friends rejoice. Soon you will enjoy yourselves all together!"

Thatcher paused in his progress toward the elevator. "All?" he said encouragingly.

"But yes. The friends of Mr. Nicolls call. They ask if Mr. Nicolls is returned. Will he return?" The manager spread his arms in a benedictory gesture.

"And what did you say?"

"But I tell them that Mr. Nicolls is not here yet." Wide dark eyes protested. What else would he tell them? "Only last night he calls from Aghiocampos. But you are in momentary expectation of him."

"That must have pleased them."

"They were overcome with joy," Lycurgos Diamantis said firmly. "Even when I say Mr. Nicolls does not sound well. They say that he will recover when he returns to wonderful Athens."

It was not surprising that "Mr. Nicolls" had not sounded well to Lycurgos Diamantis. Carl Ingraham, who had made the decoy call, had been instructed to sound like an exhausted Nicolls. He had apparently stuffed a handkerchief down his throat and succeeded in sounding like nothing human.

They bade good night to the manager and ascended.

"Bacharias is checking up, John," Gabler said as soon as they were out of earshot.

"Yes." Thatcher nodded in satisfaction. "And he's heard just what we wanted him to hear."

Gabler reviewed their activities. "Everything's arranged now. It's up to him."

In uncharacteristic heartiness, Thatcher slapped his companion on the back. "We don't have to worry about Bacharias, Everett. He's taken the bait—hook, line, and sinker!"

CHAPTER XXII

WHEN GREEK MEETS GREEK

OPERATIONS BEGAN EARLY the next morning.

"Ah, yes," said Stavros Bacharias, politeness barely veiling his contempt. "Yes, I agree that the authorities could not suspect us of anything."

Looking dispassionately at their little group, John Putnam Thatcher could only feel for his country.

The sightseeing expedition ostensibly designed to camouflage the rescue of Kenneth Nicolls had been planned, possibly over-planned, to a T. The chauffeur, currently speeding along the clogged highway to the docks in the Piraeus, had an itinerary that was paramilitary in scope. At that very moment, large numbers of people—from Paul Makris' international business-men to certain liberally inclined trade unionists—were setting stages and procuring props. Most important, Stavros Bacharias was here, sitting next to Thatcher in the Buick. Everything was going along with clockwork smoothness.

"It is to be hoped," said Bacharias in a confidential voice, "that your compatriots do not cause us any awkwardness."

Unerringly, he had put his finger on an unforeseen difficulty.

"I agree," said Thatcher with complete sincerity. The one thing he had not anticipated—and how could he?—was the unbridled zest which Kate Murphy and Lorna Jenkins were bringing to their portrayal of the American tourist.

"Well, just look at that!" Kate Murphy demanded nasally. "Mr. Gabler, have you ever seen anything like it? That man there on the corner! He's selling those cookies right on the street! Isn't that picturesque? Oh, I wish I had a camera, just to show Wilma! That's one thing you don't see in Cincinnati, let me tell you!"

Thatcher and Gabler were frozen by this improbable speech, but Stavros Bacharias seemed to feel that this was the proper mode of discourse for a home economics teacher from Ohio. At any rate, he replied with deadly courtesy:

"*Koulouria.* They are sold throughout Greece. They are very good."

Lorna Jenkins, in white gloves, a flowered hat and rhinestone earrings she had unearthed somewhere, showed that her notions of Cincinnati's whereabouts were hazy. In an accent that Thatcher pegged as Louisiana-cum-Al Jolson, she said:

"Oh, I'm sure they're delicious. But it's so unsanitary. You know, Mr. Bacharias, I just can't get used to your Greek notions of hygiene. And I don't care what you say, Kate, I wouldn't think of drinking the water..."

"You say that we can buy some nice brasses at the Piraeus?" Kate demanded, sharklike, avid.

Bacharias' smile was forced. "Yes. Yes indeed. Many interesting stores..."

"I certainly hope their prices are more reasonable than those stores on Ermou Street, or whatever you call it," Lorna said acidly. "There was this adorable rug I saw yesterday..."

While she rattled on, John Thatcher glanced at Everett Gabler who was, he could see, also apprehensive. Surely the ladies were laying it on too lavishly.

Not, it developed, for Bacharias. After pointing out an interesting fragment of wall that was worthy of attention, he turned to Gabler and Thatcher and, *sotto voce*, said:

"I think it will be best if the ladies can occupy themselves shopping—I will direct the driver—while we inquire at the docks. After all, we do not know what to expect..."

"Very wise," Thatcher agreed. There would be plenty of time for Stavros Bacharias to learn that dispensing with American women is easier said than done.

And soon he would have other things to worry about. Their descent on the Piraeus, which is the port of Athens, had been carefully timed to coincide with the arrival of the cruise ship

Capodistria. If Bacharias wanted tall, blond Americans, the *Capodistria* promised a more than ample supply.

Before leaving the hotel, Everett Gabler had foreseen that supporters of Bacharias would be in the offing.

"Do you realize that that scoundrel probably plans to have Ken shot before our eyes?"

Kate Murphy, perfecting her disguise by draping a string of large crystal beads around her neck, had been soothing.

"Don't you worry, Everett. Bacharias may have one of his sharpshooting gorillas stationed at the pier but, remember, Ken Nicolls won't be there. And by the time we're finished with Bacharias, his shooting days will be over—for good!"

Now, in her improbable Midwestern drawl, she broke into speech again.

"Oh no! We'd just love to see a ship come in. We'll shop afterwards. There's just something about a ship..."

Lorna was more explanatory. "We don't see that often, in Cincinnati."

Thatcher choked slightly but Stavros Bacharias merely shrugged and accepted the inevitable. So the Buick with its full complement continued to nose through the rabbit warren of streets to the great harbor.

When they finally reached the wharves, gay sunlight illuminated a scene rare indeed in Cincinnati. In the busy harbor, two large ocean liners were moored; surrounding them were smaller coastal vessels and small gadflies of fishing boats. Along the crowded walks were further evidence of unhygienic practice; vendors of *koulouria,* roasted nuts, and cooked fish hawked their wares, their shrill cries echoed by mocking gulls and raucous ships' whistles.

"Perhaps you ladies would care to wait in the car," Bacharias began vainly.

Kate Murphy had already flung open the door and was heaving herself out. Planted stolidly on the sidewalk, she looked around with wide-eyed interest as heavily burdened stevedores veered around her.

"Well, now, isn't this just fascinating?" she asked the

world. "What do you suppose that man was saying to me? Oh, do hurry, Lorna! This is the real Greece at last. Just like that movie!"

Bacharias was vexed. "Perhaps if we divert Miss Murphy, she would . . . er . . . draw less attention to us . . ."

Abruptly he went white. At his side, Thatcher and Gabler stiffened involuntarily. Lorna Jenkins, hard on Kate Murphy's heels, had loosed an ear-splitting scream.

"Kate! Kate, do you see who I see?"

"Where . . . oh! Well, of all people! Carl! Yoohoo, Carl!"

With loud cries, the ladies flung themselves forward against the tide of passengers debarking from the *Capodistria*. "Yoohoo! Carl!"

"I had hoped," said Stavros Bacharias, deeply moved, "that we might aid Kenneth Nicolls without attracting undue attention."

Thatcher could understand this. People planning ambushes do not appreciate audiences. Aloud he replied that the ladies did provide excellent cover.

"You are right, of course," Bacharias said, forcing a smile. "No one would ever take them for . . . oh well. Where did you say our meeting is?"

"A tobacco warehouse." Carefully Thatcher spelled out an address.

As he spoke, they were edging forward. Just then, one of the ship's officers passed near them. A heavy-set man, he had an expression of jaundiced patience that deepened when his eyes fell upon Everett Gabler. Nevertheless, he halted civilly at Bacharias' command. There ensued a good deal of rapid Greek. Then, with a sardonic smile, the bald man sketched a salute, and moved away.

Bacharias muttered under his breath. "It is just around the corner. Down an alley on the right," he reported. "I asked if he had seen a young blond American. But he does not know one American from another. And there are many of them."

Bacharias looked around with open loathing at: American

college boys, American servicemen stationed in Germany, Americans of Greek extraction visiting the old country, and American school teachers broadening their cultural horizons.

Leaving the ladies to their yoohooing, the three men followed the officer's directions. The warehouse proved to be a solid structure located amidst the factories and distilleries that cluster around the Great Harbor. Inside, years of use had impregnated the atmosphere with the rich, moist aroma of Latakia. But the building seemed empty. However, as soon as their footsteps echoed through the lofty spaces, a small man issued from a door to one side. They could see behind him a cramped office and several men bent over papers.

The small man approached in silence until he was within three feet.

"Please to pretend you are customers!" he ordered in a sharp undertone. Then his voice rang out jovially. "Ah, you have come to the right place! The Olympus Tobacco Export Company! Only the finest leaf! My card, gentlemen."

The business card was extended toward Stavros Bacharias.

"Where is Mr. Nicolls?" Thatcher whispered urgently. "Has he been here?"

"But of course. He had to leave when these others came in." Again the reversion to booming salesmanship: "And with whom do I have the honor to do business?"

From the office door two men were now watching the performance. Mechanically, Thatcher, Gabler and Bacharias all reached for cardcases and produced cards.

"We will require delivery before September 1st," Gabler said loudly. "Is that possible?"

"Of course, of course! And you need two lots, you say? There would be a substantial reduction on three. Here, I will quote you my prices."

The warehouse owner placed a piece of paper against the wall and wrote rapidly:

He has joined the American tourists' car. The large guide at Daphni will have a message for you. Go quickly! There is danger here.

In the street outside, Stavros Bacharias started to speak.

Everett Gabler, however, urged him forward. "Come! Time is of the essence!"

As they hurried back to the car, Thatcher realized he would have to keep an eye on Everett too.

"Well, there you are!" Kate Murphy yodelled. "Carl here, is our football coach at good old Mann High School! It's a small world, isn't it?"

There goes the ball game, thought Thatcher. Anything further from a high school football coach than Carl Ingraham would be hard to find. Or at least so it seemed to Thatcher. He had never seen one of these leaders of youth wearing thick glasses. And Ingraham still seemed to be taking unholy glee in assuming disguise. He vibrated in a flowered sports shirt. He was also, Thatcher noticed with pleasure, festooned with cameras, one of which he had just finished using.

"Ay-up," said Carl Ingraham with a shy smile.

Really, these classicists needed refresher courses in the geography of their native land. Ingraham had just placed Cincinnati somewhere on the coast of Maine.

"Say," Ingraham said, heavily bucolic, "you folks meet up with your friend? Or is he in one of the cars that's already gone on ahead?"

"Ahead?" Bacharias demanded.

"It's just fascinating," Lorna Jenkins announced, righting the flowered hat that had somehow been knocked askew. "Carl—and everybody—have just eight hours here. And I declare they're going to see more than Kate and I will see in five whole days. And the cruise only cost..."

Her interesting calculations were interrupted by a sudden explosion of loudspeaker orders.

"Gee!" said Carl Ingraham, "that's my car! They warned us to stick together and to be on time. We're going to see this here Daphni..."

"Daphni?" Bacharias murmured. "That explains why..."

"Then we're going to have a ding-dong tour of Athens,"

Carl Ingraham confided. "With lunch included. Then we have a whole hour free for whatever we want to do. Well, I'd better be going."

They watched him lope over to a waiting car. Clearly a whole caravan was required for the passengers of the *Capodistria.*

"It really is a small world."

Before the ladies could get well and truly launched on this original theme, Everett Gabler spoke up. "Has it occurred to you," he asked Thatcher and Bacharias, "that Nicolls may find this the safest way to get into Athens? He can go along with the group until he gets near the center of town. After all, he can't be sure that we're here to help him."

Bacharias, glancing idly at the upper story of one of the shops facing the wharves, nodded slowly. "Yes, you are right. But perhaps we can still intercept him."

Thatcher, who had noted that glance, professed doubts. "Perhaps," he said, "it would be wisest to leave him to his own devices. He certainly seems to have displayed considerable ingenuity, up until now."

"No!" Bacharias said sharply. "Pardon me, I do not wish to sound rude, but no! Remember, the closer Mr. Nicolls comes to Athens, the greater his danger. It would be wiser, I think, if we can locate him."

"You're probably right," said Everett Gabler in a fine show of being convinced. The limousine bearing Carl Ingraham left at that moment, to the accompaniment of enthusiastic adieux from Kate and Lorna, who returned to their companions in time to hear Bacharias say:

"I am sure of it. Come, we must not lose time. To Daphni!"

His voice rose as he spoke. He could be overheard by the ladies, and perhaps by some of those persons standing beyond them.

"But what about that store you told us about?" Kate Murphy lamented.

Lorna upheld the reputation of Cincinnati home economics

teachers by placing first things first. "Carl says there's a church of some sort that we shouldn't miss, Kate. I expect there are stores there too."

Faced with imperative needs, Stavros Bacharias added perjury of his immortal soul to his other sins. "Yes indeed," he assured them. "Daphni is one of the finest shopping areas in Greece!"

"Well then," said Kate Murphy brightly, "let's go!"

The monastery at Daphni is a very ancient edifice. Built at the end of the eleventh century, it has subsequently had an eventful history encompassing Frankish looting, religious animosity and architectural restoration. It has survived all this with its great mosaics relatively intact.

As Thatcher and his companions hurried past the cypresses into the body of the church, the somber eyes of Christ Pantocrater were brooding over a flock of Americans from the *Capodistria,* and a small band of Germans, helpless for once in the face of superior tourist odds. Bobbing around the whole seething mass were the blacksuited guides who prey on all visitors to Greece's historic sites.

Although undeniably an artistic jewel, the monastery at Daphni is very tiny; the day was already very hot; the overall effect was indescribable.

"Somehow," Lorna Jenkins bawled over the din, "it doesn't seem very religious. Now, our Presbyterian church back home in Cincinnati doesn't have any fancy art, but there's a feeling—if you know what I mean."

Bacharias, looking feverish, was scanning the crowd. Not surprisingly, there was no sign of Kenneth Nicolls.

"You want guide—excellent English?"

A black suit was at their elbow.

"I explain the mosaics, the battlements. Then, afterward, good lunch. Then to buy post cards..."

With a snarl, Bacharias replied in a whiplash of Greek and shook off the offending hand. With a scowl, the guide melted into a group of Norwegians who had just entered. As he left, another figure emerged, camera at the ready.

"Say, here we all are again! How about that?" Carl Ingraham was all innocent enjoyment. "I don't know if I can get the right exposure in here..."

"Now you know, Carl, that doesn't seem right to me," Kate Murphy told him virtuously. "It isn't respectful, taking pictures in church. Do you think so, Mr. Bacharias?"

In view of the steady popping of flashbulbs around them, Thatcher rather hoped that Bacharias would rebuke this fatuousness. Furthermore, Kate Murphy's accent was proving unstable; it had now slipped to an unfortunate blend of North Texas and dust-bowl Oklahoma. He reminded himself to speak sternly to her once this adventure was terminated.

But Bacharias, intent on the crowd, was not listening.

"I said," said Carl Ingraham, giving him a playful football coach's punch, "this isn't a church any more, is it?"

"What? Oh no. Daphni is a historic site. It has been secularized."

Lorna Jenkins then went too far. "Well, I swan," she said with wonder.

Everett Gabler, not a man to show emotion, passed a handkerchief over his gleaming brow.

Fortunately, Ingraham was capable of carrying on.

"Guess I've got to say so long again," he said, consulting a mimeographed sheet. "We're due in Athens."

With an effort, Bacharias pulled himself together. "Your party?" he said with a ghastly parody of a smile. "They have already proceeded?"

"Oh sure," said Carl Ingraham. "Well, see you around!"

But Bacharias plunged right after him.

"So far, so good," said Kate Murphy in matter-of-fact tones.

With audible feeling Everett beseeched both ladies to be very, very careful. Thatcher reserved his fire and concentrated upon the great solemn Christ figure.

"Nonsense," said Kate. "The man's... oh, there you are,

Mr. Bacharias. Now, where were those stores you were telling us about?"

Bacharias looked faintly unwell. He was leading a burly guide who looked oversize compared to his colleagues, most of them small, dapper men. The guide did not look like an authority on churches, nor for that matter an ex-seminarian. With a villainous wink at Everett Gabler he put a familiar hand on Bacharias' arm.

"Quiet!" he snarled. "We may be overheard. First, you can identify yourselves?"

Wearily, Thatcher, Gabler and Bacharias produced their business cards. After a fleeting inspection, the cards were engulfed in a huge fist incongruously encased by a white cotton glove. Ponderously, he relaxed his vigilance.

"Good! I've passed Nicolls on to one of our men in Athens."

"He is still with the others?" Bacharias asked anxiously.

Once again Thatcher understood: as this pursuit continued, Stavros Bacharias was facing the danger that Kenneth Nicolls and the precious microfilm might become separated. And Kenneth Nicolls now represented Bacharias' last chance at the microfilm.

The ex-seminarian looked down from his height in disgust. "Of course. They are agreed to stay with him until he is restored to his friends."

Bacharias was too relieved to speak.

"And your man in Athens?" hissed Everett, getting into the spirit of things.

The guide leaned down and began to whisper.

The chauffeur fell in enthusiastically with injunctions to hurry but, unfortunately, the road from Daphni to Athens does not lend itself to high speeds. He, and the Volkswagen trailing him since the Piraeus, proceeded at a decorous 40-miles-per-hour. The seedy commercial development unrolling was not sufficiently interesting to divert the ladies from a burgeoning sense of grievance, although they made valiant efforts to remain good-natured.

"Of course, we're just thrilled at seeing so many interesting things we might have missed," said Lorna Jenkins, sounding profoundly dissatisfied.

Kate Murphy seconded her. "Yes indeed. And of course, it's a privilege to get to really *know* the people..."

The atmosphere in the car was so charged that Thatcher momentarily missed the significance of this last, emphasized as it was. But the only Greek present, Stavros Bacharias, alternately peering out the window or checking a showy wrist watch, was anything but gratified by the tribute.

"But," said Kate Murphy, weightily, "we had hoped to pick up a few things. I certainly will be sick if I can't get my niece Gladys a little something. Gladys is really crazy about really nice things..."

"And I told Mrs. Evers—she's my landlady, and a really lovely person—that I'd try to find one of those lovely rugs for her. She wants to put it in the dining room, Kate. You know, where the braided rug is."

"That would be lovely," Kate said firmly. "Just lovely. And those beautiful bags. Now they'd be just perfect for Syl and the girls."

Thatcher was not surprised to see the thrust of American woman bent on shopping penetrate even Bacharias' preoccupation. As a banker, he would back the American woman *qua* consumer against anything short of a tidal wave.

They were nosing into Athens proper amidst the inevitable chaos of local traffic, Bacharias leaned back, and said hollowly, "I will be most happy to show you some very fine shops..."

"Not too expensive, I hope," Lorna said militantly.

"No, no!"

Thatcher turned aside to conceal a smile. This was the first and only time he felt any sympathy for Bacharias.

But Everett Gabler was implacable.

"First," he said flatly, "it really is necessary for us to stop at the National Archaeological Museum."

Miss Murphy became the American woman incarnate.

"You know," she said, thinking deeply, "you can overdo this sightseeing!"

Thatcher did not find it strange that a large group of people were milling around the sidewalk outside the National Archaeological Museum. Nor, he saw with a side glance, did Stavros Bacharias. The Americans, of course, could be explained by the *Capodistria*'s ambitious claim to show the whole Mediterranean in twelve fun-filled days. But the Greeks? Fortunately, nobody had time to wonder who they were, or why they were there.

"Hi again!" shouted Carl Ingraham, emerging from the crowd. He had calibrated the distance from stranger to friend with magnificent accuracy. "Hi, folks!"

"Every American but the American we want!" Bacharias exclaimed waspishly. "Do you see Nicolls?"

Just then the ladies, who had fallen on Ingraham, made loud noises indicating pleasure.

"Did you hear that, Mr. Thatcher?" Lorna Jenkins asked.

"I'm afraid not, Miss Jenkins," he replied at his courtliest.

She cast him a darkling glance but said: "Carl saw your friend!"

This was enough to command instant attention.

"What?" Bacharias demanded. "Where is he?"

Carl Ingraham sketched abashment at becoming the cynosure of all eyes but carried on nobly. "Tall blond fellow from California? Yup, he was here. Said he was getting pretty tired of sightseeing."

"Where did he go?" Bacharias sounded hoarse.

Ingraham dug something out of a pocket on that vivid shirt. "Yeah. This little Greek was going around, passing these out..."

Without apology, Bacharias snatched the card from Ingraham's hand.

Thatcher already knew what it said:

Costa Votsonis
Greek Handicrafts
Objets d'Art
24 Appolonas Street Athens

"Oh, doesn't that sound interesting," trilled Kate Murphy.

"So this fellow said he was going to cut out of the tour. To tell you the truth, he could use some new clothes. Terrible mess, what he had on. Anyway, said he was going to do some shopping. And we do have our free hour after this here museum." Ingraham was droning on very satisfactorily.

"But why on earth have they passed Nicolls to this place?" demanded Everett at his most negative. "Why not—?"

"Who knows?" said Bacharias imperiously. "But we must go after him!"

Thatcher let himself get swept back to the Buick but judged it expedient to introduce reasonable reluctance. He said irritably: "This is a wild-goose chase, it seems to me. I think we should simply go back to the hotel and wait for Nicolls to come to us."

This was enough to remind Stavros Bacharias that his role, after all, was aid and support to the Sloan Guaranty Trust, not leader of a posse.

With an embarrassed laugh, he replied: "Who can tell, Mr. Thatcher? It may not be safe for him at the hotel. Perhaps..."

"Well I think it's just grand," said Kate Murphy largely. "This sounds like just the sort of out-of-the-way place that tourists usually miss..."

Carl Ingraham, who had joined forces with them, chimed in. "That's one thing you don't get on a cruise, Kate. The little out-of-the-way places."

Whatever else Costa Votsonis might have been, he was the answer to a shopper's dream. His shop, located after some difficulty in the cluttered labyrinth of the old Turkish Quarter, was an uninviting doorway next to a suspiciously picturesque taverna where loud Greek folk music and tourists from Doncaster were both much in evidence.

The gentlemen of the party hesitated and looked up and down the crowded thoroughfare where no one—not even the driver of the Volkswagen—seemed to be taking the slightest notice of them. Carl Ingraham went one step further, displaying reluctance to entrust himself to the perils of commercial traffic in the mysterious Mediterranean.

The ladies yelped with pleasure and rushed indoors.

Within, shadows did not obscure a veritable cavern bursting with an Oriental profusion of goods; there were long benches heaped with cloths and bolts of sumptuous fabrics; in a corner, a mountain of gleaming rugs brought color into the darkness. The walls were strewn with long leather thongs from which brass coffee pots and trays were suspended. Large baskets contained a potpourri of oddments; small dolls dressed in the *fustanella* of the *evzone*, elaborately beaded caps, replicas of the Parthenon. At the rear of the store, a display case held trays of coins as well as bowls of semiprecious stones. Overall there hung a smoky pleasant hint of incense.

There was nobody in the shop.

Stavros Bacharias raised his voice. "Ho! Is anybody here?"

From somewhere behind the bead curtain that covered the inner doorway there was a tinkle, followed by a gentle shuffling. An old man, his face deeply seamed, appeared.

"Say," said Carl Ingraham in a stage whisper as he readied one of his many cameras, "this sure is colorful."

The ladies agreed, without removing themselves from the piles of colorful scarves.

Bacharias stepped forward and rattled off a fusillade of questions. The old man looked impassively at him. Then, with the malicious deliberation of extreme age, he replied. At Bacharias' staccato rejoinder, he merely shrugged and turned to shuffle back to his quarters in the rear.

Bacharias could not keep his temper in check. "Old fool!" he snapped. "He's just waiting for the owner. He's been asleep, and he doesn't know who has been here..."

At that moment, a musical voice filled the room.

"Welcome to Costa's," it lilted. "Just look around to your heart's content. I won't bother you unless there's anything—at all—that I can do to help."

As he stood framed in the small square of light in the doorway, Costa Votsonis might have been a classic statue come to life. Vibrant curls covered a well-shaped skull; his high-bridged nose and sensitive mouth duplicated the most golden Athenian youth. Dark green eyes sparkled against honey gold skin.

He neared Thatcher, Gabler and Bacharias. "Unless there's anything special I can do for you?" he said insinuatingly.

He was beautiful. He was also wearing a deceptively simple sweater designed by Pierre Cardin. With a graceful gesture, he removed it from his shoulders and tossed it over a nearby chair.

"Some of our best goods," he informed them, "are all packed up. You know we're opening the Mykonos shop next week, and things are *so* confused. Have you looked at these sports jackets? They're going to be very big next season. I've sent twenty to New York..."

Everett was genuinely bereft of speech. Bacharias, who had presumably intended to ask his questions in Greek, was momentarily taken aback. Thatcher merely reflected that Paul Makris could summon some very odd reinforcements.

"We're not interested in sports jackets," he said.

"No?" said Costa much disappointed.

Clearly he felt that they should be.

"Perhaps something in our ceramics. We've got some absolutely charming designs."

"...not at the moment," said Thatcher, trying for a firm tone.

"We are looking for friends who came here today," said Bacharias abruptly.

Costa simply smiled radiantly. "Sooner or later, absolutely everybody comes to Costa's," he said without false modesty. "Our things are really authentic. None of that terribly artsy craftsy stuff they sell up in the hotels. Lenny comes by whenever he's over. And of course, Larry simply adores our handwoven cloths. Do you know he's done over his breakfast room..."

Bacharias was brutal with these ingenuous confidences. "Our friend was here today. Probably within the last hour."

"*Not* the tall blond American?" Costa said. "Don't say he's *your* friend!"

He appeared to find it incredible.

"Why not?" demanded Everett Gabler testily. He was rewarded with an alarming look of pure wickedness. Before things could get out of control, Thatcher took a hand.

"We're most anxious to get in touch with him. You don't happen to know where he went after he left here, do you?"

He could feel Bacharias holding his breath.

"Well, I don't know where he is now, but I do know—"

He was interrupted by a sudden detonation of sound. Four men had rushed into the shop, bringing with them the great hurly-burly of the streets. Of variegated sizes and shapes, they had none of Costa Votsonis' high finish. On the contrary, they were clearly of the people. Earthy. Ready to break into a Greek dance, given to tears, to laughter, to smashing glasses after drinking—and it was clear that they had been doing just that.

In short, they too had seen that movie.

There ensued one of those complex impromptu parties which lurks in the corners of all Greek gatherings. One of the newcomers, a tall thin man, detached himself and unsteadily teetered over to find out what Lorna and Kate were studying. In minutes, he had draped two yards of green linen around his shoulders and was imitating Hollywood's version of the simple, great-souled Cretan free spirit.

"*Hopa!*" he sang, snapping his fingers inexpertly.

"Say, isn't this something!" Carl Ingraham yelled from behind his camera, delirious with delight.

The three others descended on Costa Votsonis who was sputtering with rage.

"American? Good! Good!" one bellowed in an overpowering waft of garlic-borne affection. He pounded Everett Gabler on the back.

"Friends, friends!" his companions echoed after a moment of befuddled blankness. Then they too flung themselves into demonstrations of affection. Thatcher found himself heartily embraced, then flung aside. With the misguided determination of the inebriated, the newcomers converged on Stavros Bacharias.

"American, good!"

"Pitssburgh!"

"Nea Iorkee!"

Costa Votsonis was impotently dancing around the outskirts, plucking at shirts that had not been designed by Cardin. Stavros Bacharias was forced to defend himself. Bellowing with rage, he tried to detach himself from the bearish embraces of his tormenters.

"The real Greece!" breathed Lorna Jenkins.

"Sure beats Cincinnati," Carl Ingraham agreed, clicking steadily.

When wild Greek shouts finally convinced the celebrants that Stavros Bacharias was not an American, they were ludicrously chagrined.

Falling back, they first looked at each other, then at Costa Votsonis.

Votsonis launched into a falsetto denunciation.

Overcome by embarrassment, the latecomers nodded sheepishly, sent weak smiles at Bacharias, then attempted apologies.

Bacharias replied with a vicious monosyllable.

Costa Votsonis was equally angered. "Barbarians, *vlachos*! This is what I have to put up with. I build an international reputation. Nothing but the best people! And what happens!"

Whatever happened, it happened in Greek.

During the bill of complaints, the invading quartet inched backward. Finally, with a last bedraggled salute, they melted through the doorway.

With an effort, Costa Votsonis recaptured his aplomb.

"My brother," he said bitterly. "What can one do?"

Bacharias, smoothing a rumpled lapel, was beside himself.

He could not even summon the energy to speak English. In a ferocious undertone, he was blaspheming steadily.

But Costa Votsonis, with a tremendous effort, had pulled himself together.

"Now, what was it you were saying?"

Thatcher reminded him of their quest.

"Oh yes, your friend. How glad I am he wasn't here—well, he did mention where he was going. He and his friends are expecting you."

To save him from being throttled, Thatcher asked where. It was, not surprisingly, an apartment in Kolonaki.

Bacharias, who had abandoned the pretense of civility, collided with Carl Ingraham in the doorway.

"Say, I hope you folks will understand, but I'm going to have to leave you," said the American.

Bacharias uttered a short ugly sentence.

Kate Murphy was standing next to Thatcher. He heard her muttered rejoinder:

"Oh yes, but the one who burns in hell will be you!"

Aloud she said: "But we haven't finished here! There are so many things to see..."

Thatcher took up his cue. "Mr. Bacharias and I unfortunately must hurry on to another appointment. But Mr. Gabler, I'm sure, is eager to continue looking at rugs."

Without waiting for a reply, Bacharias and Thatcher left for the waiting car. As they glided away from the curb, they could see the ladies in vigorous conversation with Everett.

"This is madness," said Bacharias distractedly. He looked out the rear window—looked in vain for the Volkswagen which had disappeared. Paul Makris' men, including Costa Votsonis, were nothing if not efficient. "There will be more cretins, more imbeciles at this apartment in Kolonaki! Things have been mismanaged!"

"Oh, I wouldn't say that," Thatcher rejoined.

Bacharias took a grip on himself. "You will comprehend that I grow impatient."

Thatcher nodded understandingly. Perhaps Bacharias, if he

had been in the mood for dispassionate observation, might have thought *too* understandingly.

Once they reached Kolonaki, the pace quickened again. The elevator operator at the apartment house barely gave them time to clear the door.

"I have the key," he said mysteriously. "I am instructed to admit you."

"There is no one there?" Bacharias asked despairingly.

"You are to wait," the elevator operator insisted. "Then the ladies will come."

"Ladies?"

Bacharias was taken aback. Did the operator think they were someone else? Had they perhaps strayed into . . . ?

But they were at the apartment now. The elevator operator ushered them in, then removed himself immediately.

"Now that we are alone—" Bacharias began. He broke off and stiffened. There was a sound of movement within. "Did you hear that?"

The footsteps were growing nearer. Somewhere in the distance a window was banged shut.

The bedroom door opened and a man appeared.

CHAPTER XXIII

TELL ME, SOCRATES

"GOOD AFTERNOON, Mr. Bacharias."

Kenneth Nicolls spoke quietly as he entered the room and closed the door behind him. Nevertheless the simple words conveyed the hiss of sword blades as duelists saluted each other.

"I do not understand." Bacharias stared, open-mouthed. He recovered himself and, turning to Thatcher, went on stiffly: "I was given to understand that Mr. Nicolls was in some distress."

"We have been guilty of some deception. Mr. Nicolls rejoined us several days ago."

With difficulty Thatcher was suppressing surprise of his own. For Kenneth Nicolls had been miraculously restored to his pre-revolution sobriety. In every respect he was the twin of the man who had left the Hellenus project—or for that matter, the Sloan Guaranty Trust—several weeks ago.

Unknown to Thatcher, both Lorna Jenkins and Kenneth had been busy in the last twenty-four hours. Lorna, with the scholar's eye for detail, had not forgotten, during her visit in Sounion, to demand restoration of the wardrobe stolen from the Hotel Britannia. As for Kenneth, he had been goaded beyond endurance at hearing the cleaning woman refer to him as "that cinematic gentleman." Rightly attributing this insult to his flowing golden locks, Ken had cast prudence to the wind. Ready to risk death rather than dishonor, he had raced down to the street and into the first barber shop. Now he stood before them in all the glory of a ruthless crew cut and conservative Wall Street tailoring.

The sight did not elicit any enthusiasm from Stavros Bacharias. With an air of injured dignity he said:

"It is not wise to trifle with a representative of the Greek Government. What, then, has been the meaning of this morning's charade?"

Thatcher settled himself into an easy position. "I think the Greek Government might be astonished to learn the capacity in which you have presumed to represent it."

Bacharias' confidence remained unshaken.

"Mr. Thatcher, it is time that you stopped play-acting with me. In part, I can understand your motives. There has not been entire frankness between us about the documents Mr. Nicolls has been delivering for his friends, has there? No wonder the so-famous Sloan Guaranty Trust chooses to be reticent." Here he turned sternly to the younger man. "I have been shocked, Mr Nicolls, deeply shocked to learn of your activities since I left you at Salonika. It is not thus that we expect visitors in Greece to conduct themselves."

Before Ken could answer the accusation, Thatcher took up the challenge.

"*Left?*" he queried. "Perhaps *delivered* would be more accurate. Let us say since you *delivered* Mr. Nicolls to your colleague at the newsstand in the Salonika railroad station with instructions about a certain Red Cross pin."

If anything, Bacharias was amused.

"So! That little masquerade has been penetrated, has it? But surely you do not delude yourself that anyone will believe that tale. When it is revealed to the Government authorities that Mr. Nicolls has been acting as courier for subversive forces, they will expect him to fabricate some defense. It is the habit of criminals caught in the act, the world over. That his tale should be so fanciful will be merely a reflection on his powers of invention."

By now, Bacharias was openly smiling. Ken, who prided himself on being a man of peace, yearned to wipe away that smugness with his bare fist. He had to control his breathing as he said:

"It may interest you to know, Mr. Bacharias, that the microfilm is no longer in my possession. Nor is there any evidence to show it ever was."

The man from the Ministry shrugged philosophically. "That has been a possibility for weeks now. True, I had high hopes this morning that no further intervention on my part would be necessary, other than summoning the police at the critical moment. But let me remind you that you are still wanted for police questioning. I have been prepared for this eventuality ever since that accursed earthquake. Happily the police—as well as myself—now know that Dr. Ziros reduced his treasonable documents to microfilm. I have only to conveniently remember Mr. Nicolls' suspicious behavior in the railroad station. The officer in charge will be most interested to hear how your Mr. Nicolls deliberately sought a seat by Dr. Ziros."

"And will you be believed?" Thatcher asked with real interest.

Bacharias' teeth gleamed against his dark skin. "But assuredly. I am a professional civil servant. I have no known political affiliations. *I* will be as deeply shocked as everyone else. And with Mr. Nicolls in custody, it is only a matter of time before the police trace his movements, discover how he passed the microfilm and apprehend his accomplices."

As he finished speaking, he leaned back in his chair, assurance in every movement.

"Splendid!" said Thatcher cordially.

In spite of himself Bacharias was startled. With considerable enjoyment Ken watched his confidence evaporate as Thatcher continued:

"I relied on your being too cautious to associate openly with any political group—especially one that might find itself *persona non grata* with the present regime. My plans would have to be more complicated if you were an avowed rightist. But *no known political affiliations*, Mr. Bacharias? This could scarcely be better for my purposes."

"Your jest is ill-timed," said Stavros Bacharias haughtily.

"On the contrary. By your own admission you knew where

this microfilm was; yet you neglected to tell the police. Simple explanations always have strong appeal for authorities, Mr. Bacharias. Since you did not assist the police, the authorities will reason that it was because you wanted the microfilm delivered as Dr. Ziros intended. Hence, you are a subversive leftist. No Army officer could resist the conclusion."

"Ridiculous!"

"I think not. For a man of no known political affiliations, you have a surprising amount of inside information about leftist activities. As well as a marked disinclination to share this information with the Army. They will notice that you have carefully delayed your story until after the microfilm has been delivered."

Bacharias gritted his teeth. "An absurd contention! I can explain all that."

"Possibly. But can you explain away the further proof I will offer?"

"Proof!" Bacharias exclaimed wildly. "How can there be any proof? It is all untrue!"

Ken Nicolls had been waiting for this moment. "Appearances," he said gently, "can be very misleading."

Thatcher returned to his antagonist. "You asked the meaning of this morning's charade. If that is Everett Gabler at the door, you will see for yourself in a moment."

It was indeed Everett Gabler. He was fresh from the darkroom and carried a set of photographs, still damp and curling from hasty processing.

Everett had had some difficulty escaping from Carl Ingraham. The photographer had wanted to know if there was any chance of full-time employment with the Sloan. Banking, he said, seemed to offer more excitement than secluded academics realized. It would be very dull going back to Mycenean inscriptions after all this.

"Here they are," Gabler announced. "The enlargements came out in very clear detail. Naturally I have placed another set in safe-keeping, along with the negatives." The final shot was aimed at Stavros Bacharias, who seemed to be contemplating some mad assault on the limp pile of eight-by-tens.

Thatcher spread the pictures out on the coffee table and directed their guest's attention to the salient features.

"The men you are embracing in these shots," he explained kindly, "are two notorious members of ASPIDA. They are currently wanted by the police. And the banner on the wall behind you—it has come out very clearly in the enlargement, hasn't it?—contains the most warlike of ASPIDA's slogans. Dear me, it seems to call for an immediate insurrection. Those crates beside you, with the cabalistic markings, contain hand grenades and small arms. As the police would very rapidly discover, if their attention were ever drawn to these photographs."

Bacharias stared at the prints, unwilling to believe his eyes. Dim memories of the morning's crowded activities returned to haunt him—memories of protracted exchanges, indiscriminate embracings, anonymous boxes and crates strewn over dusty floors. Suddenly he stiffened and leaned forward eagerly, only to sink back in immediate despair.

Gabler watched him in disapproval. He knew what Bacharias was looking for. Did he think that the Sloan was so incompetent? The pictures were works of art. There was no sign of Thatcher or Gabler, of Lorna Jenkins or Kate Murphy, of Paul Makris' nameless minions. The pinpoint exposure had assured absolute clarity for the principals in each photograph. Behind them ranged dim, unfocused figures suggestive of a faceless crowd.

"That banner!" Bacharias said hoarsely. "It was not in the store when I was there. This picture has been falsified!"

Thatcher shook his head. "It was there, all right. True, it was mounted on a spring hanger, like a window shade, and only lowered when your back was turned, but it was there. It is there still, and the picture is absolutely genuine."

A small shudder coursed through the Greek's frame. He made several false starts before he actually enunciated his protest.

"This is absurd. I am a rightist! My friends will speak for me."

It was Everett Gabler who punctured this delusion with his usual precision. "Of course the photographs are eminently satisfactory, but the crux of our case would be Dr. Ziros' microfilm."

"The microfilm Mr. Nicolls had?"

Gabler became reproachful. "It seems most unlikely that such an object could ever have been in the possession of any member of the Sloan. I mean the microfilm describing a number of arms dumps, the microfilm which presently rests in the center of one of your business cards. The microfilm with only your fingerprints and those of these two men—" here he paused to tap the picture of ASPIDA's desperadoes—"on it."

Bacharias was white. "You mean—" he paused to absorb the enormity of the situation. "You mean, you took one of my cards and put that microfilm in it!"

"You gave it to us," Thatcher corrected. "If you cast your mind over the events of this morning, you may remember exchanging cards at quite a brisk clip."

"My friends . . ." Bacharias began.

"Faced with these facts, your fellow reactionaries will undoubtedly feel there is nothing to be gained by dragging their organization into so unsavory a situation." Gabler spoke with conviction.

Thatcher nodded his agreement. "It might lead to suspicions that *they* were planning an armed uprising. I think your friends will expect you to immolate yourself for the cause." He went on cheerfully. "A moment ago you said criminals were the same, the world over. So are political associates. They find it fatally easy to demand self-sacrifice."

Bacharias took a deep breath. "What do you want?" he demanded.

"Not much. The Hellenus negotiations, as I am sure you remember, are due to commence shortly. The Sloan Guaranty Trust would be gravely disturbed if anything imperiled the future cooperation so necessary to the success of the venture."

"Ah! Now we see how American business behaves. Blackmailing and coercing government officials to support them!"

Gabler almost strangled in his indignation. "How dare you speak to us of coercion! After I have been savagely assaulted, kidnapped in broad daylight, subjected to gross incivility."

Bacharias could not know that gross incivility was a euphemism for brain soup, a dish Gabler did not trust himself to describe with greater particularity.

"*I* did not kidnap you!" he was stung into replying.

"You were directly responsible!"

Thatcher intervened before they all lost sight of their objective. He was no longer cheerful or good-humored. With authoritative severity, he replied:

"We are coercing you into implementing your government's policy, rather than your own, Mr. Bacharias. We are blackmailing you into representing your Ministry as it expects to be represented. It is disgraceful that intimidation should be necessary to bring an official of your seniority to a sense of his duty."

Stavros Bacharias looked at him with silent hatred.

"And I expect the Hellenus negotiations to be a great success," Thatcher concluded menacingly. "With results satisfactory to all three parties."

"I have been surprised and pleased at the rapidity with which we have finally concluded the Hellenus negotiations," said Paul Makris over two weeks later.

They were waiting at Hellenikon Airport for the flight which would carry home the men of the Sloan. The official celebrations, in the form of a triumphal banquet, had taken place the evening before. Now, less formal farewells were in progress.

"We were pleased too," Thatcher said courteously.

"But not surprised?" The Greek financier lifted his eyebrows delicately. "I can only say that it is a pleasure to do business with the Sloan."

"Now that we've started, I expect we'll be working together again."

"I sincerely trust so. As I said to Peter Chiros this morning, when he came in with the news, one can place reliance in the Sloan. No loose ends. No future possibility of unpleasantness."

Thatcher suspected a *non sequitur*, but before he could ask for enlightenment, Bill Riemer from the Embassy was extending his hand.

"Good-bye, Mr. Thatcher. I'm glad that everything has gone so well."

"So are we."

"I thought, for a while there, that we might have some awkwardness when Ken Nicolls finally showed up in Athens. But the police were very understanding, weren't they?"

"Very."

"Of course, it made all the difference, having the Ministry go to bat for him that way. The Ambassador, himself, was surprised at the amount of cooperation you got. But I said I knew the minute Mr. Gabler turned up that you'd have no trouble with Stavros Bacharias."

"He was very helpful."

"He told me at the banquet last night that he anticipates absolutely no trouble for Hellenus in the future. It's very satisfactory. Well, Mr. Makris has offered me a lift back into town, so I'll have to go. We'll look forward to seeing you in Athens again."

Thatcher said what was proper, then joined Gabler and Nicolls who were taking affectionate leave of Lorna Jenkins and Kate Murphy.

"I can't thank you enough," Kenneth was saying.

"Never mind about thanking us. In fact, forget about older women in general," Kate Murphy advised bluntly. "You just be thankful about going home to your wife and family."

Ken blushed scarlet.

"And Mr. Thatcher," Kate continued, turning away from her victim, "remember that Lorna and I expect to see you in Princeton next winter."

Thatcher promised that he would be waiting for word of their return. "I am afraid you may find the remainder of your stay in Greece a little slow now," he added.

Lorna Jenkins was cryptically amused. "Oh, I expect something will turn up," she said vaguely.

"Come now," Thatcher said good-naturedly, "you can't have many friends here who go in for this sort of activity."

Paul Makris had never been able to bring himself to discuss One-Eye and Louis the Knife with Thatcher.

"You've done us a good turn," Kate Murphy beamed at him. "We've met some old friends we hadn't seen in years. Lorna has even found some at that villa of yours."

Gabler, who took a proprietary interest in the villa at Sounion, said tolerantly that they were not bad sorts when you knew how to deal with them.

"Only one thing bothers me," he confessed. "We have destroyed Bacharias' plans for subverting Hellenus. But is the man to go scot-free? Whether or not he actually shot Elias Ziros, he was morally responsible for that murder."

"I wouldn't worry about that," Lorna Jenkins said shortly.

Everett turned expectantly to Kate Murphy. It was she who had called for Bacharias' punishment most insistently. But she was silent. Instead it was Nicolls who spoke.

"What worries me is those arms dumps. Bacharias could arrange for someone else to notify the police, and we'd never know."

"It's been a long time," Thatcher reminded him. "I'm quite sure that those arms have all been moved by now. And as we haven't heard anything, the move must have been successful."

"Yes. But should we ever have gotten mixed up with those dumps?" Nicolls insisted. "I thought non-intervention was the Sloan's policy."

"It is. But in this case, we didn't have much choice. And now, as I see a representative from the Ministry heading toward us, we had better drop this discussion."

They were all blandly discussing the Suez Canal when the official rushed up to them.

"I cannot apologize sufficiently," he began. "It was arranged that you should be seen off by Mr. Bacharias as you took leave of the Minister yesterday evening."

"And Mr. Bacharias has been delayed?" asked Thatcher, who was not altogether surprised that cordiality at this point should have been too much for the man. "Then we will assume his good wishes and ask you to convey ours."

The official flung his arms wide. "But it is not that. You have not heard, then?"

"Heard what?" asked Thatcher with dawning suspicion.

"It is the death of Stavros Bacharias that I have to report. He was struck by a car this morning on his way to the office. Right in Omonia Square. He was dead before he reached the hospital."

Shocked exclamations greeted the statement.

"Such an able man! Your Minister will feel the loss keenly."

"And in the prime of life!"

"We never expect it to happen to someone we know."

"The Minister knew that you would sympathize with us."

It was therefore a very subdued and ceremonial farewell that the official extended, but it lasted until their flight was called. There was no opportunity for any private exchange with the ladies. The three men could only look at Lorna Jenkins' spare, upright figure in surmise.

But as they plodded across the tarmac to the boarding steps, Thatcher was thinking deeply. This, of course, was what Paul Makris had been referring to. And he thought the Sloan was responsible! Incredible!

Thatcher did not share Makris' approval of this Greek predilection for extremes. He was, he supposed, too conventional; moderation in all things.

And the place to find that was three thousand miles away—on Wall Street. He looked at his two companions for agreement.

Kenneth Nicolls was following Kate Murphy's advice. As soon as the TWA jet actually stood before him, he had put everything from his mind but the vividly remembered features of his wife and the still hypothetical features of a newborn little girl. He was striding eagerly forward.

It was Everett Gabler, however, who proved that Greece teaches Man how to live. Everett was standing stock still, at the top of the boarding steps, looking back at Lorna Jenkins. Unconscious of John Putnam Thatcher, of Wall Street and of self, he spoke:

"Now there," he said in total admiration, "is a woman!"